From SECURITY BLANKET

There were faces in the quilt, too, and after a while I began to feel the faces were all looking back at me. Suddenly it seemed there were a hundred people in the twins' room—all of them staring at me—and I could swear those faces were opening their mouths, trying to tell me something. But there was only silence.

I backed away from the quilt until I hit a picture on the wall, and it fell down. I picked up the picture, and when I looked back at the quilt, it was just a quilt again. No faces, just colorful fabric filling the many squares.

I left the twins' room with a shudder and went into the living room, where the only faces looking at me were those in the smiling family photos on the wall. Then I sat at my piano and played something soothing. It had all been my imagination, I told myself. And I kept telling myself that until I almost believed it.

—

OTHER BOOKS BY NEAL SHUSTERMAN

Visit the author at www.storyman.com

DARKNESS CREEPING

TWENTY TWISTED TALES

NEAL SHUSTERMAN

PUFFIN BOOKS

PUFFIN BOOKS

Published by the Penguin Group

Penguin Young Readers Group, 345 Hudson Street, New York, New York 10014, U.S.A.

Penguin Group (Canada), 90 Eglinton Avenue East, Suite 700,
Toronto, Ontario, Canada M4V 3B2
(a division of Pearson Penguin Canada Inc.)

Penguin Books Ltd, 80 Strand, London WC2R 0RL, England

Penguin Ireland, 25 St Stephen's Green, Dublin 2, Ireland
(a division of Penguin Books Ltd)

Penguin Group (Australia), 250 Camberwell Road, Camberwell, Victoria 3124, Australia
(a division of Pearson Australia Group Pty Ltd)

Penguin Books India Pvt Ltd, 11 Community Centre, Panchsheel Park,
New Delhi - 110 017, India

Penguin Group (NZ), Cnr Airborne and Rosedale Roads, Albany, Auckland 1310,
New Zealand (a division of Pearson New Zealand Ltd)

Penguin Books (South Africa) (Pty) Ltd, 24 Sturdee Avenue, Rosebank,
Johannesburg 2196, South Africa

Registered Offices: Penguin Books Ltd, 80 Strand, London WC2R 0RL, England

"Monkeys Tonight," "Black Box," "Flushie," "Screaming at the Wall," "Alexander's Skull,"
"Same Time Next Year", "Resting Deep," and "Shadows of Doubt" first published
in the United States of America by Lowell House Juvenile, 1993.
"Riding the Raptor," "Trash Day," "An Ear for Music," "Soul Survivor," "Security Blanket,"
"Growing Pains," "Connecting Flight," and "Crystalloid" first published
in the United States of America by Lowell House Juvenile, 1995.
Published by Puffin Books, a division of Penguin Young Readers Group, 2007

1 3 5 7 9 10 8 6 4 2

"Monkeys Tonight," "Black Box," "Flushie," "Screaming at the Wall," "Alexander's Skull,"
"Same Time Next Year", "Resting Deep," and "Shadows of a Doubt"
copyright © Neal Shusterman, 1993
"Riding the Raptor," "Trash Day," "An Ear for Music," "Soul Survivor," "Security Blanket,"
"Growing Pains," "Connecting Flight," and "Crystalloid"
copyright © Neal Shusterman, 1995
"The River Tour," "Who Do We Appreciate?," "Ralphy Sherman's Root Canal,"
"Catching Cold," and foreword copyright © Neal Shusterman, 2007
All rights reserved

Puffin Books ISBN 978-0-14-240721-9

Printed in the United States of America

TABLE OF CONTENTS

FOREWORD

Once, when I was doing an author visit, a kid who had read my novel *The Dark Side of Nowhere* stood up and asked me, "Mr. Shusterman? What planet are you from?"

Thinking quickly, I answered, "It hasn't been discovered by your puny human telescopes."

I suppose people wonder where I get some of the crazy ideas for my stories. Well, I'm here to officially confirm that I am, like all of you (or at least most of you), from the planet Earth. I do get weird ideas, though, and I'm lucky enough to be able to make my living writing those ideas down. Some of them are scary, others are funny. Some are true-to-life, and others are just plain bizarre. I guess that's why I don't like sticking to a single genre—I like writing all sorts of things. I think that's the only way you grow as a writer.

The stories in this collection are of the creepy/bizarre variety, with some humor thrown in for good measure. They span half my career (I say that because I'm hoping I still have at least another half to go). For those of you who are curious as to how I came up with the stories, I've prefaced each one with an explanation of how the story came to be.

I would like to thank Jennifer Bonnell and Eileen Bishop Kreit at Penguin books for letting me creep through the darkness with this collection, as well as Jack Artenstein, who was the first publisher, way back when, to take a chance and publish collections of my short stories.

I hope you enjoy the journey, and if, after reading, you have a hard time getting to sleep, don't say I didn't warn you!

Neal Shusterman
September, 2006

DARKNESS CREEPING

CATCHING COLD

We have a psychotically impatient ice-cream man in our neighborhood. He comes down the street, playing his happy little tune, my daughters come screaming downstairs in a panic asking for a dollar each. By the time they get out the door, however, the ice-cream man is gone, and all the little kids on the street are crying, because not a single kid got ice cream. I had never seen the guy stop. In fact I had never seen him. I just heard his stupid little song.

One day we decided we were not going to stand for it anymore. We all piled into the car, we chased him down, and we cut him off, blocking traffic. Everyone who saw it applauded. He was forced to sell us ice cream. It was lousy ice cream, but to us, it tasted like victory. So you could say this story was inspired by reality. Sort of.

CATCHING COLD

History tells of a man named Pavlov.

Pavlov was a scientist who did a famous experiment with dogs. Each day he would ring a bell, then feed the dogs, ring a bell, then feed the dogs, over and over, until the dogs knew the bell meant food. Then one day he just rang the bell. The dogs, who were trained to expect the food after the bell, all began to salivate, drooling all over themselves expecting food that didn't come. They developed a physiological response to the sound of the bell. It's called *classical conditioning*.

The same can often be said of kids when they hear a certain sound wafting over the treetops in their neighborhood. A pleasant sound. A song. The song is different in every neighborhood, and in every town across the nation, but the song always means the same thing.

Are you listening?

Can you hear it now?

The music is out there, stealing through your window, echoing between closely packed rows of homes. It seems to come from the left, then from the right. It grows louder, then fades, louder and fades, until you're not sure whether the song is coming or going—and, like Pavlov's dogs, you're drooling.

You're scrambling for spare change, begging your parents for a dollar—because a dollar is all it costs to pay the ice-cream man. Just one dollar, and you can have sherbet on a stick in the shape of your favorite cartoon character, with a gum-ball nose. Hurry out that door! The ice-cream man is here!

Like you, Marty Zybeck was a victim of classical conditioning; however, no one had it worse than Marty. He kept his window open, every afternoon when the weather got warm, and kept his sizable ears tuned to that high frequency on which the tune would come.

His particular ice-cream truck played "Pop Goes the Weasel." It was one of the more annoying ice-cream truck tunes, but for Marty, it was a call to arms.

Whenever he heard it, Marty was prepared. He already had a dollar in his pocket, to give to the Creamy-Cold ice-cream man. The moment he heard the song, he would bound down the stairs and burst out the front door. His ears, like radar dishes, would triangulate the direction of the music, and he would take off, his feet pounding heavily, desperately on the pavement . . . but each day the result was exactly the same. First he would hear the music in front of him. Then he would hear it to his right. Then he would hear it passing on another street behind the row of houses to his left.

He would run until he was out of breath, and practically out of his mind, but the end result was always the same. The music would fade. The Creamy-Cold truck would leave, and he'd be left panting in the street with a dollar and no ice cream.

If only I were a little faster, he would think—but speed was

not one of Marty's strong points. He came in last in everything. He was, in fact, the very definition of "last." Not only was his the last name on any school roster, but he was also the last to finish every race, the last to turn in every test, the last to be done with dinner, and the last kid on the school bus. It only seems to follow that no matter how much he tried to get to the Creamy-Cold truck, he would be the last kid in the neighborhood out the door.

"He's an impatient one, that ice-cream man," his mother would say. "Never hangs around long." And then she'd remind Marty that maybe it was best he didn't have the ice cream anyway, as he tended toward being a husky child. "Well, it's not a total loss. All that running will do you good!"

He would sneer at his mother when she said things like that. His mother was as slender as could be—but Marty took after his father, who was not.

"I'll bet his ice cream stinks!" Marty would grumble, but deep down, he didn't believe it. In his heart of hearts, he believed that Creamy-Cold ice cream was the tastiest, most heavenly frozen treat ever devised by man—and the only way to get it was to buy it from the truck. Marty Zybeck did not have many goals in life—but at the top of that short list was catching the Creamy-Cold man.

———

Legend tells of a boy named Jim-Jim Jeffries.

Jim-Jim, as the neighborhood legend goes, was the fastest kid in little league. He could run faster than any player could throw a ball to a base, and so when he got a hit, he rarely got tagged out. He was a winner, and did not accept defeat easily. One day, long before anyone can remember, Jim-Jim went chasing after the Creamy-Cold ice-cream truck, refusing to accept that it was already leaving the neighborhood. He turned the corner, waving his dollar bill, and was never seen again.

Marty Zybeck knew the story of Jim-Jim. Children whispered it in hushed tones, but Marty had a logical, practical view of it. *Fact:* there was no one in the neighborhood with the last name of Jeffries. *Fact:* no one seemed to remember where he lived, or what he looked like. *Fact:* if anyone could confirm the story, it would be Marty's father, who was a well-respected detective with the local police force, and he flatly denied the existence of Jim-Jim Jeffries. Marty was convinced it was just a made-up story, designed to keep small children from crossing dangerous streets to get ice cream. Well, he wasn't a small child anymore. He didn't believe in Santa Claus, the Tooth Fairy, or Jim-Jim Jeffries.

Still, the rumors went round and round every summer, when the music came in on the wind, and children scraped together their change.

This was the summer, however, that Marty discovered a great universal truth that every kid in the neighborhood already knew. Marty would have known it, too, had he been just a little more observant.

It was as he sat playing video games with his friend Tyler CoyoteMoon-O'Callahan that the truth began to emerge. The

school year had just ended a few days earlier, and the two boys were filling their time playing interdimensional kickboxer. Five minutes into their third game, Marty heard the faint sounds of "Pop Goes the Weasel" through the open living-room window. Although leaving the game would allow Tyler to completely kick him into a parallel dimension, and thus win the match, he put down the video controller and stood up. He was mature enough to know that some things, like ice cream, were just more important than video games.

"Don't bother," said Tyler calmly. "He won't stop for you."

"He stops for other kids—he'll stop for me."

"Who says he stops for other kids?"

That gave Marty pause for thought. "Other kids always get ice cream from him."

"How do you know?"

"Because," said Marty, "I always see them running for the ice-cream man."

"Yeah—but did you ever actually see someone *eating* a Creamy-Cold bar?"

Marty racked his brain, trying to flip through images to find an actual memory of someone walking down the street, eating something they bought from the ice-cream man, but his memory held no such image.

"Well . . . you've eaten Creamy-Cold bars, haven't you?"

"Never," said Tyler. "Not once. Sure, I used to run after him like you do, but I never caught him, so I gave up."

They looked at each other, the only sound the music coming from somewhere outside, and Tyler said, "Everyone hears the music, but have you ever actually seen the truck?"

"Of course I have!" Marty said. But as he thought about it, he realized that the image of the ice-cream truck was only in his head. He had imagined what it would look like if he ever actually got out onto the street in time to catch it—but he never actually saw it.

"You know what I think?" said Tyler. "I think it's a ghost truck from the spirit world of our ancestors." Tyler, being half Navajo and half Irish, had a powerful belief in the ancestral spirit world and leprechauns.

"I think you're nuts," said Marty.

Tyler responded by turning to their game and kicking Marty into another dimension.

Fairy tales speak of a Pied Piper.

As the story goes, the piper's tune was so entrancing it lured all the rats from the town of Hamlin. Then, when the towns-folk refused to pay his price, the piper used his tune to lure away all the children into a mountain, where, presumably, they either lived happily ever after or died horrible painful deaths. Fairy tales can go either way.

Such a thing could never happen to large groups of children in modern times, however, because as everyone knows, large groups of modern children are much too smart for that. Between movies, sitcoms, and the colorful language of older siblings, kids know everything, or at least they think they do. Thinking they do, however, is enough to prevent an entire

mob of them from being lured by the music of a Pied Piper. More than likely they would just laugh at his funny green suit and pointed shoes, then walk the other way. No, when it comes to kids these days, there is safety in numbers, and the only ones who find themselves following the piper are the stragglers.

Stragglers like Marty.

Marty was not like Tyler. He was not satisfied to treat the Creamy-Cold man as a mystery best left alone. After all, being a detective was in his genes, and so at dinner that night, Marty tried to learn some technique from the greatest detective he knew.

"Dad, where do you begin an investigation?"

"Usually at the scene of the crime."

"What if there is no scene?"

"Then why investigate?"

"Because it's important?"

"Is there a paycheck involved?"

"No."

"Then it's not important."

His father was very good at deflecting any and all questions Marty ever asked him with logic that was so circular, it often left Marty forgetting what the question was.

"Uh . . . I want to investigate the ice-cream man," Marty said.

"Why? Did he run someone over?"

"No, he's just never there."

"You can't investigate something that isn't there—just something that is."

"What about something that *was* there, but isn't anymore?"

"That's called a cold case. Not my field of expertise."

Marty thanked his father and decided he was on his own. He spent the evening pondering the problem, starting with the things he knew for sure. *Fact*: the music comes from somewhere. *Fact*: the sound rises and it falls, which suggests that it's moving. *Fact*: if it's moving through their neighborhood, it has to pass by Fillmore Savings Bank around the corner, right?

That's when he came up with the big idea. He approached his father again the following morning.

"Dad, do you think you could get me some surveillance videos from Fillmore Savings for a school project?"

"No," his father said. "What's the project?"

"We're doing a mathematical study of how many people use the ATM machine. Can you get those tapes for me?"

"No. Why don't I just get you the bank's statistics?"

"We're supposed to write up the statistics ourselves. Can't you get me some videos?"

"No," said Mr. Zybeck. "I'll ask around."

Mr. Zybeck had so many strings he could pull around town, he was often getting tangled up in them. Getting the tapes was fairly easy—certainly easier than having to listen to Marty nag about them—which is exactly what Marty was counting on.

With a determination he rarely showed, Marty settled in to watch the surveillance tapes. The thing about the Creamy-Cold man is that he didn't come every day, and he always came at a different time. You could never predict when you'd hear that maddening "Pop Goes the Weasel" tune. Marty had no

way of knowing when he might pass by in the background. He watched hour after hour of tape, amazed at how many people at the ATM made faces at the camera, figuring no one would actually watch it. He saw one mugging, which his father claimed to already know about, but no ice-cream truck. He was about to give up when a white blur zoomed past in the background—a blur that was somehow different from all the other cars, trucks, and buses that zipped by. Marty hit the pause button so hard, the remote flew out of his hand. He picked it up and played the last few seconds frame by frame.

It was there in the tenth frame.

It was blurry, it was faint, but it was there: a speeding white truck with pictures of ice-cream selections on the side, and there was a big sign over the service window that said CREAMY-COLD.

Success! Proof positive! There actually *was* a Creamy-Cold truck. Tyler had been wrong—it was real. Maybe he was right in saying that it never stopped—but that could just be because it was driven by a psychotic ice-cream man. Sure—that was it—some lunatic who got his kicks taunting people with the promise of ice cream never delivered—but this was no ghost truck!

Then Marty let the video go one more frame—and what he saw in the next frame *really* got his attention.

The truck had progressed farther into the image. Its front end was already out of the picture, but now the entire sign above the service window could be read. It said CREAMY-COLD. CATCH ME IF YOU DARE.

Marty smiled. This was a challenge if ever there was one. He would catch the Creamy-Cold man—not just for himself but for all the kids who had ever run out into the street only to be denied the ice cream they so rightfully deserved. The Creamy-Cold man was going down!

———

Literature tells of a captain, name of Ahab.

Ahab had an unhealthy obsession with a great white whale that led to the destruction of his ship, and to his own untimely end. He had a first mate named Starbuck. I know what you're thinking, but Starbuck had absolutely nothing to do with making coffee. If he had, perhaps Captain Ahab might have kicked the whale habit and pursued the white-chocolate latte instead of the white whale. Unfortunately, as Ahab discovered, obsessions are rarely reasonable, and quite often will lead to one's personal doom. Although few involve the death of a sea mammal.

Marty's great white whale had four wheels and played a painfully annoying tune. He had no Starbuck to help him, since his first mate, Tyler, was off at the tribal casino, which, thanks to the luck of the Irish, was raking in big bucks. Therefore, in this obsession, Marty was alone.

Catching the ice-cream truck on film was different from catching it in person. It required a plan. He drew a map of the neighborhood, marking the entry and exit points. He labeled the sight lines from various key vantage spots. Then Marty took stock of the tools at his disposal. There were lots of them,

because Mr. Zybeck often brought home things from the office that wouldn't be missed. Things like paper clips, or police tape, which was good for wrapping presents if you ran out of ribbon. Mr. Zybeck brought home a few body bags once. Mrs. Zybeck found them wonderful for storing linens, although they did give Grandma quite a scare.

The various items Mr. Zybeck made off with from the police station were stockpiled in the garage. Marty systematically went through them, searching for things that he could use. There was a stun gun, but it was missing its charger. There was an entire case of pepper spray. There were batons and police lights, but none of them could be retooled for Marty's big scheme . . . until he saw the spike strip rolled up in the corner. Marty had seen spike strips before. In a police pursuit, they were rolled out in front of a speeding car to pop the tires and bring the chase to an end. Mom and Dad had used the strip once to stop Marty's older sister from sneaking out at night—but it was only effective the first time. This is exactly what he needed! Maybe he couldn't stop the ice-cream man, but four flat tires would slow him down to a crawl! With surprising stealth and cunning, Marty set his trap, and waited until he could spring it.

Fables tell of a tortoise who manages to beat a hare in a race.

The hare started out in the lead, but he was so sure of his victory that he took a nap as he neared the finish line, and slept while the tortoise slowly but surely took the gold. Of course, in reality, the hare was probably eaten by a pack of wolves, and

that's why the tortoise won the race, because, after all, nature is cruel, but it doesn't lessen the moral of the story: slow and steady (and a really hard, fang-proof shell) wins the race.

This was a lesson Marty always took to heart. He was always last. He was always behind—but in the end Marty always reached his goal—and he had a tough enough shell to ignore the bites and pecks of others who would much rather see him fail.

Marty waited with uncommon patience until July Fourth, when at 8:40 in the evening, he heard a familiar tune piercing the twilight. He wasted no time—he started his stopwatch and ran into the street.

The streets were deserted, as everyone had gone down to the lake to watch the fireworks that would be starting at any moment. It would be perfect! There was no one to get in Marty's way!

Instead of following the music, as he usually did, he ran across the street, through two backyards, until he came out onto another street. His neighborhood was like a maze—streets that wound back and forth. It was easy to get lost if you didn't know where you were going. There were only two entrances into Marty's subdivision. A vehicle moving at the breakneck speed of sixty miles per hour could wind through the streets from one entrance to another in exactly one minute and forty-five seconds.

By cutting through backyards, he got to the first entrance in fifty seconds. Sitting there, on the sloped street, was his sister's car. His sister had recently gotten her license, and was forced,

in spite of the utter embarrassment of it, to drive their mother's old Buick station wagon. Marty had promised her his dessert for three weeks if she would just park her car in this exact spot.

Now he pulled open the door, put the car in neutral, and moved away from it. It began to roll backward, where it hit a plastic trash bin resting in the gutter across the street. Marty had positioned that trash bin there, and filled it with bricks, so it would stop the rolling car. It did the job. Now the station wagon was blocking all traffic in and out of the neighborhood.

As for the Creamy-Cold truck, it had come in from the other entrance. It would try to get out this way in exactly twenty-five seconds. When it couldn't, it would have to turn around to go out the way it came. Even as he ran from the station wagon, he could hear the truck drawing nearer. But he didn't wait for it. Not here.

He took off again, stumbled over a picket fence, then crossed through more backyards, until he emerged on the other end of the subdivision. By now the ice-cream truck had tried to escape, but the station wagon would have blocked its path. It would be heading this way now. In fact, he could hear the music growing louder.

He pulled out the spike strip, which he had hidden under a hedge, and rolled it out so that it spanned the entire width of the street.

His timing was perfect, because ten seconds later, he saw with his own eyes, for the first time in his life, the Creamy-

Cold truck! It had screeched around a corner and was heading straight for him. CATCH ME IF YOU DARE, the sign had said. Now the truck would be at his mercy!

Marty stepped out of the way as it came crashing past, bringing an icy wind in its wake, then it hit the spike strip. *Boom! Boom!* All four tires blew, the spike strip flew from the street, snagging in a hedge, and the truck lost control. It spun a full three-sixty before hitting a streetlamp so hard, it blew out its light.

And there it sat with four flat tires. It was pure white, with a shiny silver grille. Its front windows were dark, so he couldn't see in. The music it always played had fallen silent, and all Marty could hear was the engine in a menacing idle.

Marty slowly approached it, ready to relish his victory. The solid steel gate of the service window was down, but as he drew near, it slowly began to rise, and fog spilled out; the icy breath of the mechanical beast. Then, inside, someone began to sing in deep, gravelly tones.

"*All around the mulberry bush . . . the monkey chased the weasel. The monkey thought 'twas all in fun . . . Pop! Goes the weasel. . . .*"

In the darkness of the truck, a figure came forward to the service window. A man. He was entirely bald, but had a bushy brown beard covered in frost. He wore a white-and-pink polka-dot outfit. The official uniform of the Creamy-Cold man. "Well, well, well," he said. "A customer!"

"I caught you fair and square. I want my ice cream."

The man leaned on the window's little silver ledge. "It'll cost you," he said.

Marty pulled out a dollar from his pocket and looked at the pictures of ice-cream choices. "I want a Cosmic Raspberry Swirl Bar. Now!"

The man reached his hand toward the dollar, but he didn't take it just yet. He hesitated, then said, "Are you offering me this money in exchange for my ice cream?"

"Of course I am."

The man smiled, his lips stretching so thin, they disappeared between the hair of his mustache and beard. "Well then. The bargain is made." He took the dollar, then turned around, reached into his freezer, and produced an ice-cream bar. He held it out to Marty. "One Cosmic Raspberry Swirl Bar."

Marty grabbed the bar, ripped off the paper, and took a bite.

It was, just as he suspected, the most marvelous, the most creamy, the most flavorful ice cream he had ever tasted. The sensation was so overwhelming it took over all his senses. Bite by bite, he devoured the bar, and when it was done, he licked the stick clean. Only after the last bit of ice cream had dissolved on his tongue did he notice that he wasn't standing where he had been standing before. He was still looking at the ice-cream man, but now Marty was standing *inside* the truck, and the ice-cream man was standing in the street. The man was smiling even wider than before.

"Wait a second," said Marty. "How'd I get in here?"

"The bargain has been made. Enjoy your ice cream." He bowed deeply to Marty, but it was more a mocking gesture than a respectful one, and when he rose from his bow, Marty

realized that the man wasn't wearing the uniform anymore. He was wearing clothes that were so small on him, they were popping at the seams. A red shirt, white pants, with a red baseball cap covering his bald head. It looked like a Little League uniform.

"It took thirty-nine years for someone to catch me. Now I'm finally free." Then he began to back away.

"Hey, ice-cream man, wait! You get back here! I demand to know what's going on!"

"Oh, I'm not the ice-cream man," he said, and pointed a long-nailed finger at Marty. "You are."

And sure enough, when Marty looked down, he saw that he was wearing a white uniform with pink polka dots.

"As for me, my name is James," said the man in the Little League outfit. "But my friends call me Jim-Jim." Then he turned and ran away.

Marty's whole body suddenly felt as cold as the ice cream he had just devoured. He tried to climb out of the service window, but the steel gate came crashing down and sealed the window shut. He went to the driver's door, but there was no handle to open it.

Then he felt a strange rising sensation. *It's the wheels!* Marty thought. *The wheels are healing themselves, and filling with air!*

In his fear, Marty found himself hyperventilating and getting dizzy, so he slowed his breathing down, closed his eyes, and tried to face the reality of his situation. *Fact:* he had made a bargain with Jim-Jim Jeffries for the ice cream in this truck. *Fact:* Jim-Jim had been trapped in this freezing place

for thirty-nine years. *Fact*: Marty wasn't going anywhere.

But that wasn't exactly true, was it? Yes, he was trapped in a cursed truck, but that didn't mean he couldn't *go* anywhere. The truth was, he could go everywhere. . .

. . . because even a cursed truck needs a driver.

When Marty opened his eyes again, he felt much calmer. Calm enough to reach into the freezer and pull himself out another ice-cream bar. That freezer was full of them. In fact, it seemed bottomless. Then he sat in the driver's seat, put his hands on the steering wheel, and stepped on the accelerator, feeling the engine rev. He didn't know how to drive, but that hadn't stopped Jim-Jim, had it?

With frost forming in his hair, he grabbed the stick shift, threw the truck into gear, and peeled out. As he did, he heard the music begin to play, blasting out of the speaker on his roof.

"All around the mulberry bush . . . the monkey chased the weasel . . ."

There were neighborhoods to visit. Hundreds of them. And there were thousands of kids to roust out of the warmth of their homes, all clutching dollar bills and spare change, running through the streets in search of an ice-cream man that they'd never catch.

Just the thought of it made Marty floor the accelerator, and he let loose a wild cackling laugh . . . because for the first time in his life, Marty Zybeck was fast!

WHO DO WE APPRECIATE?

This is one of my newest stories. My sons, and now my daughters, play soccer, and quite often I ref the games. I don't want to give away what happens in this story, but let's just say that I think we once played against the Red team.

WHO DO WE APPRECIATE?

Fair. It's a word I truly know. It's a word I understand inside and out. Fairness is the reason why I get the job. It's the reason why *they* pick me. Who are they? Well, I'll let you figure that out for yourself.

It starts on a Saturday morning. My mother figures out a way to unlock my door, as she always does, and manages to get in, pushing away the various obstacles I've put in front of the door to keep her out. The obstacles are there because every Saturday morning I hold out a thread of hope that maybe this time she'll give up, and let me sleep. Unfortunately my mother, like me, is not the surrendering type.

"Danielle, there was a call on the machine. They need you for an early game today."

I groan and put a pillow over my head. "I'm sick."

She takes the pillow away. "No, you're not."

"I've got the flu."

"No, you don't."

"But what if I do?"

She sighs. "If you're really sick, I won't make you go." She pauses to make it clear she wants the truth. I hate the Truth-Pause. "Are you sick, or aren't you?"

It annoys me that I can't lie to her when she gives me the Truth-Pause. I'm just not the lying type, as much as I'd like to be sometimes.

Instead of answering her, I sit up in bed. "So how early is the game?"

"Seven o'clock."

"*What?* I didn't even know there were league games at seven!"

"Apparently there are, and they need a referee. They need *you*."

I had thought I was going to get out of it this week. There were no calls last night. No calls this morning, and yet sure enough, there's a message on the machine, like it just magically appeared there. This should be my first hint that something's a little bit off, but I'm still not awake enough to catch it.

It was just last month that I got certified as a junior soccer referee. It's not entirely my fault. Frankly, I blame my little brother, Cody. Six weeks ago, he joined up to play in the seven-and-under peewee league. I don't know what possessed him to do it, and I don't know what possessed me to volunteer. I'm not the volunteering type, but I just happened to be there when the coach asked for refs, and I saw my hand go up. Totally bizarre. Then two weeks later, my brother quits the team, and I'm stuck. Now they call me every week, like clockwork, to ref other kids' games—and my parents won't let me quit.

"You have to learn to follow through on your commitments," they tell me.

"Yeah, well, what about Cody?"

"He's only seven."

As if that's an excuse. He quit the team, but do they care that I'm stuck reffing? No. Double standards run rampant in my family, especially when it comes to Cody. See, Cody was a preemie. He was so close to dying when he was born, I think it left my parents in some sort of permanent post-traumatic shock—and they still treat him like he could keel over at any minute. They were terrified when he asked to play soccer—it freaked me out, too, because Cody's about the most non-athletic wimp in the great history of nonathletic wimps. Even during his two weeks on the soccer team, he would run away whenever the ball came within ten feet of him. It was no great surprise that he quit. And so, as his personal purgatory, I demand under threat of death, or worse, that he come with me to every single game I'm forced to ref.

I should mention here, that in a way, refereeing has always kind of been in my nature, but until now it was never official. Any time there's a problem at school between two kids, I always seem to be the one who steps between them to resolve it. Whenever I'm working on some group project, and no one can make a decision, I'm the one who can, and the others always seem to accept it. "You're a natural referee," my parents had told me when I signed up to do this. "You were born for it." I had laughed at the time.

I quickly shower, dress in my ref uniform, then go into Cody's room and roust him out of bed. I do this by grabbing his mattress, and flipping it, with him still on it. I've gotten very good at it. Sometimes I can launch him halfway across the room.

"Daniellllllllle," he whines.

"Shut up and get dressed, I've got a game to ref."

He complains like the world is coming to an end, but he gets his clothes on. He knows he can't worm his way out of it.

We leave on our bikes for Arroyo Vista Park, where today's game will be played. I'm feeling a bit less cranky now. I'm actually beginning to look forward to it. I don't mind reffing, really. There's a certain satisfaction to being the ultimate authority, and knowing that you can handle the responsibility. I'm good at it. I'm decisive and observant. I make the right calls, and people respect this, even when the call is against them.

As for the kids, I don't mind them. They're not a problem—they're just playing the game. It's the parents who sometimes get nuts. They think that just because I'm fourteen, they can intimidate me into making calls favoring their team. Well, I don't intimidate easily.

Today, however, when I arrive at the field, there are no parents on the sidelines. Not a one. I check my watch: 6:50. Both teams are already here, practicing on their respective half of the field, but their parents aren't watching.

"That's weird," says Cody.

"Not really," I tell him. "A game this early? The parents all probably dropped their kids off and went back to bed. I don't blame them. I'd do the same if I could," and I throw him an accusing gaze, to remind him whose fault it is that we're here at this unholy hour of the morning.

I stride out onto the field to check it for safety issues—soak spots, sprinkler heads, and dangerous divots. The field is okay, except for the fact that toward one goal, the grass is turning

yellow. True, it's the fall, but around here grass stays green year-round. Next I introduce myself to the coaches. I recognize one of them. His name is Mr. Apfeldt. He was my second-grade teacher. I haven't seen him for years. He's a pretty well-liked teacher—never too hard on kids. Everyone always said the hardest thing about him was spelling his last name. I hear they even named the new elementary school gym after him.

"Hi, Mr. A," I say.

"Danielle Walker!" he says, with a grin, recognizing me immediately. "Look at you!"

I get right to business, not caring to hear all the small talk about how I've grown, and blossomed into a young woman, and all that garbage. I call over the other coach. He's a guy with an impressive beer belly, if such a thing can be called impressive. He has a towel around his neck that he uses to blot his forehead. He's sweating even though the morning is chilly.

I pull out the official scorecard. "I'll need to know your team names," I say.

The two men look at each other. "Uh . . . Our team doesn't exactly have a name," says Mr. A.

"Neither does ours," says the other coach.

This isn't unusual. Typically, the coaches have the kids pick their own team name, and sometimes it takes a while to get everyone to agree. True, it's a bit late in the season to still be undecided on team names, but hey—that's not my problem. I look at the two teams. The sweaty coach's team has red uniforms, and Mr. Apfeldt's team is in blue. "All right, then," I

tell them, and scribble on my scorecard. "The Reds and the Blues."

"Fair enough," says Mr. A.

"Fair is my middle name," I say. Actually it's Claire, but that's close enough. I notice that there's something funny about Mr. A. Something about the expression on his face. He's preoccupied. It's like the look my dad gets when some deal at work is about to go bad. It's the look my mom gets when Cody starts to cough. Come to think of it, the other coach has a similar look about him. I shrug it off. Adults' minds are always stuck in places we kids probably don't want to know about.

"Who's the home team?" I ask. Usually the home team gets to call the coin toss.

"Neither," says Mr. A.

Now I'm getting annoyed. "You mean this is neither team's home field? Neither one of you played here on other weeks?"

"Actually," says Mr. A, "this is the first game for both teams."

Great. I get stuck with late entries to the league who don't even know who's supposed to be the home team. I expected better from Mr. A.

I hadn't taken a good look at the players until now. Right away I can sense there's something strange about them. There's something about their expressions that doesn't sit right with me. See, seven-year-olds—they tend to have this vague unfocused look about them. They're easily distracted and always involved in mildly annoying activities, like kicking up dirt clods with their cleats, or running in circles when they're supposed to be standing still. These kids aren't doing those things. They're

all focused on me, waiting for the game to start. There's this intensity to them that I can almost feel. It makes me uncomfortable. I look to the sidelines. Still no parents. No one's there but Cody, who is, like I said, kicking up dirt clods, like a normal seven-year-old.

"What about assistant refs?" I ask the coaches. "I usually ask parents to act as linesmen."

"We're fresh out of parents today," Mr. Apfeldt says, offering me an apologetic smile. "You're on your own."

Now I finally begin to put things together. Late entries to the league. Kids without parents. I bring my voice down so the kids on the field can't hear me. "Are these kids from like . . . an orphanage or something?"

"Something like that," says Mr. A. "Just do your best. I'm sure you'll do fine without linesmen."

I nod to both coaches in understanding, then Mr. A says to me quietly, "A word to the wise . . . make this the best reffing job you've ever done." There's that slim, preoccupied grin again from him. I tell him that sure, I will, and that I always ref my best, which is true. Then I hurry to the other side of the field, to grab my stopwatch from Cody.

"So, do you know any of the kids on these teams?" I ask him.

"No."

"Not in any classes with them?"

"No."

"Don't recognize them from Cub Scouts or something?"

"No."

"A lot of help *you* are."

"Can I go home now?"

Now it was my turn to say "No."

I turn to go back to the midfield line for the coin toss, but before I do, Cody stops me. "Danielle," he says. "Be careful, okay?"

It's such a weird thing for him to say, I have to laugh. "Of what?"

"I don't know . . . just . . ." He struggles, trying to put whatever he's feeling into words, then lets his shoulders sag. "Nothing. Forget it."

"Nutcase," I tell him, and hurry out to the center circle, checking to make sure all the players' shin guards are on and shoes are tied. Then I call for the team captains for the coin toss. The Red captain is this scrawny towheaded kid, with hair so fine and blond it looks like peach fuzz on his head. His eyes are blue, but a weird shade. Like glacier ice. It's unsettling, so I don't look in his eyes again. He also smells funny—like maybe he had a hard-boiled egg for breakfast, and it got smeared all over his face. The Blue team captain has curly brown hair, a little too long in the back, so it falls over his neck in a goofy little mullet. I like his eyes better. They're light brown. Sure, they're as intense as the other kid's eyes, but somehow softer. I like him in spite of the mullet.

I pull my special half-dollar out of my pocket and flip it. "Call it," I say. Forgetting that I didn't say specifically who should call it.

Both the Red captain and the Blue captain call "Heads." I try to catch the coin in midair—so the toss gets voided before

it can become an issue—but I miss, and the coin hits the turf. It shows heads.

"I win the toss!" announces the Red captain.

"No, I win it," says the Blue.

"I called heads!"

"So did I."

"Well, I said it first!"

"Did not!"

"Did, too!"

Well at least they're finally starting to act like seven-year-olds. I glance over at the coaches, waiting on the sidelines for the game to begin. Since I like Mr. A better than the other guy, I make a decision. "Blue calls it."

"Why?" demands the Red captain.

"Because I said so." You can do things like that when you're a ref. It's almost like being a parent.

"No fair!"

Then his coach yells from the sidelines: "Alastor, just get it over with, okay?" I smirk. Fancy name for an obnoxious kid.

He scowls at his coach, then turns to me crossing his arms. "Fine."

I flip the coin. The Blue captain calls heads again. It comes up tails.

"Ha!" says the Red captain.

"Watch it, '*Alice.*' I call penalties for bad sportsmanship."

"That's Alastor," he snaps.

I can't wait until I call his first penalty.

From the moment the game begins, I know this is no ordinary game. First of all, these kids don't play like seven-year-olds. Usually the seven-and-under games are all about beehive ball: a whole mess of kids buzzing around with the ball in the middle, and the kids generally kicking one another more often than getting a foot on the ball.

These kids are different. They play like pros—I've never seen anything like it. They have awesome kicks, they head the ball with full force, and they don't fall down crying. They put such power behind the ball, I have to hit the ground a few times to keep from having my head taken off. I'm actually getting winded running my diagonal across the field, which never happens in these games.

As they play, I begin to notice a definite difference in style between the two teams. The Red team is good. That is to say, each player is phenomenal—but each player is also a ball-hog. There's no passing, everyone wants to be a star, and they fight one another for the ball. More than once I call a penalty on Red players for pushing—and usually it's their own teammates who they push.

As for the Blues, they're not quite as skilled as the Reds individually. None of them are standout players, but they make up for it with expert teamwork. It's a treat to watch the way they pass and dribble, moving the ball downfield. The whole is greater than the sum of the parts. The problem is, no matter how good their teamwork, there's always some Red ball-hog

who steals it away, and brings it back toward the Blue goal.

As I watch them play, I find myself doing something that a ref is never supposed to do. I find myself rooting for one team over the other.

"Danielle, I want to go home."

"So go," I tell Cody. But for once I want him to stay. Not to punish him, but because I've started to feel so alone out there on the field, having him there gives me a little bit of comfort. Of course I won't tell him that. It's the end of the first quarter. There's no score—but there will be soon. The Red team seems to keep getting angrier, and the angrier they get, the better they play. It's only a matter of time before they start scoring.

"I want you to go, too," he says. "I want us both to go. Tell them you can't stay. Call off the game. Let's just go!"

"You know I can't do that!"

Then he gets quiet. "There's something . . . wrong with them. Can't you feel it?"

"I don't feel a thing," I tell him, but that's a lie. The feeling is as heavy as the clouds that have begun gathering in the sky. It was a clear day when the game began, but now there are huge cumulus clouds hanging overhead, looking as heavy as anvils. "Let's just get through this," I tell him. "It's just one game."

"Look at the grass!" he says.

"Huh?"

"Just look at it, and *then* tell me you don't want to get out of here!"

I look at him like he's crazy—an expression that I've got pretty well mastered when it comes to Cody—then I blow the whistle and call the teams back for the second quarter.

As I jog out onto the field, I can't help but notice the grass, because now the thought of it is stuck in my head, thanks to Cody. I wish I hadn't looked . . . because now I can see that all the yellow patches on the field are in the shape of small, seven-year-old footprints.

Six minutes into the second quarter, a Red player with hair almost as red as his shirt trips a Blue player and sends him flying five feet, at the exact moment Alastor kicks the ball into the goal. The Reds start cheering. Technically I saw the trip and the goal at the same time. Arguably the goal could count. It's completely in my discretion whether or not to call it back—and if it were any other game, I'd warn the tripper, and give the team their goal. But this isn't any other game. I blow my whistle.

"Tripping!" I call. "No goal!"

All the Reds instantly cry out in disbelief, throwing their hands up into the air and looking at me with their terrible eyes. Up above I hear distant thunder volleying in the clouds. On the sidelines I can see Cody shaking his head at me, silently begging me to give them their goal, but I'm not a wimp like him. I stand by my calls.

The kid with red hair storms up to me. "I didn't trip him!" he shouts. "It was an accident!"

"No goal!" I say again.

"Troian!" the coach shouts. "Don't talk back to the ref!"

Troian storms off, but Alastor is there to take up where he left off.

"You're cheating," he says. "Just like you cheated on that math test."

My head nearly spins around at that. "What?"

Alastor shrugs. "I didn't say nuthin."

"You'd better watch yourself!" I tell him—and he sticks his tongue out at me. That's all he needs to do. I reach into my pocket and pull out the yellow card and show it to him—that's the official first warning. Next comes the red card, and he's thrown out of the game. No one ever really uses the yellow or red cards for kids this young, but somehow I feel it's appropriate today.

On the sidelines his coach throws up his hands. "You see what you did, Alastor? You see?"

But Alastor just smirks, like it was worth it. Like he can feel me squirming. He marches off, and as he does, I notice his feet leave yellow footprints in the grass. It's not just him, it's the entire Red team.

I take a deep breath that ends with a shiver, and bring the ball out to where Alastor had shot it from.

There's no possible way that he could have known about the math test. And it was only one answer—and I did it by accident—I didn't even mean to see Randy Goldman's answer sheet, but I *did* see the answer to a question I couldn't answer myself. And I *did* use that answer. It had been bugging me all week, because, like I said, I'm all about being fair, and doing the right thing. This rotten little kid could not have known.

It was just coincidence. He was just grasping at straws to rattle me.

What happens next is something you never see in competitive sports—not even in little-kid soccer. The play resumes, but the Blue players don't play. They just stand there like pegs in a pinball machine. The Reds dribble around them, one of them shoots, and scores on a goalie who doesn't even move to stop the ball. The Reds cheer again. I expect Mr. A to get on his team's case for just allowing the goal, but he doesn't. With no choice, I call the goal good, and retrieve the ball to put back on the centerline.

As I do, the Blue captain—the one with the brown curls—comes up to me and says quietly, "We gave them back the goal you took away. Play fair, okay?"

"I am playing fair."

He touches my arm gently, and gives me the Truth-Pause, like my mother does. "This time play fair for real."

I feel all squirmy again, like I did after speaking to Alastor—but with this kid it's different. It's not a bad feeling. Suddenly it's like I feel okay about the math test. Like it only happened to remind me how important it is for me not to cheat. Like it only happened to prepare me for today. Then he lets go of my arm, and the feeling goes away.

"Uri, don't talk to the ref, just play the game," calls Mr. A from the sidelines.

Uri, I think. There's something about the names of the Blue players that sticks with me, like I've heard them before. Uri, Mikey, Gabe, Raffi, Remi, Ari, and the kid they just call

"Zap." For the life of me, though, I can't figure out where I've heard those names. As Uri runs off to the centerline, I notice that his feet don't turn the ground yellow. If anything, his footsteps make the grass more green.

I start the game again, and follow Uri's recommendation. I play the fairest that I possibly can. Even though the Red team scores two more goals. Even though the clouds have gotten so dark up above, it looks as if night is starting to fall at 7:30 in the morning.

Three to zero at halftime. For all their teamwork, the Blues can't punch a single hole in the Red defense. As the kids hurry off to their coaches for midgame snacks and water, I silently swear that this is the last game I'm ever going to ref.

Cody sits alone on the sidelines, halfway down the field from the Blue team. "Still feel like leaving?"

He nods. "I feel like it," he says. "But I don't want to anymore."

This is odd for him. Usually when he wants something he nags until he gets it. I expected him to spend halftime begging me to leave. "Why not, the game's too exciting?"

"The game's too important," he says. "There's gotta be a spectator."

"Important, how?" I ask.

He shrugs. "Don't know."

I want to deny what he's saying, but I can't. Something's going on here that is beyond the workings of a soccer game—

and although Cody says he needs to be a spectator, I sense there are already spectators—tons of them, watching from places we can't see. The thought makes me feel even colder, so I change the subject. "C'mere," I say to him. "I want to introduce you to somebody." I haul him over to Mr. A.

"Mr. A, this is my brother, Cody. Cody, this is Mr. Apfeldt. I had him for second grade."

Cody stares at him like a deer in the headlights of a semi. Cody's always been uncomfortable with teachers. Mr. A smiles, and holds out his hand to shake.

"Hi, Cody. I think I was supposed to have you in my class this year. But I guess that didn't work out."

Cody looks at Mr. A's hand. I nudge him, and he shakes it.

"Nice to meet you, sir."

Mr. A goes off to his team, and Cody looks at his hand—the one that shook Mr. A's—like it might be radioactive or something.

"What's wrong with you?"

"Nothing," he says. "So that's Mr. Apfeldt?"

"Didn't I just tell you that?"

"Just wanted to make sure I heard you right."

I'm about to go onto the field and start the second half when Cody stops me.

"Danielle, there's something you oughta know."

"What?"

"They named the gym after Mr. Apfeldt."

"Yeah, I heard."

Then Cody takes a deep breath, looks around to make sure

no one else is close enough to hear, and says, "They named it after him because he died over the summer."

I open my mouth to say something back to him, but find I have nothing to say.

"It was a car accident," Cody says. "I had a substitute the first week of school until they found a new teacher."

I want to tell him that he must have gotten it wrong. He always gets stories wrong. This time, though, I think he's telling the truth. I can't look him in the face. Instead I look up at the sky. Now I can see lightning sparking deep within those mountainous clouds. "Maybe ..." I say, "maybe it'll rain. Maybe I'll have to call the game, and this can all be over."

Cody shakes his head. "The storm won't start until the game ends."

I know he's right about that, too. I put my arm around him and give him a kiss on the cheek. I don't think I've kissed him since he was a baby.

With the wind blowing, and the electric smell of ozone in the air, I stride out and blow my whistle calling the teams back onto the field.

———

I ref my heart out that third quarter. I try to pretend it's just any old game. The Blues score. The Reds are winning three to one.

"Way to go!" screams Mr. Apfeldt to his team. "Way to go!"

I have to hold back my cheers, but Cody doesn't—he shouts from the sidelines, like a one-man cheering squad. The team give one another high fives, but they're quiet about it. They know they're not home yet. It will take two more goals to tie, three to win.

With the wind roaring as if there's a tornado on the next street, it's hard to hear my whistle when I end the third quarter. As the teams take their breaks, I go over to Mr. A. I stand there for a moment, as he talks to the team, giving out new positions. Then, when he's done, I have to say something. I have to know.

"What's going on here, Mr. A.?" I ask. "How can you be here . . . and who are these kids?"

He thinks about his answer for a long time. "I'm here because I'm here," he says. "And as for the teams, they're not kids. Or maybe they've always been kids, I don't know. All I know is that once in a very, very long while they have a contest. A battle. And who wins and who loses . . . well . . . that decides . . ."

"Decides what?"

"Decides . . . everything."

I look to the two teams out on the field waiting for me to start the final quarter. I've always sensed there were opposing forces in the world. Light and darkness, order and chaos, good and evil—call them what you want, but it doesn't change the fact of it. How and why these beings chose this battleground I don't know, but I can no longer deny the truth. The fate of the world is about to be decided by a suburban peewee soccer game. And I am the judge.

"What happens if the Red team wins?" I ask Mr. Apfeldt.

He's not too comfortable with the question. "I'm not exactly sure," he says. "They've never won before. But maybe it's best if we don't think too much about it now."

Easy for him to say; he's already dead.

I return to the field to do the job I was given. The job I was chosen for. I blow the whistle that may just begin the end of the world.

Red gets possession. Troian takes it downfield, but it's stolen by his teammate Loki, who then gets it stolen by another teammate, Seth—and finally as it gets close to the goal, Alastor takes it away, and drives toward the goal. Mikey defends expertly, and takes it, passing it to Gabe, who passes it to the twins, Remi and Raffi, who take it down toward the Red goal. But now the Red defensive players are arguing. Those Reds just can't get along, and that could be their undoing. They're so involved in battling one another that Remi dribbles the ball right past them and scores.

The Blues are only down by one now. Four minutes left. The Reds are furious. They yell at one another, they yell at the coach. I show the yellow card to two more kids for poor sportsmanship, but no one gets the red card. It's like they know exactly how far they can go before being ejected from the game. That's the nature of evil, I guess—to always be at the brink of being caught—almost, but not quite being exposed for what it really is.

One more minute of play. I'm shivering. The leaves that have been hissing in the roaring wind are finally being torn from their branches and disappearing into the blackening sky.

The field is yellow everywhere now, and both coaches look scared—not just Mr. Apfeldt, but the Red coach, too—as if he never really wanted his own team to win.

And then something happens. Something that changes everything.

The ball is moving toward the Red goal again. It looks as if Blue will score—Uri comes in for the shot, but Alastor is there to block it. He gets to the ball first, they collide, and Uri loses his balance, flying into the hardwood frame of the goal. The goal shudders, Uri yells out in pain and hits the ground. I blow the whistle and race to him.

"Take a knee!" I call out to the players. Everyone, even the Reds, go down on one knee as I go to examine the injury.

It's bad. Really bad. Uri's arm is broken—twisted at a horrible angle—but as I look away from it, I see through the corner of my eye, not an arm, but feathers. White feathers on a wing bent backward over itself. I quickly look at it again, but it's just an arm.

Uri moans in pain. Coach Apfeldt is there in an instant, assessing the damage. He tries to move Uri's "arm," but Uri yells the second he touches it.

Then from behind me I hear a cold, calculated voice. "Looks like the game's over." Standing over me, Alastor looks much taller than his four feet. From this angle, I can see two little bumps beneath his hairline that look like the slightest hint of horns.

"It's not over yet," I tell him. "There's still three minutes to play."

Alastor puts his hands on his hips, all cocky and gloating. "Rules say seven players on a team. Now they got six."

"So what—they can play with less than the regulation number."

Then he smiles. "Not if we call for a forfeit."

"But . . . but no one ever does that!"

"So what? It's the rules. We can if we want."

And the thing is, he's right. If they call for a forfeit, I have no choice but to call the game and declare them the winners.

I look down to Uri. "I'm sorry," he says weakly, grimacing in pain. "I'm so sorry . . ."

Coach Apfeldt looks at me desperately, but what can I do? I have to ref. I have to follow the rules.

Alastor turns to his coach. "Call a forfeit."

Their coach, as big as he is, seems somehow smaller than the kid. "C'mon, Al—let's just finish the game. Six players— you'll beat 'em easy . . ."

"*Call a forfeit!*" Alastor yells, his voice blending with the thunder, his eyes reflecting the lightning still caged within the clouds.

His coach looks to me, tears in his eyes, and says: "I officially request that the Blue team forfeit. They have less than the regulation number of players, and by league rules—"

"I'll do it," says a meek voice behind me. "I'll play for the Blue team."

I turn to see Cody standing behind me.

"I'll take Uri's place," he says.

I'm stunned speechless. I look at the other players. These

aren't just little kids, they are creatures of immense power. I try to imagine what Alastor and Loki and all the others will do to him once he gets on that field. "Cody, you can't."

Although Cody looks scared, he won't back down. "I have to. You were brought here for a reason, Danielle. I think I was, too—and I guess it wasn't to watch from the sidelines."

Alastor scowls at not getting his forfeit—then he looks my brother over, and laughs. He turns to Loki. "This oughta be fun," he says, and raindrops begin to fall. Not enough to call the game, but enough to remind us that the storm is only minutes away. Three minutes, to be exact.

"Cody . . ."

"I know what I'm doing."

I don't feel right about it at all, but then I don't feel right about any of this. Everything feels Wrong with a capital W. But my only choices are to give the game to the Reds or to let Cody play. So I let the game go on. Cody takes his position as left midfielder.

If Cody had been out of his element among other seven-year-olds, he's completely lost on the field now. He can't even turn his head fast enough to keep up with where the ball is. Now the ball comes his way—a powerful line drive. I expect him to treat it like it's a game of dodgeball, but he doesn't. The ball comes flying in his direction, and instead of blocking it with his hands—which would make me have to call a hand ball if it hits him—he lowers his hands and stops the ball with his chest. I can see Cody beginning to double over, the wind knocked out of him, but somehow he stays on his

feet. He passes the ball to Mikey, and Mikey takes it downfield. No goal. It comes back toward Cody again. The Reds are intentionally sending the ball in Cody's direction, because they know he's the weak link. Each time the ball comes to him, he doesn't flinch. Sometimes he gets hit hard by the ball, other times it flies past him. Sometimes he tries to get his foot on it, and can't—but just as often he kicks it accurately and directly downfield, right toward one of the Blue players. Maybe it's my imagination, but he seems to be getting better by the second. Certainly he's nowhere near as good as anyone else on the field, but he's good enough to hold his own.

Alastor kicks the ball downfield, but Cody's there to stop it. He dribbles a little bit, drawing the Red midfielders toward him, then he passes to Gabe, who delivers a power kick over the Red goalie's head. Goal! Tie game! The Blue team doesn't take time to celebrate—it's right back to the line. Not even Cody cheers. He's focused. The Reds are furious at one another, blaming one another for the goal. Quickly I put the ball down, blow the whistle, and play resumes. One minute. The rain is still just a drizzle, but lightning has begun to flash everywhere. The thunder is so loud it feels like it could tear the earth apart. Maybe it will. But not yet. Not yet!

Thirty seconds. Alastor drives toward the goal at full force, but Cody is in his way. He doesn't care, he barrels through Cody, sending him flying, just as he sent Uri flying—but Cody, bruised and shaken, picks himself up. By simply standing in the way, Cody has stopped Alastor's drive. Mikey gets the ball and takes it toward the Red goal. Cody races along with him, out of breath but keeping up. Mikey shoots. But it's stopped by a Red defender, who boots it with incredible force. Right at Cody.

"I've got it!" Cody shouts. It's coming right at his head. He's going to head the ball—a ball that's flying toward him like a black-and-white-checkered bullet!

He angles his head to receive it, but his judgment is off. It doesn't hit the top of his head, or his forehead—it nails him in the face, bouncing right off his nose.

"AAAHH!" he screams.

This is it, I think. This is where he crumbles, and the Red team drives past him to score the goal and win.

But then I follow the path of the ball. It had bounced right off Cody's face . . . and toward the goal! The goalie dives for it, but he wasn't expecting it, and he's an instant too late. The ball bounces past him for a goal! I can't believe it!

Lightning crashes again, and I look at my stopwatch. Six seconds, five, four—the Red team's scrambling to get the ball to the centerline so they can kick off. Three . . . two . . . one!

I put the whistle to my mouth and blow those three wonderful long blasts signaling the end of the game.

Now—for the first time—the Blue team begins to cheer. They race to Cody, lifting him up. He's almost weightless in their arms.

"We knew you could do it, Cody!" his teammates say. "We all knew it."

Only now do I notice the blood. There's blood all over my brother's face. "Cody, are you all right?"

He looks at me with a smile still as wide as his whole face, wondering what I'm talking about. Then he touches his nose, finally seeing the blood for himself. "It's just a bloody nose," he says.

"But what if it's broken?"

"So it'll heal."

This from a kid who always screams at the prospect of Bactine and a Band-Aid.

Mr. Apfeldt comes over with the winning ball, and looks at it. He rubs his finger over a spot on the ball. There's a small red smudge on the ball, already turning brown: the spot where it connected with Cody's nose.

"Looks like it took a blood sacrifice to win the game," says Mr. A. "How about that!"

He hands the ball to Cody, telling him he can keep it. A souvenir for saving the world.

That's when I realize that Uri is with them, jumping up and down, and holding Cody high, using the same arm that was broken . . . and I realize that it was never broken at all.

When the excitement settles a bit, I ask Uri why he did it. "With the game so close, why did you pretend to be hurt, and let my brother play?"

Uri just shrugs. "He needed to win more than I did."

"But . . . how did you know he *would* win?"

"I didn't," said Uri. "I guess you could say it was an act of faith."

Remi razzes him when he says it, but doesn't contradict him.

Across the field, the Reds grumble, curse and blame, but their blustering means nothing now. Even the lightning and thunder have stopped.

"Look at them," says Mr. Apfeldt. "How could a team like that ever expect to win?" Then he gathers his own team together into a huddle. "Okay, guys. You know what to do."

The Blues—Cody included—put their hands in the center, and they chant *"Two, four, six, eight, who do we appreciate? Reds! Reds! Yaaaaaay!"*

But the Reds are gone. They've vanished along with their coach. They didn't even have the courtesy to echo back with the traditional "one, three, five, nine," rhyme.

Mr. A and his players come over to say good-bye. Some shake my hand, others are too cool for that—they just punch knuckles with me and Cody. Then Gabe says, "Hey, could I try out your whistle?"

I take it off my neck and hand it to him. He takes a deep breath and blows. It begins as a shrill sound, but mellows until it sounds like a horn. Nothing so refined as a trumpet or anything. Something more earthy, like he's blowing into a ram's horn—and as he blows, the clouds above boil away into nothing. Bright sunlight begins to fill the field, and by the time his lungs have forced his last bit of wind through the whistle, the grass that had gone completely yellow is green again.

"Yeah, that's a good one," he says, handing it back to me. "You should hold on to it."

"I think I will," I tell him. But I don't think I'll use it for just any old game—because after Gabriel the archangel has blown

into your whistle, it's probably best to save it for *really* special occasions.

Cody is practically dancing, his feet barely touching the ground. I give him my sleeve to wipe his bloody nose. "Does it hurt?" I ask

"It's a good hurt," he answers.

When I turn to Mr. Apfeldt and his team, they're gone. Uriel, Michael, Gabriel, Raphael, Remiel, and the rest have all vanished, just as the Red team had. There's another coach walking onto the field now, and I can see a new set of kids arriving. Kids with parents. "Are you our ref?" the coach asks.

"Nah, I just reffed a game. I'm sure yours'll be along in a minute." And then I add, "I'm surprised people are showing up—what with the lightning and all."

He looks at me as if he hasn't heard me right. "What lightning?"

I stammer for a moment, and realize that perhaps I should finally take Mr. A's advice, and not think too much about it. "Never mind," I say. "Have a good game."

Cody and I head to our bikes. His bleeding has stopped, but his nose is swollen and turning purple. "So what should we tell Mom and Dad about it?" he asks.

I think about the answer, and how I can never lie to my parents. "Tell them the truth," I answer. "Tell them the team needed an extra player, and you made the winning goal with your face."

He laughs at that, and so do I. Sometimes the truth is exactly what parents need to hear.

SOUL SURVIVOR

I have always been intrigued by ghost stories. I very rarely write them, though, because I always find one ghost story to be much like another. It was the character's voice in this story that got me to want to write it. When I'm experimenting with a new style, and new storytelling voice, I usually experiment by writing a short story.

The goal here, as was the goal in my novel *Everlost*, was to come up with a ghost story that was unique, and didn't feel like "just another ghost story."

This story helped me to explore the world of ghosts, and laid the early groundwork for *Everlost*.

SOUL SURVIVOR

What I tell you now you can never tell another living soul.

It began as a dream—or what I thought was a dream. I was floating—rising higher and higher. Then, when I looked back, I could see someone lying in bed. It was a boy. Not just any boy—it was my own self, and I was lying in the stillness of sleep.

This was one of those dreams where you know you're dreaming—where you have your whole mind, not just part of it, to think things through and make sense of everything. An out-of-body experience—that's what they call it. And as it turns out, I picked just the wrong time to have one.

The room I was floating in was bright and clear, because dawn had already broken, and light was pouring in through the blinds. Then I heard a noise growing louder. I should have realized something was wrong by the way it sounded. It grated against the silence of the morning, but I was so wrapped up in floating around the room, I didn't notice until it was too late.

There was a mighty roar and a shattering of wood and metal. Then something hot and silver passed through me, and in an instant it was gone.

So was my body.

So was the entire second story of our house.

A moment later, the blast of a great explosion shook the air.

When we had first moved to this house, my parents had asked me if I wanted the bedroom upstairs or downstairs. I had chosen upstairs. Big mistake. With the second floor of the house torn away, I could see my parents below in their roofless bedroom, screaming. They weren't hurt. No, they were terrified—still not knowing what had happened, and not understanding why there was morning sky above them instead of their ceiling fan.

But I knew exactly what had happened. A jumbo jet had taken off half of our house just before slamming into the ground two streets away.

As for my body, well, I'm sure it felt no pain because it was over so quickly. Anyway, I wouldn't know because I wasn't there to feel it. Perhaps if it hadn't happened so quickly, I might have been drawn back into my body to die with it, but that's not what happened.

Now I'm alive, but with no body to live in.

Perhaps that's how ghosts are made.

I remember drifting into school the next day, going up to my friends and screaming into their faces that I was still here. But they couldn't see me or hear me. I also remember hovering among the flowers at my funeral, thinking that being there was the proper and respectable thing to do.

For many weeks after that, I drifted through the rooms of

my uncle's house, where my parents were staying now that our house was destroyed. I stayed there, sitting on the couch and watching TV with them. I sat on an empty chair at the dinner table, day after day, yet they never knew I was there . . . and never would.

Soon my parents' grief was too much for me to bear. There was nothing I could ever do to comfort them. So I left.

You can't imagine what it's like to have lost everything. Losing your house, and your things, and your friends, and your family is all bad enough—but to lose yourself along with it—*that* was beyond imagination. To lose my thick head of hair that I never liked to brush. To lose those fingernails that I still had the urge to bite. To lose the feeling of waking up to the warm sun on your face. To lose the taste of a cold drink, and the feel of a hot shower. To just *be*, with no flesh to contain your mind and soul. It was not a fun way to be.

I drifted to the lonely basement of an old abandoned building, and lay there for weeks, not wanting to go anywhere, not wanting to face a world I could not be part of. I just wanted to stay in that lonely place forever.

Perhaps that's how buildings become haunted.

It was months before I could bring myself to look upon the light of day again, and when I did, it was like coming out of a cocoon. Once I could accept that my old life was gone, I began to realize that I did have some sort of future, and I was ready to explore it.

I began testing my speed. I was just an invisible weightless spirit of the air, but I could will myself to move very fast. I practiced, building my skill of flight the way I had built my swimming speed in the pool—back in the days when I was flesh and bone. It wasn't that different, really, except now I didn't need muscles to make myself move, only thoughts.

Soon I could outrace the fastest birds and fly higher than the highest jets. I could turn on a dime and crash through solid rock as if I were diving through water. These were times I did not miss the heavy weight of my body.

And, wow—were there ever places to explore! I dove through oceans, and actually moved through the belly of a great white shark. I dipped into the mouth of a volcano, racing through its dark stone cap—right into red-hot magma! I plunged deeper still, beyond the earth's mantle to hit its superdense core. It wasn't as easy to move through as water and air, but I did it. I did all these things.

And each time I would slip into one of these great and magical realms, I would play a game with myself.

"I am this mountain," I would say. Then I would expand myself like a cloud of smoke, until I could feel my whole spirit filling up the entire mountain—from the trees at its base to the snow on its peak.

"I am this ocean," I would say. Then I would spread across the surface of the water, stretching myself from continent to continent.

"I am this planet," I would tell myself, stretching out in all

51

directions until I could feel myself hurtling through space, caught in orbit around the sun.

But soon the game lost its joy, for try as I might, I could never stay in the place where I had put myself. I did not want to be a mountain, immense and solitary, moving only when the earth shook. I did not want to be a sea, rolling uneasily toward eternity, a slave of the moon and its tides. I did not want to be the earth, alone and spinning in an impossibly vast universe.

And so I dared to do something I hadn't found the nerve to do before. I began to move within the minds of human beings.

———

Like anything else, it took practice.

When I first slipped inside a human being, all I could see was the blood pumping through thousands of veins and arteries. All I could hear was the thump of a heartbeat. But soon I would settle within someone and begin to pick out a thought or two. And soon after that, I could hear all of that person's thoughts. Then I began to feel things the way that person felt them, and see the world through that person's eyes—without ever letting on that I was there.

It was almost like being human, and this hint of being human again drove me on with a determination I'd never felt before.

After many weeks of secretly dipping into people's minds, I discovered I could not only hear the thoughts of these people but change those thoughts. I could make them turn left instead of right. I could make them have a sudden craving for an ice-cream sundae. Have you ever had a thought that seemed to come flying out of nowhere?

Perhaps someone was passing through you.

I moved daily from person to person, taking bits of knowledge with me as I went, taking memories of lives I'd never lived. I got to dive off cliffs in Mexico, experience the excitement and terror of being born, and I even blasted into space in a rocket, hiding deep within the mind of an astronaut.

This was a game I could have enjoyed forever . . . if I hadn't gotten so good at it. You see, I came way too close to the minds on which I hitchhiked.

———

"Who are you?"

The voice came as a complete surprise to me. I didn't know what to do.

"Who are you?" he demanded. "And why are you in my head?"

I was in the mind of a baseball player. I'd been there for a few weeks, and this was the first time he'd spoken to me.

He was a rookie named Sam "Slam" McKellen—I'm sure you've heard of him. They called him Slam because of the way he blasted balls right out of the stadium at least once a game. I know because I swung the bat with him.

"You'd better answer me," his thoughts demanded.

McKellen was the first one to know I was there. I was thrilled . . . but also terrified.

"My name is Peter," I said, and then I told him about the

plane crash. I explained how I had lost my body, and how I had survived for more than a year on my own. I must have gone on babbling for hours—it was the first time I had someone to talk to.

McKellen listened to all I had to tell him, sitting quietly in a chair. Then, when I was done, he did something amazing. He asked me to stay.

"We have batboys in the dugout to help us out," he told me. "Who says I can't have a batboy on the *inside* as well? Heck, I'm important enough." He began to smile. "Sure," he said, "someone to pick up my stray thoughts that happen to wander off. Someone to remind me when I'm late, or when I forget something important. Sure, stay, kid," he said. "Stay as long as you want."

I don't need to tell you how it changed my death. It's not everyone who gets to live inside a major-league baseball player. I mean, I was with Slam every time he swung that bat, every time he raced around those bases, every time he slid into home. And when he came up to accept his MVP trophy that year—it was *our* hands that held it in the air.

When we went out to eat, sometimes he would let me take over, giving me total control of his body. That way I could be the one feeding us that hot-fudge sundae—and tasting every last bit of it.

At night we would have long conversations about baseball and the nature of the universe—a silent exchange of thoughts from his mind to mine. In fact, we did this so often our thoughts were beginning to get shuffled, and I didn't know which were his thoughts and which were mine. Pretty soon I figured our two sets of thoughts and memories would blend together forever, like two colors of paint. As far as I was concerned, that would be just fine.

But then he offered to do something for me that I never had the nerve to ask him to do, and it changed everything.

"I'm gonna write your parents a letter," he announced. "I'm gonna tell them that you're alive and well and living inside my head."

I should have realized how that letter would have sounded, but I was too thrilled by the offer to think about what might happen. So we wrote the letter together and mailed it. Then, three days later, the world came collapsing down around us like a dam in a flood.

You see, my parents were never much for believing anything they couldn't see with their own eyes. When they got the letter, they called the police. The police called the newspapers, and suddenly the season's star MVP was a nutcase who heard voices.

Sam "Slam" McKellen became the overnight laughingstock of the American League. It's funny how that happens sometimes . . . but it wasn't funny to us.

I tried to get him to shut up, but he insisted on telling it like it is, getting up in front of the microphones and explaining to the world how a kid was renting space in his brain. We even went to see my parents, and although I kept feeding him facts about my past that only I could know, my parents were still convinced McKellen was a madman.

We were sent to doctors. Then we were put in hospitals and filled with so much medication that sometimes it seemed like there was a whole platoon of us in here, not just two.

In the end Slam finally broke.

"Peter, I want you to leave," he told me as we sat alone in the dark, in the big house our baseball contract had bought. Our hair was uncombed and our face had been unshaven for weeks.

"The doctors are right," Slam announced. "You don't exist, and I won't share my mind with someone who does not exist."

I could hardly believe what I was hearing.

"I order you to leave and never come back," he said. "Never look for me. Never talk to me. Never come near my thoughts again." And then he began to cry. "I hate you!" he screamed—not just in our head, but out loud. "I hate you for what you've done to me!"

I could have left then. I could have run away to find someone else who wouldn't mind sharing his life with a poor dispossessed soul like myself. But I realized that I didn't want to leave.

And I didn't want to share anymore, either.

"I'm not leaving," I told him. "*You* are."

That's how the battle began.

A tug-of-war between two minds in one brain is not a pretty sight. On the outside our face turned red, and our eyes went wild. Our legs and arms began convulsing as if we were having an epileptic fit.

On the inside we were screaming—battling each other

with thoughts and fury. His inner words came swinging at me like baseball bats. But I withstood the blows, sending my own angry thoughts back like an iron fist, pounding down on him. Yes, I smashed that thankless baseball player with my ironfisted thoughts again and again, until I could feel myself gaining control. This was my body now. Not his. Not his ever again.

I pounded and pounded on his mind and filled his brain until there was no room for him anymore. But try as I might, I could not push him out. I could only push him *down*. So I pushed him down until the great baseball player was nothing more than a tremor in my right hand.

I had control of everything else . . . but even that wasn't good enough. As long as any part of him was still there, he could come back, and I didn't want that. I had to figure out a way to get rid of him—for good.

That's when I remembered the dolphins.

In all my travels through air, land, and sea, there was only one place I knew I had to stay away from.

The mind of a dolphin.

I came close to the mind of a dolphin once. I had thought I might slip one on for size—but the place is huge! A dolphin's brain is larger than a human's, and its mind is like an endless maze of wordless thought.

When I had first neared a dolphin, I had felt myself being pulled into that mind, as if it were a black hole. I resisted, afraid I would get lost in there—*trapped* in there, wandering forever through a mind too strange to fathom.

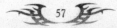

And so I had turned away from the creature before I had been caught in its unknowable depths.

But now I had to find a dolphin again.

———

With the baseball player's spirit still making my hand quiver, I made a two-hundred-mile trek to Ocean World—a great marine park where they had countless dolphins in captivity. The whole time I didn't dare sleep, sure that the baseball player would fight his way back in control of my new body.

I arrived at midnight, on a day when a full moon was out and the empty parking lot was like a great black ocean.

With the strong body of the athlete I possessed, I climbed the fence and made my way to the dolphin tanks.

The plan was simple—I had worked it out a dozen times on my way there, and I knew that nothing could go wrong. I was stronger than the baseball player—I had already proven that. All that remained was getting him out of this body forever. Then, and only then, would it truly be mine.

I held on to that thought as I dove into the frigid water of the dolphin tank. Then, as I began to sink, I let Slam climb back into my mind. He was crazed now, screaming in anger and fear. He did not know what I was about to do, because I had kept my thoughts from him.

Suddenly there was a dolphin swimming up to us. It appeared to be just curious as to what was going on in its tank. As it drew nearer, and nearer still, I waited. Then, when it was right up next to us, I blasted the baseball player out of my mind.

Though I'd tried many times to do that, this time it wasn't hard at all. In fact, it was as easy as blowing a feather out of my hand—because *this* time there was a place for his spirit to go. It went into the dolphin . . . and there it stayed.

But the dolphin clearly did not want that kind of company. It began to swim around the huge tank, bucking and twisting as if it could shed this new spirit that had merged with its own. But the dolphin's efforts were useless. Slam was now a permanent resident in the dolphin's mind.

And as for me—I was free! I was the sole owner of this fine body! All I had to do was swim back to the surface to begin my new life.

All I had to do was swim.

All I had to do . . .

That's when I discovered that this strong athletic body, this body that had hit a hundred fastballs over the right-field wall . . . had never learned to swim.

Slowly panic set in. I moved my hands, I kicked my legs, but the muscles in my body had no memory of how to behave in water. They thrashed uselessly back and forth, and my lungs filled with the icy water. Meanwhile the dolphin swam furiously around the tank, not caring about me or my new body, but trying to rid itself of the foreign spirit that had entered its mind.

I felt death begin to pound in my ears with the heavy beat of my slowing heart, and I knew that if I didn't leave this body soon, it would be too late.

I had to leap out of it. I *had* to give it up. If I stayed in

this body a few minutes longer, I might not have been able to escape it—I might have been bound to it the way normal people are bound to their bodies. But my will was strong, and my skill at body-jumping well honed.

And so I tore myself from my new body, letting my spirit float to the surface like a buoy . . . while there, at the bottom of the dolphin tank, the soulless body of the great baseball player drowned.

———

I don't know what happened after that, because I left and didn't look back. I have heard tales, though, of a dolphin that leaped out of its tank so often that they had to put a fence over it. But who knows if stories like that are ever true?

And that brings me to you.

You see, I've been with you longer than you think. I've been sitting on your shoulder watching what you do, what you say, and even how you say it. I know the names of your relatives. I know your friends. We've already shared several hot-fudge sundaes together.

And if someday very soon, you wake up only to find yourself walking toward a dolphin pool in the dead of night . . . don't worry.

Because I know you can swim.

BLACK BOX

There was this light switch in my house. It was in a weird place—a little too high, and in the middle of a wall. It didn't turn off any lights, or turn on a disposal. As far as I knew it wasn't connected to anything. I got to thinking about mysterious switches and buttons. What if you were told never to flick a switch, or press a button. Would you be able to resist? No matter what the consequences?

Black Box

The old man wore a playful smile as he beckoned them closer. Karin and her cousin Randy stepped across the yellowing floor of the immense den, deep within their grandfather's ancient house. They were paying their respects to the old man, as their parents had insisted.

On a cherrywood table rested a menagerie of colorful origami animals—a folded-paper zoo. Karin wondered whether her grandfather spent all his time making them or if he had folded the animals to impress her and Randy, the way he used to when they were five.

He always spoke to them in Chinese first, as if his speaking the language would magically make them understand it better. Karin understood a little bit, but she knew that Randy didn't speak a word—he just squirmed and looked annoyed. For his sake she said, "You have to talk English, Grandfather."

"English!" spat their grandfather, then waved his hand as if swatting the thought away. "Ah! You children lose everything. All the old ways, you lose. How can you call yourselves Chinese?"

"We're not Chinese," Randy said defiantly. "We're American."

Karin gave Randy a sharp elbow to the ribs.

"Don't get him mad!" she whispered.

The old man looked at Randy with hardened eyes, and then he laughed. "Yes. American." He chuckled. "Apple pie!" Then he laughed and Karin elbowed Randy again.

"Don't you know not to say things like that to him?" she said. Randy never did learn how to deal with Grandfather. Still, her cousin was right. They were both born in America; even their parents had been born in America. How much more American could they get?

Grandfather laughed a little too long, and Karin began to feel uncomfortable.

Finally, he shook his head and wiped the tears from his eyes. "Yes. American." He sighed. "The old world is gone. My world—gone. Soon nobody will be left to remember."

"I'll remember," offered Karin

Grandfather smiled. "Sweet girl," he said. "But stupid."

Randy snickered.

"You should not laugh," said Grandfather, wagging an arthritic finger at him. "Next to you, she looks like a genius."

Karin smiled and gave Randy a smarter-than-you look, then she turned back to the old man. He looked very serious for a moment, then he glanced down at the dark cherrywood table and the collection of paper animals. He picked up a paper cat. "This world of new things—you think it is strong like a lion, when in truth it is fragile like paper."

He crumpled the origami cat in his hand and flicked it with his fingers across the room. "There. Destroyed by a single finger."

Then Grandfather let loose a hacking cough that rattled the room so much Karin wondered how his lungs could stand it. When his coughing fit was over, the old man turned to a shelf filled with old knickknacks and pulled down a black box about the size of a shoe box. At first Karin thought it held tissues, but there was no opening on it. Anywhere.

"This is very old," Grandfather said, brushing his finger across the smooth, ebony surface. "Even older than me. Hard to believe anything is older than me, hah?" And he let out a laugh that sent him into another coughing fit.

Karin and Randy looked at the box.

"What is it?" Karin asked as Grandfather handed it to her.

"Puzzle box," answered the old man.

Randy grabbed it from her and pawed his fingers all over it, leaving dull fingerprints on the shiny lacquered surface. "There's no way to open it," he said.

Karin grabbed it back from him and examined it again herself. Randy was right—it was solid all the way around!

Grandfather gently took it back from her. He tapped the top twice, then placed three fingers on one side, two on the other, then pressed inward with his thumbs. A panel slid open. Karin was amazed.

"No way!" said Randy, his eyes wide.

"Way," Grandfather said simply. He pressed and prodded different pressure points, deftly and skillfully, as if playing an instrument. The box began to open up with dark, textured surfaces. When Grandfather was done it looked more like a black flower than a box, and in the center of that flower was another, smaller box, even blacker than the first one. It was perfectly square, about two inches wide.

Karin and Randy just stared. "Another puzzle?" asked Karin.

"No," answered Grandfather. "A solution."

Grandfather held the inner box in his hand and placed his fingertips on it. Instantly, a lid opened, revealing a carved jade panel, and in the center of all that sparkling green jade was a bright gold button. Not the kind of button you wear, but the kind of button you press. Tiny Chinese characters were carved into the jade all around the gold button, but Karin couldn't read them.

"Oooh!" said Karin.

"It must be worth big bucks!" said Randy.

"Never mind that," snapped Grandfather. He put the little box down on the table. Randy and Karin couldn't take their eyes off it.

"I want to give this to the right person before I die," Grandfather said. "Your parents and your older brothers and sisters—they are worse than you. They hate the old ways, and the old things. They want to forget them. This is how I know that one of you must get this gift."

"Thanks!" Randy reached out his hand, but Grandfather slapped it away.

"Not so fast." He picked up the little box and handed it to Karin. Her eyes lit up, and she gazed at it as if it were a diamond ring in a jewelry box.

"You are the trustworthy one. Your cousin Randy here, he would trade this for a baseball card, yes?"

"No!" said Randy, but Karin knew that it probably depended on how good the baseball card was.

Grandfather turned his gaze back to Randy. "I bring you here, Randall, so you will always remember the honor you did not receive from me. Someday you will learn to respect old things."

Randy scowled and pouted, and then said under his breath, "I don't want it. It's a girl's thing, anyway." But he knew that it was not.

Karin moved her finger across the rough jade and around the smooth gold button, then her fingertip came across the button and she started to press it. Grandfather gasped and pulled her finger away with his bony hand.

"You must not!" he cried out. "Can't you read?"

"It's in Chinese," she said, looking at the Chinese characters written around the button.

Grandfather sighed.

"This has been in our family for forty-nine generations," he said. "Fifty-one, now that I pass it on to you. It has been our family's task all these years to guard this button with a clear heart, and a clean mind. Show no one. Tell no one. And never, *ever* press it."

"But what does it do?" asked Karin.

Grandfather leaned closer, speaking in a raspy whisper.

"This," he said, "is the button that ends the world."

———

That evening Karin sat on a lumpy bed in one of the many upstairs bedrooms of her grandfather's huge house. She puzzled over the puzzle box, practicing how it opened and closed. She had only seen her grandfather do it once, but once was all it took for her to memorize it.

Randy, who lay on the floor tossing a ball at the high ceiling, watched in disgust at how easily Karin could now open the box. She had a photographic memory, and she knew that it irritated Randy no end.

"He gave it to me because he knows I'll take care of it."

"*And* because you kiss up to him."

Karin closed the puzzle box and practiced opening it again. There wasn't much for the two of them to do on these annual family get-togethers. The other cousins were all either much younger or much older than Karin and Randy. The young ones were all asleep in the maze of bedrooms within Grandfather's immense house. All the adults were downstairs, babbling about nothing important. Their jumbled voices drifted up the great staircase and echoed down the winding halls.

"You don't believe any of that stuff about that stupid button, do you?" scoffed Randy, tossing his ball and watching how close he could come to hitting the light in the center of the ceiling.

Karin pulled out the little box from the center of the puzzle box.

"No . . ." she said.

Randy smirked. "You *do* believe it—I can tell." He tossed the ball again. "You're as loony as he is."

"I believe some of it," said Karin. "You remember last year I showed everyone that genealogy I did?"

"Genie-what?"

"Genealogy—the family tree."

"Oh yeah, that thing."

"Well, our family does trace back to some sort of royalty. I'll bet that this box really *was* passed down from our ancestors."

"And do you believe it could destroy the world?"

Karin flipped open the little box. She regarded the gold button. It seemed so harmless, and yet . . .

"No," she said. "Of course I don't believe it. But it's strange to think that people *did* believe it, maybe for thousands of years."

"You think anyone's ever pressed it?"

"Probably not," said Karin. "They wouldn't press it if they believed in it."

"This is what I think," said Randy. "A thousand years ago, we had this ancient Chinese nerd relative, and one day his friends gave him this box as a practical joke—and that idiot believed the joke."

Karin tilted the little black box in her hand, and the button reflected a pinpoint of light that danced across the peeling wallpaper.

"I'll bet you don't even have the guts to press it," said Randy, and then his ball went a bit too high, hitting the light above him and smashing it. Randy rolled out of the way just as the glass showered down to the warped wooden floor. Karin froze, closing her eyes and gripping the little black box.

In the silence that followed she could hear shouts from downstairs and the sound of feet running down the hallway toward them. Several people were wailing—it seemed a bit much just for some broken glass.

Randy's father appeared at the door first.

"I'm sorry," said Randy in a panic. "I didn't mean it—it was an accident."

But Karin could tell that her uncle wasn't looking at the glass.

"Randy, Karin," he said, not looking at all well. "I'm afraid something terrible has happened. It's your grandfather."

Grandfather's funeral was held just a day later.

It was more convenient that way, since the whole family was already in town for the annual reunion. No one had expected him to die that night, especially the way it happened. He had fallen through a termite-eaten floorboard, right in front of all the relatives. Leave it to Grandfather to make such a dramatic exit from the world.

Karin's mom had cried hysterically for most of that night. She had been talking to him when it happened. "Just like that," she kept telling everybody. "He was talking to me—he was in the middle of a sentence, *in the middle of a word*—and then suddenly he wasn't there. All that was left was a hole!"

To Karin this was more than an accident. Somehow the old man knew his time was coming. It made Karin wonder what else he might have known.

At the funeral, Karin watched as Randy, on the far side of the casket, squirmed away from his parents and came around to her. His mind, like hers, seemed to be less concerned with Grandfather and more concerned with what Grandfather had left behind. Randy began whispering to Karin while an old woman spoke a Chinese eulogy.

"Do you have it?" whispered Randy.

She knew what he was talking about. "Yes."

"Where?"

"It's in my purse. Leave me alone," said Karin.

"Are you carrying it with you everywhere now?"

Karin sighed, and her parents threw Randy an angry look. Randy shut up, for a little while.

When the ceremony was over and everyone was walking back to the cars, Randy pulled Karin off on a detour through a maze of high tombstones—a place Karin didn't want to be, but she didn't resist. She didn't want to think or talk about the button anymore, and yet at the same time, she wanted to talk about it more than anything.

"You must be curious," said Randy.

"I thought you didn't believe in the button," Karin said.

"I don't, but I can still be curious about it, can't I?"

Karin reached into her purse and pulled out the little black box. She opened it to reveal the gold button.

Randy stared at it, practically drooling. He wanted that button, and Karin was beginning to wish that their grandfather had given it to him instead.

"I mean, look at it," he said. "It's not attached to anything.

If we took it apart, it would probably just be a gold button and a hollow box. Nothing but air inside."

"You are *not* taking it apart," Karin said sternly.

Randy leaned up against the back of a huge black stone and crossed his arms. "So what do you think it's supposed to do? You think it's supposed to send off nuclear missiles or something?"

"Don't be dumb," said Karin, chalking up another mark on her list of Stupid Randy Comments. "When this button was made, there were no missiles."

"So then how is it supposed to end the world? Is it supposed to release evil spirits or something? Or send out poisonous gas? How?"

"I don't know," said Karin, and then she smirked. "Why don't you go back to the grave and ask Grandfather?" And then she whispered, "Put your ear close to the ground. He might answer you."

Randy punched Karin in the arm for that, and Karin whacked him back, hard.

"I don't believe in that dumb thing for a second," insisted Randy. "It's not scientific. I don't believe it."

"Well, whether you believe it or not," said Karin, "you don't have to worry about it anymore, because you're never going to see it again."

"Why not?"

"Because I'm putting it away for good, just like our ancestors did. I'm putting it in a safe place where no one will ever find it, until it's my turn to pass it on."

Karin slipped the little box back into her purse, thinking of all the places she could put it where it would be safe until she was about ninety years old. The problem was, she didn't know of such a place.

───────

That night was their last in Grandfather's house. No one wanted to stay there anymore. It wasn't just that he was dead, it was the way wood creaked when you walked on it—as if it could give way any moment the way it did beneath Grandfather. It was frightening to think that a house so big, which looked so sturdy, could be so fragile.

Karin did not sleep that night—not because of Grandfather's death, and not because of the termite-eaten floorboards. She couldn't sleep because of the box. If a box could have a spirit, then it was beginning to possess her. It seemed Randy had the same problem.

When he crept into her room an hour before dawn, Karin was sitting up, holding the little box in her hand and staring at the button.

"I knew you'd be awake," said Randy.

She was glad he was there, because she couldn't go on sitting alone any longer. She just had to tell somebody. She had to talk about it.

"I can't stop thinking about it," she told him. "I put it back in the puzzle box, and then I put the puzzle box under my bed, but I could still see it there in my mind. It's like a photograph that won't go away. Then I put it in the hall, but that didn't help, so I snuck outside when everyone was asleep and put it in our car. But no matter where I put it, I still kept seeing it."

"So you went back out to get it?" asked Randy.

Karin nodded. They both stared at the button. Its gold face now seemed silvery blue in the dim moonlight.

"I don't want it anymore," said Karin. "You can have it."

Randy shook his head. "You keep it."

They stared at the button in silence.

I'm not going to push it, thought Karin, although every fiber of her body told her that she was going to do just that. It was like trying not to look at her grandfather's body when they opened the coffin in the chapel. No matter how hard she tried not to, she just had to look.

Randy seemed to read what she was thinking.

"Let me do it," he said.

"No." Karin pulled the box a few inches away from him. "I mean, it's just a superstition, right?" said Karin.

"Right."

"And if we push it, nothing will happen, and we can stop worrying about it and get back to sleep, right?"

"Right."

Karin slipped her finger across the smooth, cold surface. She rested it on the button.

She could hear her heart pounding, and swore she could hear Randy's as well. Silently, she cursed her grandfather for giving her the button.

"Get it over with," hissed Randy.

Karin took a deep breath, felt the cold metal beneath her fingertip . . . and pressed.

She held the button down, gritting her teeth, closing her eyes.

But nothing happened.

No explosions, no demons, nothing. Only the silence of the night, and faint snores coming from the other rooms.

Feeling stupid, they both breathed a deep sigh of relief. This was what Grandfather wanted, Karin was sure now. He wanted to show them how weak they truly were. He had called them stupid—was this his way of proving it?

Karin stared at the button a moment longer, her finger still firmly pressing it down. Finally, she relaxed and took her finger off it.

"Well," she said as the button snapped back up, "I guess that's it. I guess nothing's going to hap—"

RESTING DEEP

A friend was telling me a story he had read about a father who takes his son fishing with a storm on the horizon. Immediately, I constructed an entire plot about why they were going fishing and what would happen in the story. That story, of course, went in a completely different direction—the only similarity was a fishing boat going out in a storm. Many times we are inspired by other authors. The trick is to take that inspiration and create something that is uniquely your own.

RESTING DEEP

My parents dropped me off at his house late last night.

Greaty's house.

That's what I call him, "Greaty"—short for Great-Grandpa. He's the oldest in the family. He's buried two wives, two sons, and one daughter.

His house is small: a living room, a bedroom, and a tiny kitchen. It's really a shack in a row of other shacks, where ancient people cling to their last days.

It smells old here. It smells salty, like the sea. And Greaty's always eating the fish he catches.

"Good to see you, Tommy," he said to me at the door, smiling his long-toothed smile.

Whenever I see his smile, I run my tongue along my braces, feeling the crooked contour of my own teeth, wondering if one day mine will look like his, all yellow and twisted.

"Ready for a good day of fishing tomorrow?" he asked.

"Sure, I guess."

My parents left me here to spend a night and a day. They do this every year, four times a year. It started when I was little. It had to do with my fear of water. Mom and Dad decided that the best way for me to get over it was to send me out with

Greaty on his big fishing boat. Then I'd see how much fun water could be.

But it didn't work that way.

Greaty would always tell tales of sharks and whales and mermaids who dragged fishermen down to their watery graves. Going out with him made me more afraid of the water than I had been before, so afraid that I never learned to swim. Still, I went out with him and continue to go. It's become a family tradition. Sometimes, I'm ashamed to say, I hope for the day when Greaty joins his two wives, two sons, and one daughter so I don't have to go out to sea with him ever again.

It is an hour before dawn now. Greaty and I always set out when everything is cold, dark, and still, and my veins feel full of ice water. I watch him as he prepares his boat. It's an old fishing boat, its wooden hull marred with gouges from years of banging up against the dock. When a wave lifts it high against its berth, I can see the barnacles crusted on its belly. It has been years since Greaty has bothered to have them scraped off.

He calls his boat the *Mariana*, "named after the deepest trench in the ocean," he once told me. "That trench is seven miles deep, and it's where the great mysteries of the world still lie undiscovered."

I sometimes think about the trench. I think about all the ships and planes that have fallen down there in wars. I imagine being in a ship that had seven miles to sink before hitting bottom. That's like falling from space.

We set out, and by the time dawn arrives, we are already far from shore. I can tell that the day is not going to be a pleasant one. The sun is hidden behind clouds. There is a storm to the north, and it's churning up the surf.

Greaty heads due north into the choppy waves. He stares at the horizon and occasionally says something to me just to let me know he hasn't forgotten me.

"Today's going to be an exceptional day," he tells me. "One day in a million. I can feel it in my bones."

I can feel it in my bones, too, but not what Greaty feels. I feel a miserable sense of dread creaking through all of my joints. Something is going to happen today—I know it, and it is not something good. I imagine giant tidal waves looming over us, swallowing us in cold waters and sending us down to the very bottom, where it's so dark the fish don't have eyes.

———

Half an hour later, the shore behind us is just a thin line of gray on the horizon. Greaty has never taken me out this far before. Never.

"Maybe we'd better stop here," I tell him. "We're getting kind of far from shore."

"We'll stop soon," he says. "We're almost there."

Almost where? I wonder. But Greaty doesn't say anything more about it. His silence is strange. I don't know what he's thinking—I never do.

And then something suddenly strikes me in a way that it has never struck me before—I don't know my great-grandfather. I've spent days and weekends with him every few months for my entire life, but I don't *know* him. I don't know what he thinks and what he feels. All I know about him is the way he baits his hooks, the way he talks about fishing. I can't get the feeling out of my head that suddenly I'm out on a boat with a stranger.

"You know how many great-grandchildren I have, Tommy?" he asks, shoving a wad of chewing tobacco into the corner of his mouth. "Twelve."

"That's a lot," I say with a nervous chuckle.

"You know how many of them I take fishing with me?" He stares at me, chewing up and down, with a smile on his crooked, tobacco-filled mouth.

"Just me?"

He points his gnarled bony finger at me.

"Just you."

He waits for me to ask the obvious question, but I don't.

"You want to know why I take only you?" he asks. "Well, I'll tell you. There's your cousins, the Sloats. With all the money they've got, they can buy their kids anything in the world. Those kids are set for life. Then there's your other cousins, the Tinkertons. They've got brains coming out of them like sweat. They'll all amount to something. And your aunt Rebecca's kids—they're beautiful. All that golden hair—they'll get by on their looks."

"So?" I ask.

"So," he says. "What about you?"

What about me? I take after my mother—skinny as a rail,

a bit of an overbite. And I got my father's big ears, too. Okay, so I'm not the best-looking kid. As for money, we live in a small, crummy house, and we probably won't ever afford anything better. As for brains, I'm a poor student. Always have been.

The old man sees me mulling myself over. "*Now* do you know?" he asks.

I can't look at Greaty. I can only look down, feeling inadequate and ashamed. "Because I'm ugly . . . because I'm poor . . . because I'm stupid?"

Greaty laughs at that, showing his big teeth. I never realized how far the gums had receded away from them, like a wave recedes from the shore. He should have had all his teeth pulled out and replaced by fake ones. The way they are now, they're awful, like teeth in a skull.

"I picked you because you were the special one, Tommy," he says. "You were the one *without* all the things the others have. To me that makes you special."

He turns the wheel and heads toward the dark storm clouds on the horizon.

"I was like you, Tommy," he tells me. "So you're the one I want to take with me."

———

The waves begin to get rough, rolling up and down like tall black hills and deep, dark valleys. The wind breathes past us, moaning like a living thing, and I feel seasickness begin to take hold in my gut.

Greaty must see me starting to turn green.

"How afraid of the water are you, Tommy?" he asks

"About as afraid as a person can get," I tell him.

"You know," he says, "the ocean's not a bad place. When I die, I would like to die in the ocean." He pauses. "I think I will."

I swallow hard. I don't like it when Greaty talks about dying. He does it every once in a while. It's like he sees the world around him changing—the neighborhood being torn down to build condos, the marshes paved over for supermarkets. He knows that he'll be torn off this world soon, too, so he talks about it, as if talking about it will make it easier when the time comes.

"Why are we heading into the storm?" I ask Greaty.

He doesn't say anything for a long time.

"Don't you worry about that," he finally says coldly. "A man can catch his best fish on the edge of a storm."

We travel twenty minutes more, and as we go I peer over the side, where I see fins—dorsal fins, sticking out of the water—and I'm terrified.

"Dolphins," says Greaty, as if reading the fear in my face.

Sure enough, he is right. Dolphins are riding along with the boat. As I look into the distance, I see dozens of them, all running in line with us, as if it is a race. And then suddenly they stop.

I go to the stem of the boat and look behind us. The dolphins are still there, but they wait far behind. The bottle tips of their noses poke out of the water, forming a line a hundred

yards away, like a barrier marking off one part of the ocean from another.

I look down at the waters we've come into and could swear that, as black as the waters were before, they're even blacker now. And the smell of the sea has changed, too.

Greaty stops the boat.

"We're here," he tells me.

He gets out his fishing rod, and one for me. Then he pulls out bait, impaling the small feeder fish onto tiny barbed hooks.

Suddenly the boat pitches with a wave. It goes up and down like an elevator—like a wild ride at an amusement park. My stomach hangs in midair and then falls down to my toes.

The water rises around the boat, almost flowing in, but the boat rises with it.

"You know why a boat floats?" he asks me.

"Why does a boat float, Greaty?"

"Because it's too afraid of what's under the water," he says, completely serious.

Greaty throws his line in, and we wait, he sitting there calmly, and I, shivering, with sweaty palms. I watch lightning strike in the far, far distance.

Greaty knows what he's doing, I tell myself. *He's been fishing his whole life. He knows how close you can get to a storm and still be safe . . . doesn't he?*

I haven't thrown my line in yet. It's as if throwing a line into the water brings me closer to it, and I don't want to be closer to it. I watch my feeder fish, sewed onto the steel hook, writhe in silent agony until it finally goes limp. Greaty watches the fish die.

"Dying is the natural course of things, you know," he says. "Bad thing about dying, though, is having to die alone. I don't want to die alone." Then he turns to me and says, "When I go, I want someone to come with me."

He takes my line, casts it into the water, and hands me back the rod. I feel the line being pulled away from the boat as the hook sinks deeper and deeper. Lightning flashes on the distant horizon.

"The person who dies with me, though, ought to be someone I care about. Someone *special*," he says.

"I gotta use the bathroom," I tell him, even though I don't have to. I just have to get away, as far away as I can. I have to go where I don't see the ocean, or the storm, or Greaty.

I go down to the cabin, and there I feel something cold down on my feet. I look down and see water.

I race back up top. "Greaty," I say. "There's water down below! We're leaking."

But he isn't bothered. He just holds his line and chews his tobacco. "Guess old *Mariana* decided she's not so afraid of the ocean after all."

"We gotta start bailing! We have to do something!"

"Don't you worry, Tommy," he tells me in a soft, calm voice. "She takes on a little water now and then. It doesn't mean anything."

"Are you sure?"

"Of course I'm sure."

Then Greaty's line goes taut, and his pole begins to bend. He skillfully fights the fish on the other end, letting out some line, then pulling some in—out, in, out, in, until the fish on the other end is exhausted.

In the distance behind us, the dolphins watch.

I hear the snagged fish thump against the boat, and Greaty, his old muscles straining, reels it in.

At first I'm not sure what I'm seeing, and then it becomes clear. The thing on the line is like no fish I've ever laid eyes on. It is ugly and gray, covered with slime rather than scales. It has a long neck like a baby giraffe, and its head is filled with teeth. It has only one eye, in the center of its forehead—a clouded, unseeing eye.

Greaty drops the thing onto the deck, and it flops around, making an awful growling, hissing noise. Its head flies to the left and then to the right on the end of its long neck, until finally it collapses.

Greaty looks at it long and hard. Far behind us, the dolphins wait at the edge of the black waters.

"What is it, Greaty?"

"It doesn't have a name, Tommy," he tells me as he heads into his tackle room. "It doesn't have a name."

He comes out of the boat with a new fishing rod—a heavy pole, with heavy line and a hook the size of a meat hook. He digs the hook into the thing he caught and hurls it back into the ocean, letting it pull out far into the dark waters.

What could he possibly be trying to catch with something that large?

"Greaty, I want to go home now." I can hear the distant rumble of thunder. The storm coming toward us is as black as the sea. When I look down into the cabin, the water level has risen. There is at least a foot of water down there, and the boat is leaning horribly to starboard.

"Greaty!" I scream. "Are you listening to me?"

"We're not going home, Tommy."

I hear what he's saying, but I can't believe it. "What?" I shout at him. "What did you say?"

"Don't you see, Tommy?" he tells me. "There are places out here—wondrous places that no one has ever charted. Places deeper than the Marianas Trench! Bottomless places where creatures dwell that no man has ever seen."

The boat pitches terribly. Water pours in from the side.

"We're going to be part of that mystery, Tommy, you and me, together. We're going to rest deep."

"No!" I scream. "You can't do this! I don't want to die out here!"

"Tommy, you're not doing anyone else on this earth any good," he explains to me. "You won't be missed by many, and even then you won't be missed for long. I'm the only one who needs you, Tommy. So I won't be alone."

"I won't do it!"

Greaty laughs. "Well, seeing as how the boat is sinking and a storm's coming, it doesn't look like you have much of a choice. Not unless you can walk on water."

A wave lifts the boat high and water pours in, filling the cabin. And then something tugs on Greaty's line so hard that

it pulls the rod right out of his hand. It disappears into the water.

"I think it's time," he says.

I scramble into the flooding cabin and find a life jacket. I put it on, as if it can really help me.

When I come out, the water gets calm, and I feel something scraping along the bottom of the boat—something huge.

I look up to the sky, wishing that I could sprout wings and fly away from the sea. Then something rises out of the water in front of us—a big, slimy black fin the size of a great sail, and beneath that fin, two humps on a creature's back—a creature larger than any whale could possibly be.

"Look at that!" shouts Greaty.

The fin crosses before us, towering over our heads, and then submerges, disappearing into the black depths.

It gets very quiet. Much *too* quiet. Greaty puts his hand on my shoulder.

"Thank you," he whispers. "Thank you, Tommy, for coming with me."

Somewhere below, I hear a rush of water as something coming from very, very deep forces its way toward the surface, getting closer and closer. The water around us begins to bubble and churn.

"No!" I scream, and climb up to the edge of the sinking boat.

I never thought that I would leap into the ocean by choice, but that's exactly what I do. My feet leave the gouged old wood of the *Mariana*, and in a moment I am in the sea.

The water is icy cold all around me, salty and rough. I break surface and gasp for air. My life jacket is all that keeps me from sinking into this bottomless ocean pit. A wave washes me away from the boat.

Then I hear a roar and the cracking of wood. A great gush of water catches me in the eyes, making them sting. I turn back, and see it only for an instant. Something huge, black, and covered with ooze. It has sharp teeth, no eyes, and a black forked tongue that has forced its way through the hull of the boat, searching for Greaty like a tentacle . . . and finding him. The thing crushes the entire boat in its immense jaws. Its roar is so loud, I cannot hear if Greaty is screaming.

A wave hits, and I am under the water again. When I break surface, the beast, the boat, and Greaty are gone. Only churning water and bubbles remain where they had been.

Far away, I can see the dolphins waiting at the edge of this unholy water. I move my arms and kick my legs, teaching myself to swim.

I will not join you in your bottomless grave, Greaty. I will not let you take me with you. You will be alone. And even though I am out in the middle of the ocean at the edge of a storm, I will not die this way. I will not.

Something huge and smooth brushes past my feet, but I don't think about it. Something rough and hard scrapes against my leg, but I only look forward, staring at the dolphins lined up a hundred yards away. Those dolphins are waiting for me, I know. They will not dare come into these waters, but if

I make it back to them, I know that I will be all right. They will carry me home.

And so I will ignore the horrors that swarm unseen beneath me. I will close my ears to the roars and groans from the awful deep. And I will get to the dolphins. Even if I have to walk on water.

SECURITY BLANKET

I was once at a garage sale where an old woman was selling a quilt that meant a lot to her. The quilt, she said, was full of scenes from her life. There was a little girl ice-skating, and a picture of a cabin on a lake. A lot of the squares had faces on them. When sheheld it up, it was as if the faces were all looking at me. Or maybe it was just my imagination . . .

SECURITY BLANKET

I finally snapped on the day we found the quilt.

It was 7:30 on a Saturday morning as we drove in the van searching for garage sales. As usual, Timmy and Maddie, my twin brother and sister, were fighting like Velociraptors in the back of the van, gouging each other's face, ready to draw blood. I knew the fight would go on until one bit the other hard enough to make them let out a scream that could shatter bulletproof glass.

Dad had the music turned up full blast. It was his defense against Timmy and Maddie's little war. Today it was about their stupid yellow blanket. There used to be *two* stupid yellow blankets, but last year one got lost. Ever since, the surviving one was fought over constantly.

"Mom, can't you shut them up?" I asked.

Mom turned around and said something totally useless to the twins, like "You stop that now," then she went back to looking out the window for garage-sale signs.

"Mom, I swear, if they don't stop screaming, I'm going to gag them with that miserable blanket," I warned.

"Have some patience, Marybeth," Mom said, as she always says. "They're only five; they'll grow out of it." That's what she said when they were four, and when they were three, and when they were—

Two minutes later, Timmy bit Maddie, who then let loose a wail that rattled my brain. And that's when I did it: I grabbed their stupid yellow blanket, balled it up, and hurled it out my window. We were driving over a bridge, and the blanket went sailing like a comet over the edge of the guardrail, down to the creek below.

Now they both began to cry hysterically, and Mom looked at me, horrified. "Marybeth, how could you do that? How could you be so cruel?"

I shrugged. "Maybe it's genetic," I said. Mom had yet to come up with a good comeback line to that one.

We continued on in a whimpering sort of silence until hand-painted signs led us into a neighborhood I didn't know. We found the garage sale at the end of the street.

A man and woman had all the leftovers of their life spread out on their driveway. They smiled when they saw us coming. People who give garage sales love when people drive up in nice big vans like ours. Vans can haul off a lot, and often we did.

It used to be that we mostly picked things up for the church thrift shop. But ever since Dad lost his job, we've been picking up things for ourselves. Usually people just get rid of junk at these sales, but every once in a while you can find something great. That's how we found my piano last month. It cost two hundred dollars, but the same one would have cost at least a thousand in a store.

But there were few such bargains at this garage sale.

"Most of the stuff we just pulled out of the attic," said the pale, thin woman who owned the house. "We hadn't been up there for years. It's funny the things you collect."

Yeah, I thought. *It's funny the things people try to get money for, too.*

Mostly it was clothes—old bell-bottom pants, stained blouses, moldy things that smelled of mothballs, and children's clothing. In fact, there were all kinds of children's things—toys, picture books . . . and a child's quilt.

The quilt was just draped there, over a little white rocking chair, and my eyes were immediately drawn to its lively colors. At first I thought it was because the sun was hitting it, shining through the trees, creating a patch of bright light that made the quilt seem to glow. But then I realized that the morning sun was still behind the clouds.

I stared, unable to take my eyes off the bright colors of the little blanket. *How could someone have sewn something so beautiful?* I wondered. And then I remembered how my grandmother used to sit hour after hour, working on patchwork quilts in tranquil silence. I'm not a sentimental type—things that are cute or quaint usually make me sick. But that quilt went beyond being quaint . . . it was masterful.

"Have your children grown and left home?" my mother asked the woman who lived there. "Is that why you're selling all of this?"

The woman just stared at her, blinking. "No, we don't have any children," she said.

"So what's the deal with all these toys?" I asked.

The woman shrugged uncomfortably. "I don't know. They were all up in the attic."

"They must have been left by the previous owners," my mother suggested as she looked at the toys.

"Yes," said the woman. "Yes, that must be it." And then she went to help some other customers.

At the edge of the driveway, the twins bounced up and down on a plastic teeter-totter. But it wasn't long before they began teasing each other, and Dad had to pull them apart before they tore each other to shreds.

By now, the quilt had caught Mom's attention. "How beautiful," she said, lifting it off that little white chair. She unfolded it, revealing swimming colors and hundreds of bright patches of fabric. Then she turned to the woman and held it up. "How much for this?" she asked.

"Five dollars," the woman suggested.

"Sold," Mom said. Then she turned to me. "Pay for it, Marybeth. I believe you owe the twins a replacement blanket."

On Monday, during lunch, I sat with my friend Corinne in the cafeteria. We were scarfing down ravioli that was so salty, it made our eyes water.

"My little brother's a nuisance, too," Corinne said. "He gets into my things and makes paper airplanes out of my homework. Then, when I yell at him about it, he cries, and I end up getting in trouble. Is that what it's like with the twins?"

"It's different with them," I said. "It's not that they get

into my things, it's just that they're, well, *there*."

"I wish my brother was just *there*," said Corinne. "Actually . . . I wish he *wasn't*." And then she laughed, smiling with a ravioli-filled mouth as if she were just making a joke. But I knew she meant what she said, even if she didn't know it . . . because lots of times I felt that way, too.

When I got home that day, as I was walking down the hallway toward my room, I thought I saw something move. It was something about the size of a cat—or maybe it was just my imagination. Still, I had to investigate.

Mom was off at work, Dad was at a job interview, and the twins were at day care, so I was totally alone. Maybe I should have been scared as I stepped into the twins' room, looking for that moving shape, but I wasn't. Not yet, anyway.

As my eyes scanned the room, I saw that the blinds were drawn, casting diagonal slits of light against the wall. I also noticed that the quilt, which had been folded at the end of Timmy's bed when I left for school, wasn't there anymore. And then I saw it.

There, in the corner of the room, something was peering out at me. It was a creature with a dark face and many legs, like a scorpion—at least that was what I thought before my brain kicked in. Then I realized it was just a trick of the light. I quickly fumbled with the blinds, and they rose with a clatter, letting in the late afternoon sun. That's when I saw that there was no creature on the floor. It was just the quilt, crumpled into a random pile of hills and valleys that, when lit just right, seemed to be a living thing.

Still, I hesitated before I reached for it. Then I realized how silly I was being, so I grabbed it and shook it out to convince myself there was nothing hiding beneath it. Of course, nothing did shake out but a fine spray of dust that drifted in and out of the shafts of sunlight. I spread the quilt across Timmy's bed, then stood back to admire the way the light was hitting it.

There was something about the quilt that I hadn't noticed before. It wasn't simply a random patchwork of designs—each square was a scene. I had to look at it for a long time to really see it, but once I did, I couldn't deny that there were almost a hundred different scenes on that blanket. There was a winter scene of children playing in the snow, and a summer scene of children playing on the beach. Another square, which at first glance seemed to be just brown strips across a blue background, was actually someone crouching in the branches of a tree against a clear sky.

There were faces in the quilt, too, and after a while I began to feel the faces were all looking back at me. Suddenly it seemed there were a hundred people in the twins' room—all of them staring at me—and I could swear those faces were opening their mouths, trying to tell me something. But there was only silence.

I backed away from the quilt until I hit a picture on the wall, and it fell down. I picked up the picture, and when I looked back at the quilt, it was just a quilt again. No faces, just colorful fabric filling the many squares.

I left the twins' room with a shudder and went into the living room, where the only faces looking at me were those in

the smiling family photos on the wall. Then I sat at my piano and played something soothing. It had all been my imagination, I told myself. And I kept telling myself that until I almost believed it.

———

It was only a matter of time until Maddie and Timmy had a fight over the quilt. They had shared it for three whole days before they got tired of sharing. It was actually a record for them.

It began at dawn.

"It's mine!" yelled Maddie.

"No, it's mine!" screeched Timmy.

"No, it's *mine!*"

"No, it's MINE!"

"NO, IT'S MINE!"

It would have gone on like that for hours if someone didn't stop them, so I scraped myself out of bed and went into their room.

"Will you two just SHUT UP!" I roared as Mom came into the room as well.

"Marybeth," she said, "we don't use the S-word in this house."

I smirked at her. "That's not the S-word," I said.

"Yeah," said Timmy. "'Stupid' is the S-word."

"It's MINE," said Maddie, returning to the war at hand. "It's for *me* to sleep with at night." She wrapped herself in the quilt, but Timmy grabbed a corner and tugged until Maddie spun out of it like a top and hit the wall with a *thud*.

"I've got an idea," I said, leaving the room and returning with thumbtacks. I pulled the quilt away from Timmy and tacked its four corners to the wall.

"Wonderful," said my mother, smiling at me with approval. "It was too pretty to sit on a bed anyway."

The twins began to whine about it, and that's when I left for my own room, where I dressed and left for school as quickly as I could. All the while I was trying to push what I was thinking out of my mind. It was something I heard—not with my ears, but in a place deep within my head that my ears couldn't reach.

It was coming from the quilt. The moment that I had driven those four thumbtacks through its corners, I had heard the quilt scream.

The next night Mom and Dad had a fight. Dad was doing his taxes and had papers spread across every table in the house. He always got irritable around tax time, but this year was worse than any other, because he had been out of work for so long.

He and Mom argued that night about money. They argued about how hard Dad was looking for work, and they argued that Mom didn't get paid enough. They also argued over the fact that they were arguing. Finally I heard my name mentioned, and I stood at the edge of my doorway looking out into the living room, listening to what they were saying.

"We can't have both," said my dad. "It's got to be one or the other."

"We can't just take it away from her," said my mom. "She's wanted one for so long."

"Well, then, what are we going to do?" asked my dad in frustration. "Let the twins run around in the street after kindergarten?"

I knew what they were talking about. My piano. Ever since I was ten, they'd promised me I could have one, and just one month ago I finally got it. Now they were talking about selling it to pay for the twins' day care.

I didn't want to stand there and listen to their decision. I knew what it would be. The twins always got what they wanted. They were always taken care of first. And as for me, well, I would just have to share in Mom and Dad's money misery, because misery loves company, right?

Then Mom and Dad began to whisper so quietly that I couldn't hear, and I heard them coming into my room. I jumped onto my bed and pretended to read.

Mom, I could tell, almost had tears in her eyes. Dad looked pale and tired. *This is all the twins' fault*, I thought. Dad had lost his last job because he had to spend so much time at home when they had the chicken pox.

"Your father and I are going out," Mom said. "You'll watch the twins for us, okay?" She didn't so much ask me as tell me.

You must be desperate if you're asking me, is what I wanted to say. They never trusted me alone with the twins, because they said I was too mean to them, and they're probably right.

"Sure," I said. "I'll watch them."

As soon as the twins heard that they were being left with me, they began to whine.

"No!" Timmy yelled. "Marybeth will play tricks on us!"

"She'll play scary games," Maddie cried. "She'll make us cry. Marybeth hates us."

"Don't be silly," Mom said. "Marybeth's your sister. She loves you." And with that, she and Dad left.

Now, I wouldn't say I'm the nicest person in the world, but I would never call myself evil. At least not until that night. I'm not sure what came over me, but as soon as Mom and Dad left, I turned to the twins with a big smile that was not meant to comfort them.

"All right, you two," I said. "Would you like to play a game?"

They looked at me with wide eyes that were getting wider by the second. "What kind of game?" they asked in unison.

"The monster game," I replied.

"No!" they cried. "We hate the monster game! We hate it!"

"Well, tough," I told them. "That's the game *I* want to play."

Immediately the twins ran into the living room and ducked under the coffee table, as if hiding there would keep them safe.

"Please, Marybeth," Timmy whimpered. "Please don't scare us!"

I dug through my closet until I found this wonderfully hideous rubber Halloween mask. Then I put it over my face and stomped out into the living room.

"*Grrrrrowl!*" I roared, shoving my monster face under the

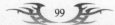

coffee table. The twins ran screaming into our parents' room, and I stomped after them.

"I'm the monster that eats bad little boys and girls!" I growled, finding them in Mom and Dad's bed, hiding their faces with pillows.

"*Grrrrrowl!*" I roared again. They screamed, leaped out of the bed, and ran. I stomped after them and found them in their own room. They were fighting to get underneath the quilt, which now lay crumpled in the corner of Timmy's bed, like a creature ready to spring.

That's odd, I thought. *Mom must have pulled it down from the wall.*

They grabbed the quilt and managed to wrap both of themselves in it from head to toe. I began to laugh at the way they quivered beneath it. I mean, did they think that a puny little blanket could protect them?

"Are you scared?" I growled at them.

"Yes, yes, we're scared."

"Are you *really* scared?"

"Yes!" they yelled. "Please stop, Marybeth!"

"Good!" I bellowed. "That's what you get for ruining everything for everyone."

Then they started to cry, and I realized I had gone too far. I took the dumb old mask off. "Oh, stop whimpering," I said. "It was just a game. You can come out now."

But they didn't come out.

"Come on," I coaxed. "You can't hide under that blanket all night!"

"We're not hiding," said Timmy. "We can't get out!"

I watched as the two of them struggled to unravel themselves from the blanket.

"Don't be ridiculous," I said. But as I watched them struggle, I could see that blanket stretching around them, pulling tighter and tighter—actually straining to keep them from struggling out.

"Help us, Marybeth!" they cried. "The monster—it has us! It's eating us!"

That's when I saw the eyes. They were attached to all those faces—hundreds of them—all staring out of the quilt . . . and this time I knew it wasn't just my imagination.

They were all the faces of children.

"Help us, Marybeth!" the twins kept shrieking.

Panicked, I ran across the room and, in the process, stepped on the thumbtacks that had held the thing to the wall. Wailing in pain, I fell to the ground. That's when I noticed that the twins' cries seemed to be getting weaker. I *had* to get them out.

I crawled to the bed, where the quilt had them wrapped up tighter than ever. I could see that, all bundled up, the thing did look like a creature . . . but like no creature I had ever imagined. I bit back my own fear, reached for the terrible quilt, grabbed hold of an edge, and tore it off the bed.

But there was nothing beneath it.

There in my hand was a mere blanket, a limp quilt that was still warm to the touch.

"No!" I cried.

I ran to my room with the horrible quilt clutched in my hand and got a pair of scissors. I was ready to cut the thing into a million pieces. But as I brought the scissors to the fabric I knew that I couldn't do it—because of something I saw *inside* the quilt.

There, at the very corner of the fabric, was a new patchwork square. Two ovals of tan velvet on a purple cotton background. And, when I looked at it hard enough, those ovals became two faces—*their* faces. I could see my brother's and my sister's eyes, just like all the other eyes, silently staring out at me from inside the quilt.

———

The following Saturday, Mom and Dad had a garage sale.

"Look at this!" said a woman who rummaged through the piles of children's clothes and children's toys. "It's a double stroller!" She was talking to her husband, who held newborn twins in his arms. "Just what we need," the woman went on, and then she turned to my mother. "I guess your twins have outgrown it," she said, giving the stroller a friendly pat.

My mother just stared at her, blinking. "No, we don't have twins," she said.

The woman glanced around at the piles of clothes. "But you seem to have two of everything, so I thought—"

"The stroller was in the garage," my mother said with a shrug. "I don't know how it got there . . . maybe it was from the previous owner."

And then Mom walked off to help some other customers. I

almost said something, but what good would it do? I was the only one who remembered the twins. To everyone else, it was as though they had never existed.

"You're lucky," said my friend Corinne, who was rummaging through our stuff as well. "You're lucky you're an only child. I have to share everything with my little brother."

And then Corinne picked up the many-colored quilt, which lay folded across a plastic teeter-totter.

"I should give this to my brother to replace that disgusting old security blanket he carries around the house," said Corinne. "How much do you want for it?"

I thought about it. I thought about it a long time. And in the end I let her have it.

"Take it," I told her. "It's free."

And why not? Who was I to stop the quilt on its journey through this world? And besides . . . misery loves company.

SAME TIME NEXT YEAR

I love time-travel stories, but there's something about them that always bothers me. There is one very simple fact about time and space that time-travel stories always ignore. I wanted to write a story that would take that fact into account, and show what would *really* happen if time travel were possible....

SAME TIME NEXT YEAR

In a vast universe, toward the edge of a spinning galaxy, on a small blue planet flying around the sun, in a place called Northern California, lives a girl who is quite certain that the entire universe revolves around her. Or at least she acts that way. In fact, if an award were given out for acting superior, Marla Nixbok would win that award.

"I was born a hundred years too early," she often tells her friends. "I ought to be living in a future time where I wouldn't be surrounded by such dweebs."

To prove that she is ahead of her time, Marla always wears next year's fashions and hairstyles that seem just a bit too weird for today. In a college town known for being on the cutting edge of everything, Marla is quite simply the Queen of Fads at Palo Alto Junior High. Nothing and nobody is good enough for her, and for that reason alone, everyone wants to be her friend.

Except for the new kid, Buford, who couldn't care less.

Buford and Marla meet on the school bus. It's his first day. As fate would have it, the seat next to Marla is the only free seat in the bus.

The second he sits down, Marla's nose tilts up, and she begins her usual grading process of new kids.

"Your hair is way greasy," she says. "Your clothes look like something out of the fifties, and in general, you look like a Neanderthal."

Several girls behind them laugh.

"All else considered, I give you an F as a human being."

He just smiles, not caring about Marla's grade. "Hi, I'm Buford," he says, ignoring how the girls start laughing again. "But you can call me Ford. Ford Planet."

Ford, thinks Marla. She actually likes the name, against her best instincts. "Okay, F-plus—but just because you got rid of the 'Bu' and called yourself 'Ford.'"

"Didn't you move into the old Wilmington place?" asks a kid in front of them.

"Yeah," says Buford.

The kid snickers. "Sucker!"

"Why? What's wrong with the place?" asks Ford innocently.

"Nothing," says Marla, "except for the fact that it used to belong to old Dr. Wilmington, the creepiest professor Stanford University ever had."

Ford leans in closer to listen.

"One day," says Marla, "about seven years ago, Wilmington went into the house . . . and never came out."

Ford nods, not showing a bit of fear.

"Personally," says Marla, trying to get a rise out of him, "I think he was killed by an ax murderer or something, and he's buried in the basement."

But Ford only smiles. "I wouldn't be surprised," he says. "There's a whole lot of weird things down in our basement."

Marla perks up. "Oh yeah? I wonder what sort of research was this Professor Wilmington doing when he disappeared."

Ford smiles, and then stares straight at Marla. "By the way," he says, pointing to her purple-tinted hair and neon eye shadow, "you've got to be the weirdest-looking human being I've ever seen."

Marla softens just a bit. "Why, thank you, Ford!"

Marla peers out of her window that night. Through the dense oak trees she can see the old Wilmington house farther down the street. A light is on in an upstairs window. She wonders if it's Ford's room.

Like Marla, Ford is trapped out of his time, only *he* belongs in the past, and she belongs in the future. It's not as if she likes him or anything. How could she like him—he is a full geek-o-rama nausea-fest. But she can use him. She can use him to get a look at all those dark, mysterious machines in his basement.

Marla smiles at the thought. Using people is a way of life for her.

And so the very next afternoon, Marla fights a blustery wind to get to Ford's house. By the time she arrives, her punked-out hair looks even worse, for the wind has stood every strand on end. She likes it even better now.

"Thanks for coming over to help me study," says Ford as he lets her in. "I mean, moving in the middle of the school year sure makes it hard to catch up."

"Well, that's just the kind of person I am," says Marla. "Anything I can do to help a friend."

Marla looks around. The furniture is so tacky, it makes her want to gag. The living-room sofa is encased in a plastic slipcover. Ford's mother vacuums the carpet wearing a polka-dot dress, like in *I Love Lucy*. For Marla, it's worse than being in a room filled with snakes.

"It's noisy here," says Ford. "Let's go study in my room."

Marla shudders. Who knows what terrors she'll find there?

"How about the basement?" she asks.

"It's creepy down there," says Ford.

"You're not scared, are you?"

"Who, me? Naw."

Marla gently takes his hand. "C'mon, Ford . . . we need a nice quiet place to study."

Ford, who has taken great pains not to be affected by the things Marla says or does, finally loses the battle. He takes one look at her hand holding his and begins to blush through his freckles. "Oh, all right."

While the rest of the house has been repainted and renovated, the basement has not changed since the day Wilmington disappeared. All of the old man's bizarre stuff is down there. Maybe Wilmington himself is down there somewhere, just a dried-out skeleton lurking behind a heavy machine. What if they were to find him? How cool would that be?

As they descend the rickety stairs, Marla grips Ford's hand tightly, not even realizing she is doing so. Ford's blush deepens.

"Gosh, I thought you didn't even like me," says Ford.

Marla ignores him, blocking out the thought, and looks around. "What is all this stuff?"

"That's what I've been trying to figure out," says Ford.

Everything is shrouded in sheets and plastic tarps. Strange shapes bulge out. They look like ghosts, lit by the flickering fluorescent light. There is a warped wooden table in the middle of it all. Ford drops his schoolbooks down on the table and a cloud of dust rises. It smells like death down there—all damp and moldy. The walls are covered with peeling moss, and they ooze with moisture.

"We can study here," says Ford, patting the table. But Marla is already pulling the sheets off the machines.

Whoosh! A sheet flutters off with an explosion of dust, revealing a dark, metallic, multiarmed thing that looks like some ancient torture device.

"I wouldn't touch that," says Ford.

Marla crooks her finger, beckoning him closer. Her nails are painted neon pink and blue with tiny rhinestones in the center of each one. She leans over and whispers in Ford's ear, "If you really want to be my friend, you'll help me uncover all these machines."

Ford, his blush turning even deeper, begins to rip off the sheets.

When they're done, a cloud of dust hangs in the air like fog over a swamp, and the machines within that dusty swamp appear like hunched monsters ready to pounce. All they need is someone to plug them in.

Ford sits at the table and studies the old professor's notes and lab reports. But Marla is studying something else—the knobs and switches on the grotesque and fantastic devices are what grab her attention. They might not find Wilmington's body down there, but Marla is happy. This is already more interesting than anything she has done in quite a while.

She joins Ford at the scarred table, going through the professor's old notes page by page.

Hyperbolic Relativistic Projection.

Metalinear Amplitude Differentials.

It makes little sense to them, and Ford has to keep looking things up in a dictionary.

At last, with the help of the professor's notes, they're able to figure out what most of these machines are supposed to do.

The one with a metallic eyeball looking down from a tall stalk is a waterless shower that can dissolve dirt from your skin by sonic vibrations. But according to Wilmington's footnote, it doesn't work; it dissolves your skin, instead of the dirt.

The device with iron tentacles growing from a steel pyramid is supposed to turn molecular vibrations into electricity. It works, but unfortunately it also electrocutes anyone who happens to be standing within five feet of it.

Another device—a hydrogen-powered engine—was supposed to revolutionize the automotive industry. According to a letter the professor received from the chairman of one of the big car companies, the engine nearly blew up half the plant when they turned it on.

In fact, none of the things Wilmington made worked

properly. Not the refractive laser chain saw, or the lead-gold phase converter, or even the self-referential learning microprocessor.

"No wonder no one from the university ever came by to collect all this stuff," Marla complains. "It's all junk."

Then Marla sees the doorknob. She hadn't noticed it before because it's in a strange place—only a foot or so from the ground, half hidden behind Wilmington's nonfunctioning nuclear refrigerator.

When Ford sees it, his jaw drops with a popping sound. "A tiny door! Do you think Wilmington's shrunk himself?"

"Don't be a complete gel-brain," says Marla, brushing her wild hair from her face. "It's just a root cellar. But Wilmington might be in there . . . what's left of him, anyway."

The temptation is too great. Together they push the heavy refrigerator aside, grab the knob, and swing the door wide.

An earthy smell of dry rot wafts out, like the smell of a grave. The door is two feet high, and inside it is pitch-black. Marla and Ford crawl into the root cellar and vanish into darkness.

Through ancient spiderwebs they crawl until they find a dangling string. When they pull it, the room is lit by a single dim bulb that hangs from an earthen ceiling six feet from the ground.

There are no dead bodies down there. The smell is a sack of potatoes that have long since gone to their maker.

But what surrounds them is enough to make their hearts miss several beats.

Razor-sharp gears, knifelike spokes, and huge magnets are

frozen in position. The entire room has been converted into one big contraption, and in the center of it is a high-backed chair, its plush upholstery replaced by silver foil.

It looks like the inside of a garbage disposal, thinks Marla.

In the corner sits a pile of dusty notes, and on a control panel is an engraved silver plate that reads:

TEMPUS SYNCRO-EPICYCLUS

"What is it?" wonders Marla. She looks to Ford, whom she has already pegged to be a whiz at this scientific stuff.

Ford swallows a gulp of rotten, stale air. "I think it's a time machine."

———

It takes a good half hour for them to find the nerve to actually touch the thing. Ford sits on the floor most of that time, reading Wilmington's notes.

"This guy has page after page of physics formulas," Ford tells Marla. "He must have thought he was Einstein or something."

"But does it work?" she asks.

Ford furrows his brow. "I have no idea."

"There's one way to find out," she says, grabbing Ford's sweaty hand.

Together they run upstairs and find the perfect guinea pig; Ford's baby sister's teddy bear, Buffy. They bring Buffy down and set him on the silver chair.

"I don't know," says Ford. "Maybe we ought to know everything about this machine before we start throwing switches."

"You can't ride a bike unless you get on and pedal," says Marla, "and you can't travel through time unless you throw the switch!"

"But—"

Marla flicks the switch. The gears begin to grind, the electromagnets begin to spin and hum. They duck their heads to keep from being decapitated by the spinning spokes. Static electricity makes Ford's greased hair stand on end like Marla's. The dangling bulb dims.

There is a flash of light, and Buffy the bear is gone, leaving nothing behind but the stinging odor of ozone in the air. The machine grinds itself to a halt.

Ford and Marla are left gasping on the ground.

"In-totally-credible!" screeches Marla. "Now let's bring it back!"

"That's what I was trying to tell you," explains Ford, catching his breath. "According to Wilmington's journal, time travel only works one way. You can go forward in time, but you can never come back."

"That's ridiculous! That's not the way it happens in the movies."

"Maybe real time travel doesn't work the way it does in movies," suggests Ford.

But to Marla it doesn't matter at all. The point is that however time travel works, it *does* work.

Ford looks to see where the dial is set.

"According to this," he says, "we sent the bear three days into the future. If the bear reappears in that chair three days from now, we'll really know if this thing works."

"I hate waiting," says Marla as she impatiently picks her rhinestoned nails.

———

Two days later, Marla's parents read her the riot act. That is to say, they sit her down and demand she change her ways, or else.

"Your mother and I are sick and tired of you being so disrespectful," says her father.

"What's to respect?" she growls at them. "Is it my fault I was born into a family of cave people?"

That makes her parents boil.

"That's it," says her father. "From now on you're going to stop acting like the Queen of Mars, and you're going to start acting like a normal human being. From now on, young lady, no more neon-blue lipstick. No more ultraviolet hair. No more radioactive eye shadow. No more automotive parts hanging from your earlobes. N-O-R-M-A-L. Normal! Do you understand me? Or else you get no allowance! Zero! Zilch!"

"You're so backward!" screams Marla, and she runs to her room and beats up her pillows.

Alone with her thoughts, it doesn't take long to decide exactly what to do. Without so much as a good-bye, she takes a final look at her room, then climbs out of the window and heads straight to Ford's house.

———

The sky is clear, filled with a million unblinking stars, and a furious wind howls through the trees. It's a perfect night for time travel.

"Marla," Ford says. "I've been reading Wilmington's notes, and there's something not quite right."

"Don't be an idiot!" Marla shouts in Ford's face. "The machine works—we saw it! We're going and that's final."

"I'm not going anywhere," says Ford. "I'm not into future stuff, okay?"

"It figures," huffs Marla. "I'll go by myself, then."

She pulls open the basement door and stomps down the stairs. Ford follows, trying to talk some sense into her.

"There's lots of stuff I'm still trying to figure out," he says.

"Oh yeah?" She whirls and stares impatiently at him. "Like what?"

"Like the name of the machine," Ford says. "It bugs me. *Tempus Syncro-Epicyclus*. I looked up the word 'Epicyclus' in the dictionary. It had something to do with Ptolemy."

"Tommy who?" asks Marla.

"Not Tommy, *Ptolemy*. He was an ancient astronomer who believed the earth was the center of the universe, and the sun revolved around it!"

"So?" she hisses.

"So, he was wrong!" shouts Ford.

Marla shrugs. "What does that have to do with a twentieth-century genius like Wilmington? At this very moment, *he's* probably in the future partying away, and I plan to join him."

Marla impatiently crosses the basement toward the root-cellar door.

"Marla, the last person to touch that machine must have been Wilmington—and it was set for three days! If he went three days into the future, *why didn't he come back?*"

"What are you getting at?"

"I don't know!" says Ford. "I haven't figured it out yet, but I will! Listen, at least wait until tomorrow. If the bear comes back on schedule, you can do whatever you want."

"I can't wait that long. I've got places to go!" shouts Marla.

"You're crazy!" Fords shouts back. "You're the type of person who would dive headfirst into an empty pool, just to find out how empty it is!"

Marla pulls open the root-cellar door, but Ford kicks it closed. The house rattles and moss falls from the peeling walls.

"This is my house, and that means it's my machine," he says. "I won't let you use it, so go home. Now!"

Marla turns her Day-Glo-painted eyes to Ford and grits her teeth. "Why you slimy little sluggardly worm-brain! How dare you tell me what I can and cannot do! You think I care what you say, you *Leave It to Beaver* dweebistic troll? Marla Nixbok does what she wants, *when* she wants to do it, and if you won't throw the switch on that machine, I'll throw it myself!"

Still, Ford refuses to budge, so Marla takes her nails and heartlessly scratches his face, a maneuver she often uses when words no longer work.

Ford grabs his face and yelps in pain. Then he takes his foot away from the door.

"Fine," says Ford. "Go see the future. I hope you materialize right in the middle of a nuclear war!" With that, he storms to the stairs.

Good riddance, thinks Marla. Maybe she ought to travel fifty years into the future, just so she can find Ford as a shriveled old man and laugh in his wrinkled face.

Marla bends down and crawls into the root cellar.

At the top of the basement stairs, the truth finally strikes Buford Planet with such fury that it nearly knocks him down the stairs. If Marla uses that machine, her future won't be nuclear war. It'll be far, far from it.

"No!" he screams, and races back down the stairs.

In the root cellar, Marla turns the knob to *One Year*. One year is a good first trip. After that, who knows? Decades! Maybe centuries! At last she'll be free to travel to whatever time and place she feels she belongs. The Queen of Time. She likes the sound of that.

Ford crawls into the root cellar, out of breath.

"Marla, don't!" he screams.

"Get lost!" she shrieks back.

"But I figured it out!"

"Good. Does the machine work?"

"Yes, it does, but—"

"That's all I need to know!" Marla flips the switch and leaps into the silver chair. "See you next year!" she calls.

"Noooooooooo!"

But Marla never gets to see the horror in Ford's eyes. Instead she sees a flash of light and is struck by a shock of pain as she

is propelled exactly one year into the future, in this, the most exciting moment of her life.

In an instant she understands it all—and it is much worse than diving into an empty pool. Now she knows what Ford has been trying so desperately to tell her, because she is now very, very cold.

And she is floating.

Ford was right: the machine works all too well. She has traveled one year forward in time.

But she isn't the center of the universe.

And neither is the earth.

Suddenly she remembers that the earth revolves around the sun, and the sun revolves around the center of the galaxy, and the galaxies are flying apart at millions of miles per hour. Everything in the universe has been moving, except for Marla Nixbok. Marla has appeared in the *exact* location in space that she had been in one year ago. . .

But the Earth has long since moved on.

Even the sun is gone—just one among many distant stars.

Now she knows exactly why Wilmington and Buffy the bear can never come back. And as her last breath is sucked out of her lungs by the void of space, Marla Nixbok finally gets what she has always wanted: a crystal-clear vision of her own future. Now, and forever.

THE RIVER TOUR

Just this year I spent some time speaking at schools in San Antonio, Texas—one of my favorite cities. Downtown, they have an area called the Riverwalk. The San Antonio River meanders between the streets—it's kind of like the American version of Venice. There are restaurants and hotels lining the Riverwalk, and there's a boat tour that points out historical sights. I sat at a Riverwalk café, and wrote this story about a river tour that is similar, and yet decidedly different.

THE RIVER TOUR

Welcome to the river tour! My name is Sharon, and I'll be your guide. Please, no pushing—there's room on the barge for everyone. Son, please stay away from the steering wheel. Thank you. Oh, and please, no eating or drinking on the barge. Take your seats and we can be off.

Our river tour began long before anyone can actually remember, and is one of the favorite tourist attractions in our fine city. You'll see trendy restaurants and open-air cafés up and down the river for miles—but for the best ones you'll need reservations. Ah yes, the sounds and smells of life. Garlic and barbecue, laughter and song. So seductive. So tantalizing. It makes you want to jump and swim to shore, doesn't it? Well you can't, it's against the rules—so don't even try.

Now then—on our right side you'll notice that tree. A big one, isn't it? See how the roots are pushing up the path. It's hundreds of years old, and its boughs are massive—they almost reach right across the river, don't they? Back in the old days, it was called "The Hanging Tree." That's right—391 men were hanged from that tree. Criminals, of course. They say that their bodies were carried by barge downriver, to be buried. In fact, I believe it was this very barge that took them. I remember it like it was yesterday. Uh . . . that is to say . . . I remember the first time I heard the story like it was yesterday.

To our left we're coming up on a landmark building. Do you see—the one with gargoyles on the roof? That's the Woebegone Hotel, where Angus O'Malley and his bride jumped to their deaths on the evening of their wedding. They landed right in the river. Well . . . not exactly *in* the river—they landed on a passing barge. Very messy. Ma'am, would you like me to take that picture for you so you and your husband can both be in it? Yes, I agree—this is a wonderful picture spot. And you look so lovely in that wedding dress.

Now we're coming up on the Moribund Fireworks Factory, or what's left of it. It went up in flames, and all that remains are the ruins you see here today. Fortunately it was during the middle of the night, so the only person killed was the unlucky security guard who was on duty. Uh . . . sir . . . sir—you there in the uniform—could you please stop crying, you're upsetting the other passengers.

If you'll look ahead of us, we're about to pass under the Crossriver Bridge—also known as the "Crossfire Bridge." This is the infamous spot where ruthless mob boss "Joey the Weevil" was gunned down by FBI agents—and if you look closely you can still see the bullet holes where—Sir! *Sir!* Yes, you sir, in the double-breasted pinstripe suit, I must insist that you sit down. Standing makes the boat unstable, and you could fall into the water. Believe me, you don't want to fall into these waters. I could tell you stories.

Now, around the next bend, you'll see up on the riverbank

an ambulance, right at the edge of the road, right next to a truck with a badly dented grille. That's the spot where you attempted to cross the street. Yes, you. Don't turn around—I'm not talking to the person behind you, I'm talking to *you*. As I was saying, that's where you tried to cross the street just a few minutes before you got in line for the river tour.

As I recall, your mother always told you to look both ways when you crossed. You really should have listened to her. Off our starboard side, you'll notice there's a running shoe floating in the water. Nike, I believe. Yes, that's right, it's yours. That truck was moving at seventy miles an hour, after all. No surprise that your shoe ended up all the way over here.

What was that? No, I'm afraid you can't get off the boat here. That's strictly forbidden, and besides, we've still got a long way to go. Which reminds me—I do believe you haven't yet paid me for the tour. What's that you say? You don't have any money? Oh, I think you do. If you'll just check your eyelids, you'll find a coin on each one. They are your payment for passage. After all, you can't take a river trip without paying the ferryman, can you?

And now, as we leave the lights of our fine city behind and begin the final, less well-lit part of our journey, please feel free to lean back, relax, and rest in peace. I thank you for taking the river tour. My name is Charon, your ferryman on the river Styx, and it's been a pleasure to serve you.

FLUSHIE

My parents used to live on the twenty-seventh floor of a thirty-one-story apartment building in Manhattan. The top floor was a sports club, with a pool that was almost the length of the entire floor. At the deep end, the pool ended right at a huge window. You could tread water in the deep end and look out the window at an amazing view. One day while doing just that, I came up with this, probably one of my darkest stories.

FLUSHIE

Duncan held his breath.

He always held his breath, and he had gotten quite good at it. But not good enough.

"I coulda had a C!" growled Brett Duggan when the assault began. "I needed a C on this test—I told you that!"

Duncan had squirmed and fought against Brett and Nate's powerful grip, but then Charlie had joined in.

"Hold him!" yelled Nate, his voice echoing in the tiled bathroom.

It hadn't taken the three of them long to push Duncan to his knees.

"All you had to do, Duncan, was get a B," said Brett, pretending to be calm. "You know what a B is, don't you? Anything less than ninety *percent*! But does Duncan Goldwater get a B? No. You get a *hundred and four*! Like, how does someone get a hundred and four?"

"Extra credit!" Duncan screamed defiantly. He knew the answers to all the questions on that boneheaded math test, and no one was going to force him to lower his grade on purpose. It wasn't his fault the teacher had graded on a curve.

True, if Duncan hadn't been in the class the curve would have made Brett's miserable 67 a C-minus instead of a D. But it wasn't Duncan's job to make sure morons like Brett Duggan, Nate Carver, and Charlie Mintz passed math, or science, or English.

With Duncan's head hovering over the toilet, he was completely at their mercy, and the ritual began—a ritual that was passed on from grade to grade—a ritual that kept the bullies in charge—and Brett, Nate, and Charlie were really good at being bullies. Duncan suspected it was the only thing they *were* good at.

It happened like it always happened. And Duncan held his breath.

Brett gave Nate a thumbs-up and yelled, "Flush!"

Nate lifted his foot and stomped down on the shiny metal lever.

Grrissshh! Water gushed in Duncan's face like a great flood —not from a tank, but straight from the water pipes built into the walls of the old school bathroom. The newer restroom in the science wing had more water-efficient toilets, but when you needed to deliver someone a really good flush, the first-floor boys room was the best place to do it.

"Flush!" ordered Brett.

Grrissshh!

The water swirled around Duncan's head—colder this time, coming from deeper in the pipes. Duncan could no longer hold his breath. He opened his mouth to take a gasp of air, but mostly he got a mouthful of water. It was the same lousy-

tasting water that bubbled out of the faucet and water fountains around school, but telling himself that didn't make Duncan feel any better.

"Flush!" commanded Brett. Nate stomped on the lever a third time.

Grrissshh!

The water exploded in his face again, and at last the three flushmasters were satisfied. The water found its level in the bowl, and Brett lifted Duncan's head from the toilet by his sopping-wet hair. Humiliated, Duncan stumbled to a dusty corner of the bathroom and slid to the floor like a rag doll.

At fourteen, Duncan still felt like crying whenever they flushed him, but he held the tears back. Crying was what they wanted. From the time he was six, his classmates wanted to see him break. He could not give in.

"I'm really tired of you, Flushie," said Brett, kicking the toilet seat down for emphasis. The mighty porcelain bang was still echoing when he stormed out. Charlie followed him, laughing, but Nate lingered at the door.

"Duncan," he said, "you're such a waste of life." And then he was gone, letting the door squeak closed behind him.

Duncan knew how he must have looked, crumpled there in the corner of the bathroom, wet from his shirt pocket up. Pathetic.

But I'm not pathetic! his inner voice screamed. *They make me look this way! They make me feel this way!*

What was the use? Duncan cradled his head in his hands.

He wasn't the only A student in school; there were lots of others. Maybe the walking brain-dead like Brett grumbled about the smarter kids behind their backs, but those other smart kids were respected. They were well-liked by everyone, and none of them—*none* of them—ever got the flush.

That honor was reserved for one boy alone: Duncan Goldwater.

Why me? Duncan would always wonder . . . but he was smart enough to know why.

It was because he was Flushie. He had always been Flushie. If he were a D student, he would *still* be Flushie. There would always be a reason to give him the old swirling shampoo, because from the first day that he let them overpower him, that's who he'd become. There were kids in school who didn't even know him by any other name. Just Flushie.

The door creaked open. And the humiliation continued, only now it had a different face.

It was Sandra Martell.

He didn't want her to see him this way. He didn't want anyone to see him this way, especially not her.

She stepped in slowly and gingerly, as if the white floor tiles were eggshells—as if the floor of the boys' room were filled with invisible mines that only a girl could set off.

Duncan stood up immediately. His shoes slipped on the wet floor, but he recovered quickly, grasping onto an old radiator coil.

Sandra stood a few feet away, not saying anything yet, so Duncan said something. Something stupid.

"This is the boys' room," he offered, and deep in his mind the little guy who ran things bashed his moronic A-plus brain with a hammer for being so dumb.

"I know," said Sandra. "Are you okay?"

"Yeah," said Duncan. "No problem."

Sandra still kept her distance. Duncan tried to remember if she had ever been one of the flushers before. Had she ever been there watching and laughing like so many others did—others who Duncan thought were friends? Well, maybe she had been one of them before, but she wasn't laughing now, and that was something.

"Brett, Nate, and Charlie ... they can be such creeps," she said.

"Brett, Nate, and Charlie," echoed Duncan, "have the combined IQ of a soccer ball."

Sandra laughed. "A *flat* soccer ball." She shrugged. "Still, they're not all bad. They're just jealous. I mean, remember at the science fair, how they smashed the electronics on your seeing-eye bicycle, because all they had were dumb things like baking-soda volcanoes? See—they're mad, 'cause they can't be as smart as you."

Duncan shrugged, then mumbled, "Maybe."

"And anyway," said Sandra, "someday you'll be designing supercomputers or something, and making lots of money. They'll be lucky just to work for you, right?"

"I guess," said Duncan.

"So you see, Flushie, it's not so bad."

"Duncan!" he said a little too loudly. "My name is Duncan."

Sandra backed away a bit, grimacing at her mistake. "Sorry, Duncan. It's just . . . I don't know . . . we've all gotten used to the name. It's just a nickname. It doesn't mean anything. I'll call you Duncan from now on."

She said his name as if it were a foreign word, heavy and hard to push out.

For lack of a better idea, Duncan held out his hand for her to shake. "Thanks, Sandra," he said. "Thanks for coming in and talking to me."

She looked at his outstretched hand with silent dread. His hands were still wet from being flushed, so Duncan dried them on his pants, then held out his hand again. Sandra *still* wouldn't shake it.

She took an uncomfortable step back. "I've never been in a boys' room before," she said. "I'd better go."

She left much more quickly than she had come in, and Duncan dropped his arm.

Did she really care what happened to him, or was it just pity? Was he really that untouchable to a girl like Sandra? He had seen her dissect a frog in science class, and on a field trip he'd seen her dig for clams in briny muck up to her elbows. But his hands she would not touch.

Outside, the sound of feet heading to fourth period gave way to the second bell, and then silence.

In that silence Duncan thought about how he would get back at them. He would get back at all of them. There was no doubt of that. The very thought made him feel much, much better.

Duncan got up and stood before the warped bathroom

mirror. He pulled a comb from his pocket and combed his hair, determined to step out of the bathroom with some dignity.

———

Cheshire Tower stood majestically at the corner of Second Avenue and Eighty-fourth Street. Anywhere else on the planet its twenty-seven floors would have been impressive, but this was New York, so it was dwarfed by taller skyscrapers on three of its four sides.

Duncan's apartment had never had a chance at a decent view, being on the second floor. "Your mother's afraid of heights"—that was his father's excuse for putting their home nose level with the diesel exhaust pipes that rumbled by on the street all day long. "You want a view?" his father would say. "Then go up to the pool on the roof." But Duncan had better things to do today.

His pockets stuffed with allowance money he had been saving for weeks, Duncan left the building and turned up Eighty-fourth Street, where the beige bricks of Cheshire Tower gave way to the dark bricks of the old five-story low-rises that filled the rest of the street. Now that summer was just a week away, the pavement was teeming with activity. Duncan didn't know any of these people; they were just faces he passed on his way to his school every day. But he knew about Eugene. Everybody knew about Eugene.

Eugene was only twelve but was almost ready to shave. He was nearly two years younger than Duncan, but his voice was

already changing. Eugene was simply never born to be a kid.

As always, Eugene was out on his stoop as if he were waiting for something. He usually was.

"Do I know you?" he asked in a thick New York accent when he saw Duncan approach.

"You're Eugene, right? You sell stuff, don't you?"

"I don't sell stuff," said Eugene, looking around cautiously. "I sell *items*. You need an item?"

"I hear you got great fireworks—I need some for Fourth of July."

"Well, why didn't you say so?"

A minute later they were down in a basement, where Eugene revealed a regular arsenal of fireworks. He walked around, pointing things out to Duncan. "You got your Roman candles, you got your M-80s, you got your blockbusters—and none of those namby-pamby legal ones—this is the old-fashioned stuff. These Roman candles here will blow a hole in your face the size of a baseball. Pretty cool, huh?"

"What about the blockbusters?"

"You kiddin' me?" He pointed to a collection of colorful cylinders, an inch in diameter and about two inches long. "Quarter stick of dynamite in each one—make a blast you can hear all the way to Jersey. Guaranteed to make a big splash with your friends."

"How much for the whole box?"

Eugene raised an eyebrow. "How much you got?"

"I can't believe it," said Brett. "I must be dead or something. Flushie actually got a C on the math final!"

Duncan overheard the conversation. Mr. Carbuckle, the math teacher, wanted to talk to him about the test, but Duncan didn't care. Carbuckle tossed out the lowest grade anyway, and this was definitely Duncan's lowest grade.

"You did it on purpose, didn't you?" asked Sandra, but Duncan just shrugged. "Maybe I just didn't study." He headed out into the hall, following Brett and his entourage of friends.

Brett spotted him and put his head into a headlock—Brett's idea of a friendly gesture. "Jeez, Flushie, you didn't have to do that bad on my account."

"Least I could do for you, Brett," said Duncan. "After all, you haven't flushed me for a whole month."

As everyone laughed, Duncan reached into his backpack and pulled out a bundle of envelopes. "Listen, everybody. Since we'll all be going to different high schools next year, I wanted to have a party for Fourth of July. You can see the fireworks from the roof of my building."

Duncan reached into his backpack and handed Brett the first invitation.

The sports club on the top of the Cheshire Tower had a fifty-foot indoor swimming pool—not all that big, but big enough for the twenty-seventh floor of an apartment building. There were windows all around it, but most impressive was the big window at the deep end, just six inches above the waterline.

132

There was no deck at the deep end, and anyone who could bob his head high enough would get a glorious view of the city from the pool.

It had cost Duncan's father a small fortune to rent out the entire pool for the Fourth of July. Duncan promised to work all summer to pay it off, and by the time school ended, he had already lined up some odd jobs tutoring math and walking an old lady's five poodles. The work helped to pass the time from the end of school to the Fourth of July—two weeks that, to Duncan, seemed to stretch on forever.

Then, on that long-awaited Saturday evening, his schoolmates began to arrive in droves. Duncan couldn't believe that they all came!

"I never knew you had so many friends," remarked his mother.

"Yeah. It's amazing what pizza can do," said Duncan. And pizza there was. Everywhere. There was even one floating on a platter in the pool, looking like a jellyfish with pepperoni on it.

"This is great, Duncan," said Trevor—another flusher who had never said anything nice to him before. A girl named Melissa, who was famous for spreading vicious rumors about Duncan behind his back, scarfed down pizza and told him that he was the best.

But there was one guest who was not having a good time. Sandra sat in her green party dress, alone on the edge of a chaise longue.

"You didn't tell me it was a pool party!" she said.

"Sorry, I forgot," Duncan lied. "If it makes you feel any better, I won't go swimming either."

Sandra smiled politely at his offer.

"You could help me ref the water-volleyball game," he suggested. Then he looked at his watch. It was already twenty minutes before nine, just the right time for the game. It would definitely be the best game ever.

———

When it got dark, Independence Day exploded in the skies over Cheshire Tower like a revolution. Duncan helped his dad set up the volleyball net across the width of the pool, and everyone except Duncan and Sandra played.

Brett, who was self-proclaimed captain of the deep-water team, hogged the ball and held several people underwater until they came up coughing. This strategy seemed to work, because they creamed them. It was 8:56.

Duncan began to get just a bit edgy. "Rematch!" he called, but there were complaints that the sides weren't fair, and people began hopping out of the pool. To Duncan, that was completely unacceptable.

It was then that he slipped on the wet tiles of the deck. He didn't fall in the pool, but the sight of old Flushie slipping was enough to plant a seed in everyone's mind. It only took one suggestion from Brett for that seed to take root.

"Taking up diving, Flushie?" razzed Brett. Everyone laughed, and Brett heaved himself out of the pool, heading around the deck toward Duncan. The others looked at one another and began smiling.

"Sure, I'll bet you could be an Olympic diver," said Charlie, jumping out of the pool.

And then Nate said what they were all thinking: "Let's throw Duncan in the pool!" There was outrageous commotion in the water as everyone climbed out and headed toward him. Panicked, Duncan looked for his parents, but they were probably out on the sundeck watching the fireworks.

Sandra saw what was happening and tried to stop it. But there were simply too many of them. Then she slipped, too, falling hard on her knees.

"*Flush-ie, Flush-ie, Flush-ie!*" they chanted as they approached. The useless lifeguard pointed and blew his whistle, but nobody listened. *Not now!* thought Duncan, looking at his watch. It was exactly one minute until nine!

Naturally, Brett was the first one to reach him, and the look on his face reminded Duncan why he had thrown this "party" to begin with. Brett looked like a lion about to devour an antelope. It was how he looked whenever he flushed Duncan.

Brett grabbed Duncan hard. Duncan resisted, but then he felt hands all over him, lifting him off the ground, moving him closer to the water.

"*Flush-ie, Flush-ie, Flush-ie!*"

"No!" yelled Sandra, but she got tangled up in the mob as she tried to get them off Duncan.

"*Flush-ie, Flush-ie, Flush-ie!*"

They all heaved at once, and the force created enough mo-

mentum to take them all in, like a single beast with a dozen arms and legs.

Far away a church bell began to chime out nine o'clock, and an odd sound echoed under the surface of the Cheshire Tower pool, like a submarine struck by a torpedo. The big window just above the deep end rattled violently.

By the time everyone came up for air, it was clear something strange was going on. The water was moving all by itself.

While the others floundered, wondering what was going on, Duncan swam with all his might to the nearest ladder, held on with all his strength, and watched.

It didn't happen the way he had imagined it. He had thought there would be a whirlpool spinning around and around, but there wasn't. Instead, there was a wave in the deep end that rolled like the ocean surf but never got any closer. The water in front of that wave was dragged beneath the churning water like a powerful undertow.

"Wow, a wave pool!" shouted Charlie.

Nate, who was right underneath the big window at the deep end, was the first to find out exactly what was going on. First his head bobbed on top of the great rolling wave, then he was pulled beneath it. Without even having a chance to scream, he was pulled deep down in the pool, and before he knew what was happening, he was out in the cold night air, falling toward the taxicabs twenty-seven floors below.

Everyone caught on quickly when Charlie disappeared, too. Then the screaming began. They all tried to fight the riptide pulling them to the deep end, but it was hopeless. One by one

their screams were silenced, and they were pulled under as if into the mouth of a shark, then ejected from the building through a huge, jagged hole in the side of the pool.

Duncan watched with a sense of power he hadn't felt since the week before, when he had finished building the time bomb—the very bomb that had now blown a hole in both the pool and the outer wall of the building. It had been easier to build than any of his science projects. *I'll bet they heard that in Jersey, huh, Eugene?* he thought when the blast first went off.

The lifeguard and adults, who had rushed back to the pool, could do nothing but gawk and shriek as they watched kid after kid go under.

Melissa went, dragging the volleyball net with her, followed by several others. It was then that Sandra came floating by, her green party dress rippling around her like a lily pad. Duncan could not let *her* go. He had never intended for her to be in the water at all. He reached out his hand and she grabbed it—this time with no reservations. That in itself was something! He pulled her toward him and helped her hook her arms around the chrome pole of the pool ladder.

Now do you see? he thought. *Now do you see why I didn't want you to swim? You're the only one worth saving, Sandra. The only one!*

There was a roaring blast like the sound of a whale's blowhole, and they both turned to see that the water level had dropped far enough to reveal the top lip of the gaping hole. The rolling wave was gone, and all that remained was the

water pouring down a bottomless waterslide that spilled into the sky above Eighty-fourth Street.

Brett bobbed past Duncan, holding out his grubby hand. He locked eyes with Duncan. This time, Brett's eyes were the eyes of the antelope. "Help me," he pleaded.

Duncan held out his hand toward Brett, but instead of taking Brett's hand, Duncan closed his fingers into a fist and gave Brett a thumbs-up.

"Flush!" Duncan sneered. With that, the current caught Brett and pulled him into the hole, where he was permanently expelled.

Duncan looked at Sandra, who was screaming and shivering as she clung to the ladder.

"It's okay," he said.

He wanted to stop her from crying. He wanted to kiss her. Would she let him do that, knowing how strong he really was? Strong enough to beat his enemies—strong enough to win once and for all. Duncan took one hand from the ladder and moved it toward her trembling cheek.

That's all it took.

His foot slipped from the rung, his hand slipped from the bar, and he was suddenly moving farther and farther away from Sandra. "Duncan!" she screamed. He tried to swim back to her, but it was too late. The current had him, and he felt himself being pulled toward the final flush of his life.

Trevor was still in the pool, fighting a battle with the foaming white water—a battle he lost. Trevor went down, then at last the hole locked its sights onto Duncan, pulling him

toward it like a tractor beam. Helpless, he stopped fighting its powerful gravity and accelerated toward the black hole. Then, as if in slow motion, it ejected him out into . . . city lights! All around, dazzling him! Wind, filling his ears, eyes, and mouth!

Far below, the traffic had already come to a screeching halt. Honking horns, screaming bystanders, and bursts from the fireworks filled the night. Duncan took in the amazing view as he fell, and he let out a final cry of victory, for he knew that all the others had gone before him. At least that was something!

As the ground raced up to meet him, Duncan threw out his arms and legs, riding the wind like a skydiver.

And he held his breath.

Monkeys Tonight

When my son was about three years old, we made the mistake of showing him *The Wizard of Oz*. It got to the scene with the flying monkeys, and he ran from the room in terror. From that moment on, he was terrified of monkeys. Shortly thereafter he had a dream that there were monkeys in the house, and he had us check, not just his room and the closet and under his bed, but in the garage, the backyard, and the refrigerator. We thought we had convinced him that the house was safe from a monkey invasion until he looked at the fireplace. We had been talking about Santa coming down the chimney, as it was close to Christmas, and he decided that if Santa could come down the chimney, then monkeys could as well. After that night, I just had to write a story about those monkeys. . . .

MONKEYS TONIGHT

My sister wakes up screaming at the top of her lungs—a sharp, shrill sound, like an alarm, or a teakettle boiling to death. The awful noise rips me out of the deepest of sleeps. I twist through space until I feel the blanket around me and the coldness of my feet. She screams again, and I pull the blanket over my head, trying to cram it into my ears.

Then I hear the panicked footsteps of my parents as they race down the hall. I glance at the clock. It's almost four in the morning.

Mom and Dad bound into the room as Melinda empties her lungs again, even louder than before.

"Shut her up!" I croak to my parents in a raspy night voice. Mom and Dad ignore me and race to Melinda's bed. They shake her and shake her until she comes out of her nightmare. Her screaming fades into a whimper, but when she sees Mom and Dad above her, she begins to sob. Dad takes her into his arms as she cries.

"I'll get her some water," says Mom.

"Bring some for me," I say, knowing that Mom doesn't hear me. She never hears me when Smellinda is crying. Smellinda: that's what I call her, because as far as I'm concerned, she stinks.

141

"Can't you shut her up?" I plead, trying to stretch the blanket over my freezing feet.

"Ryan, just go back to sleep," says Dad.

Easy for him to say. He doesn't have to share a room with a human air-raid siren. There is something wrong when a twelve-year-old boy is forced to share a room with his eight-year-old sister. There ought to be a law against it.

Dad picks up Melinda and rocks her gently. "What is it, honey?" he asks.

"Monkeys," whimpers Melinda.

I groan and bury my head in my pillow as Mom brings water for Melinda and nothing for me. Why did I know it was going to be monkeys? It's always monkeys.

Monkeys. Of all the dumb things to be afraid of. I mean, there are plenty of *really* scary things to be afraid of, aren't there? Mummies, and skeletons, and spooky graveyards, and vampires. But personally, it's spiders that freak me out. Sometimes I imagine these big, three-foot-long spiders with hairy black legs the size of human arms. They drink your blood, spiders do. Well, not human blood—fly blood. But I suppose if spiders were big enough, they could go for human blood, too. Just the thought of them makes my skin crawl and my heart start to race. But *monkeys?* Who in their right mind is scared of monkeys?

Smellinda, that's who.

Dad holds her and walks back and forth on Melinda's side of the room, full of dolls and rainbow wallpaper. It's the side of the room my friends make fun of when they come over to visit, as if I had anything to say about it.

"There are no monkeys in here," Dad tells Melinda. "It was just a dream. Just your imagination."

"They came down the chimney," she cries. I start to laugh to myself. A few weeks ago we saw a television show about how they transport zoo animals by plane. One of the animals they showed was a monkey. Ever since then, every time a plane flies by, Melinda is certain that a monkey is going to jump out of the plane like a hairy paratrooper and head straight for our chimney.

"There are no monkeys in the room, sweet cakes," says Mom, flicking on the light, blinding me. "See?"

I roll over and bury my face in the pillow.

"The closet," says my sister.

Dad opens the closet to reveal clothes and a messy pile of toys.

"The bathroom," says Melinda.

Dad steps into the bathroom, peeling back the shower curtain to reveal just a leaky faucet and a bathtub ring.

"The kitchen," insists Melinda.

Dad carries her down the hallway, and I hear him and Mom inspect every inch of our house. Closets, cabinets, the oven, the fireplace—they even check under the furniture.

Finally, ten minutes later, they come back with Melinda happily asleep in Dad's arms, satisfied that the house has been purged of the banana-eating menaces. They gently tuck her in, turn off the light, and go back to bed.

Melinda, her nose stuffy from crying, snores away. Even after her monkey fit, she can sleep. But I'm not so lucky. I can

hear everything around me. I hear the awful ticking of her Mickey Mouse clock. I hear the *whap!* as the paperboy throws newspapers on driveways long before the sun comes up. When I open my eyes I see shadows and get spooked. The shadows are like fat spiders, with legs stretching along the walls and floor. Darkness creeping, inch by inch toward my bed. I know that it's only clothes piled in the corner, and stuffed animals on the shelves, and patterns cast by the window blind, but still, I see spiders. Once I've got the spider creeps, I know I won't sleep for the rest of the night, no matter how much I want to.

But there's Melinda across the room, sleeping happily with her dolls and purple ponies and fluffy teddy bears. She sleeps peacefully, probably dreaming of a beautiful fairy-tale castle. And I silently wish for her dream castle to be invaded by baboons.

On the drive to school in the morning, Melinda and I sit in the backseat. Melinda plays with Deep Space Barbie, who has blue hair and green skin. I just sit there like a zombie who didn't get enough sleep. How I wish I could go back to bed!

Mom drives, listening to the news, hoping to hear a traffic report. Instead, we hear a story about the zoo.

Tragedy struck the Central Zoo yesterday, begins the reporter, *when an angry gorilla apparently broke through its cage, grabbed a man, and ripped off—*

CLICK!

Mom quickly turns off the radio, pretending she didn't hear the reporter.

Melinda looks at me with a face that's turning almost as green as Deep Space Barbie. "Ripped off what?" she asks.

"Probably ripped off his arms," I tell her.

"Ryan!" my mother warns.

"Maybe his head, too. Gorillas are known to do that."

"Mommy, what do you think the gorilla ripped off?" Melinda asks tentatively.

"I think it ripped off his wallet," says Mom, "so it could treat Mrs. Gorilla to a fancy dinner."

Melinda laughs.

"Maybe he got his legs, too," I tell Melinda. "Apes are strong. Monkeys are, too. I'll bet if they wanted to, all the gorillas and baboons and orangutans and chimps could break out of their cages and escape in a matter of minutes. Hey, Mom, how far is the zoo from our house?"

"Never mind that!" says Mom.

I snicker, and in a flash of inspiration, I grab Melinda's Deep Space Barbie. "This is probably how it looked at the zoo yesterday." I insert Barbie hair-first into my mouth and bite off her head.

"*Mommmmyyyyyyyy!*" screams Melinda.

Mom glares at me in the rearview mirror. "Ryan, stop it!" she yells.

I spit it out and the little plastic head ricochets off the window and lands in Melinda's lap. She puts the head back on, but she can't stop crying. I, on the other hand, can't stop laughing.

It's a full moon tonight. The kind that brings out the were-wolves—if you believe in that stuff. Our house doesn't get werewolves, though. Tonight, we get something else.

I'm fast asleep when I first hear Melinda. She's not scream-ing, she's calling my name. "Ryan," she whispers. I'm dragged feet first out of my dream, and twist through space back into my bed, where I open my eyes and see Melinda looking toward me in the dim blue of the moonlit room. It is four o'clock again. I sigh and wish there were a Sister Fairy who would come in the night to take Melinda away, leaving a quarter beneath my pillow. Fair exchange.

"Ryan," she whispers. "Do you hear that?"

Scrape, scrape, scrape. It could be coming from anywhere.

"It's probably just a stray cat," I tell her. "Go to sleep." But the sound gets louder. Scrape! Scrape! Scrape! Now I can hear the hiss and rattle of falling debris.

"It's coming from the chimney!" says Melinda.

"Naah, it's probably just Dad making some weird late-night snack," I say, but now the sound has got me worried, too.

I sit up and listen. There's a noise coming from the hard-wood floor in the living room. The squishy sound of bare feet—plod-plod-plod—but then the sound is gone. *It's in the hallway,* I tell myself. *It's walking on the carpeted hallway, si-lently.*

It's much too quiet. I can hear the ticking of the clock pounding in my ears like a woodpecker. I am about to an-

nounce to Melinda that it was just her imagination when a shadow leaps into the room, howling.

It's a monkey—laughing in a crazy, screeching, evil voice. I see it, but I don't believe it. I am too shocked to scream.

"Ryan?" Melinda's high-pitched panicked voice is like a squeaky wheel. "No . . . no," she whines. She tries to scream, but it's like her throat is all closed up in fear. She starts batting the air around her. "Go away! Go away!"

A second monkey runs into the room, jumps up on a shelf, and begins throwing books everywhere.

Another monkey comes in through the window and terrorizes Melinda, flailing its hands in her face and making awful noises. Melinda gasps, unable to catch her breath in fear. Then she screams, and so do I. That's when the room explodes into a mad monkey house. The closet door flies open and they leap out like commandos—not just monkeys, but apes like chimpanzees and orangutans, too. They charge out of the closet as if the closet is a doorway to another world. Small monkeys with long tails and white faces climb out from the dresser drawers and leap from wall to wall. A single gorilla growls in the doorway, making sure we can't get out. Both of us scream and scream. *Where are our parents? Why can't we hear them coming down the hall?*

One baboon with wild, fiery eyes and sharpened teeth smiles and speaks—*he actually speaks!* "Your parents won't wake up." He sneers. "They won't wake up until morning. We won't let them."

I try to help Melinda, but hairy hands grab me and throw

me back against the wall. I can only watch as they torment her, tearing apart her stuffed animals, chewing them to bits, shredding her books, leaping across her bed, and swinging wildly through the room. They pull at her arms and tug at her hair as she screams. An orangutan plays her head like the bongo drums. A chimp makes hideous faces at her, and Melinda keeps screaming in terror, until she finally screams herself out. Soon her voice is gone, but her mouth keeps screaming silently. This is her nightmare—but how did it get out of her head? *How?*

Finally the raid ends, and the apes and monkeys begin to leave. Some climb out of the window, others vanish into the closet, some climb into the dresser drawers and disappear, and others race out of the room and scurry up the chimney. I look to Melinda. She is pale. She looks straight ahead, frozen, but does not see.

"Melinda?"

She will not answer me. It's as if she's gone far away and doesn't even hear me.

"Melinda?"

But she won't talk at all. I think she may never talk again.

The last monkey—the baboon with sharpened teeth—looks around the ruined room, at the night's work. He leaps up to the windowsill to leave, and I say a prayer of thanks that it's all over. But then he turns to me before he disappears into the night. He smiles at me, showing his terrible teeth. I pull my blanket over me, but it won't cover me no matter how hard I try.

"Pleasant dreams, Ryan," he rasps in a deep, scratchy voice. Then he says, with an awful wink:

"Tomorrow night, spiders."

SCREAMING AT THE WALL

One of my all-time favorite songs is "Synchronic-ity 2" by the Police. I'm sure you know the song, even if you don't know it by name. It's about, among other things, the Loch Ness Monster rising from the depths, and an equally frightening family situation about to unfold many miles away. (The monster, you come to realize as you listen to the song, is a metaphor for what's happening in the family. Man, those guys were brilliant!)

Well, this story has absolutely nothing to do with that.

However . . . the first two lines of the song are *"Another suburban family morning, Grandmother screaming at the wall."* Every time I heard Sting sing that line, the image got to me. Grandmother scream-ing at the wall. Why is she doing that? In the song you assume she must be crazy. . . but then I started thinking—what if Grandmother's not crazy at all? What if something else is going on . . . ?

SCREAMING AT THE WALL

"Of course I love you," says Grandma. "I love you very, very much, Leslie."

Grandma stands inches away from the hallway wall. There is not so much as a picture on the wall, just white paint.

I can see her from my room. The way she stands there talking to the wall—it scares me.

"Let me give you a hug," says Grandma. She holds out her arm and grasps the air in front of her, as if she is hugging someone. But no one is there.

She's been talking to that wall for about a month now. It's not just the wall, though. She'll get angry at someone who's not even in the room. And she treats all of us as if we're invisible.

Dad hardly seems to notice anymore. He's too busy remodeling the house, even late at night. Each night I go to sleep to the sound of saws and hammers and drills.

Mom sits on the edge of my bed, and we talk about things. Lately, we just talk about Grandma.

"Sometimes it happens like that when you get old. People just sort of wind down," Mom tells me. "It's a part of life."

I think about that: *winding down*, like old gears . . . like our grandfather clock in the hall, which can never keep the right time. But Grandma's not a machine; she's a human being.

I think back to the times when Grandma was okay, before her mind started to slip. She was wonderful and warm and loving. She would take me to the movies and we would talk like the best of friends. But that was a long time ago. Now she's very different. My friends laugh at her, but there's nothing funny about it.

I hear a hammer banging away in the garage. In the kitchen, Grandma sits in the dark. I can hear her talking about the ice cream she's pretending to eat, and then she sings "Happy Birthday" to the empty room. I remember that my birthday is coming up next month.

"That's all right, honey," she says to the dark, empty room. "I don't mind wearing a party hat."

"Who is she talking to?" I ask Mom. "What is she seeing?"

"I don't think we'll ever know," says Mom.

I know what my birthday wish will be. I'll wish that Grandma had her mind back.

———

It is midnight. I hear Grandma. I leave my room and go into the living room, where Grandma sits in the green velvet chair, watching TV by moonlight. But the TV isn't on.

"They call this music?" she says. "A lot of noise, if you ask me. And look at them—grown men with pink hair."

She reaches down beside her and moves her hand back and forth. It takes me a moment to figure out what she's doing. She's petting a dog. But we don't have a dog.

"And what's the point of smashing the guitars?" she says, pointing at the dark TV. "This isn't music; it's a circus."

"Grandma, can you hear me?" I ask.

She looks through me as if I'm not even there. Then, suddenly, she gasps in shock and jumps to her feet. She feels around the walls as if she's blind.

"I'll go get the candles," she says, and then shakes her head with a sigh.

"All this rain," she says. "I've never seen it rain like this." But outside the stars are out and the moon is bright. It isn't raining—not a drop.

Dad works hard every weekend, building our new rec room. He pretends that nothing is happening. Grandma is his mother; it must be hard for him to see her like this.

Anyway, he doesn't like to talk about it, but I keep asking because I want answers. I miss the way Grandma used to be.

"It started about five years ago," Dad finally says, resting from his work and drinking a Coke. "I remember, I first noticed something was wrong when she started laughing at a joke before the punch line. She just walked away, not even hearing the rest of the joke. Then she would start waking up at all hours of the night. She would go and make herself breakfast and talk at the breakfast table as if we were all there at two o'clock in the morning." He shook his head. "Anyway, pretty soon she was living in a whole different world from us."

Dad wipes the sweat from his brow. "She needs us to take care of her now. Okay, Leslie?"

I nod quietly, sorry I made him talk about it.

Dad goes back to his work, burying himself in the room he's adding on, trying not to think about Grandma. I watch as he takes a heavy sledgehammer and swings it at the hall wall, over and over, creating a huge hole that will become the doorway to our new rec room.

One night before the rec room is finished, Grandma starts screaming at the wall again.

"How dare you!" she screams. "I'm your own flesh and blood!"

The others race in to find her standing in the unfinished rec room. "You're going to put me in a sanitarium?" she screams at the drywall in the corner. "That's what you're going to do? I'm not crazy!"

"I can't take this anymore, Carl!" my mom screams at my dad. She storms out of the room in tears.

Dad follows her, trying to calm her down, and I'm left alone with Grandma.

There's no electricity in the rec room yet. The only light comes from the hallway and from the bright, full moon. I watch Grandma staring out of the picture window, as if she can see something in the dark, as if she can see the river that the window overlooks. All I can see is darkness.

There are tears in her eyes. Even though she is standing right next to me, she seems so far away. So alone.

"Grandma," I ask. "Do you love me?"

"I wish it would stop raining," she says, looking up at the clear, starlit sky. "All this rain, it can't be good for the soil."

"Could you just give me a hug, Grandma—just one hug, like you used to?"

Then, for a moment, I get the feeling that we have had this conversation before. But the feeling is gone in an instant.

———

For my thirteenth birthday we have a small party with just a few friends. Dad tries to get us to wear stupid party hats, but no one wants to. Grandma sits alone on a folding chair out in the unfinished rec room, staring at the unpainted wall across the room, occasionally chuckling to herself.

We all eat ice cream and everyone sings "Happy Birthday"—everyone except Grandma. A few minutes later I notice that one of my dumb friends has put a party hat on her. I go into the rec room and take the hat off.

"Have you ever seen the river like this?" Grandma says to the dry, sunny day. "All swollen from the rain? It has to stop raining soon."

For a strange moment, as I hold that party hat in my hands, I get the feeling again that I've done this before . . . but I know I haven't.

Party hat, I think. *Wasn't Grandma talking about a party hat a few weeks ago?* But everyone calls me back into the living room to open my presents, so I don't think about it anymore.

For my birthday I get a puppy.

The next night it begins to rain. Troubled by the thunder and lightning, I stay up late and watch TV with Mom and Dad in the living room. Magoo, my new dog, sits by the side of the green velvet chair. On TV a rock band plays wild music. Mom and Dad think it's awful, but I kind of like it. And then I notice . . .

The guys in the band all have pink hair . . . and at the end of the song they smash their guitars.

A chill runs through my body. I look for Grandma, but she is not in the room.

"What's wrong, Leslie?" asks Mom. "Are you all right?"

"I don't know," I say. "I just feel . . . funny."

Bam! The thunder crashes at the same moment the lightning hits, and the house is plunged into darkness.

Dad is up immediately. "I'll get the candles," he says. He feels around for the walls in the dark, like a blind man.

A few minutes later, with a candle in my hand, I search the house for Grandma. I find her in the garage, looking through boxes of old photos.

"Can't leave these behind," she says. "Have to take them with me."

"Grandma," I ask, just beginning to understand. "Where are you? What do you see?"

"Barry, you and your family should never have come to visit with the weather like this," says Grandma. "You should have told them not to come, Carl. You can do what you like, but I'm not taking the chance. I'm getting my stuff, and I'm getting out. Before it's too late."

I can tell she's talking to my dad and Uncle Barry—but Uncle Barry and his family live a thousand miles away in Michigan, and they haven't visited us for years. Yet Grandma's talking to them like they're in the room.

And suddenly I realize what's wrong with Grandma.

"Grandma," I say. "I know what's happening. I understand now."

———

"Leslie, your imagination is running away with you," says Dad. He's sitting in the rec room holding a candle. The lights have been out for an hour now. I stand at the entrance to the rec room. Mom and Dad sit in a corner. They're talking about putting Grandma into a home or a sanitarium.

"No!" I insist. "It's true. Grandma is living in the future. She's not crazy."

"Get some rest," says Mom. "You'll feel better in the morning."

"No, I won't!" I shout. "Don't you get it?" I stand in the doorway of the rec room. "This doorway used to be a wall—this used to be the wall that Grandma would talk to—but she wasn't talking to the wall, she was talking to *us* inside the rec room. Only the rec room hadn't been built yet! And when she was pretending to eat ice cream in the middle of the night, she was seeing my birthday party a month later. And when she watches the TV when it's off, she's seeing TV shows that

won't be on for a whole month. I even caught her petting the dog *before* we had the dog. And remember when she stood in the rec room screaming into the corner about your wanting to send her away? Well, she was screaming into the corner you're sitting in right now! She *saw* the conversation you're having right now, and it really upset her!"

I clench my fists, trying to get Mom and Dad to understand. "Don't you see? Grandma's body might be stuck in the present, but her mind is living a month in the future." I point to the grandfather clock down the hall. "It's like how that clock always runs too fast. At first it's just a couple of minutes off, but if we don't reset it, it could run hours—even days—ahead of where it's supposed to be! Grandma's like that clock, only she can't be fixed!"

Lightning flashes in the sky, and Mom stands up. "I think this storm is giving us all the creeps. I'll feel better when it's over tomorrow."

"No," I say. "According to Grandma, the storm goes on for weeks and weeks."

That's when we hear Grandma screaming.

We run into the bedroom to find Grandma thrashing around the room, bumping into things. She clutches the bedpost, holding on for dear life, as if something is trying to drag her away. Mom and Dad try to grab her but she doesn't see them; she just keeps on thrashing and clinging to the bedpost, like a flag twisting in the wind.

"Barry!" she screams. "Hold on! Carl! Don't let her go!"

Dad grabs her and holds her, but she is stronger than any of

us realize. There is sheer terror in her eyes, and I try to imagine what she sees. "Holly's gone, Carl—Holly, Barry, Alice, the twins, they're all gone—there's nothing you can do! Now you have to save yourself! No, don't let go! No!"

She screams one last bloodcurdling scream that ends with a gurgling, as if she's drowning. Then, silence.

And that's when I know Grandma is gone.

She's still breathing, her heart is still beating, but she is limp and her eyes are unseeing. Her mind has died, but her body doesn't know it yet. It will in several weeks, I think.

Suddenly the only sound I hear is the falling rain and the rushing of the river a hundred yards beyond our backyard.

That was almost a month ago. Now I stand in my room, shoving everything I care about into my backpack, making sure I leave room for Magoo. I don't let Mom and Dad know what I'm doing. I can't let them know, or they would stop me.

In the rec room, which has been painted, carpeted, and furnished, Mom makes up the sofa bed. "Uncle Barry and Aunt Alice won't mind sleeping on this," says Mom, patting the bed. "The twins can sleep in your room," she tells me. "You can stay with us. It's only a week—I don't want to hear you complaining."

But I'm not complaining.

"Isn't it wonderful that they're coming all the way from Michigan to spend time with us?" says Mom. "After all these years!"

"I just wish we had better weather. I've never seen it rain this much," says Dad, coming into the room. "It can't be good for the soil."

———

That night, I give Mom and Dad a powerful hug and kiss good night, holding them like I'll never let them go. Then, after everyone's asleep, I go into Grandma's room. She lies in bed, as she has for a whole month now. Not moving, barely even breathing.

I give her a hug also, and then I climb out of the window into the rain.

It is raining so hard that in moments I am drenched from head to toe. I am cold and uncomfortable, but I'll be all right.

Tonight I will run away. I don't know where I will go; all I know is that I have to leave. Even now, I can hear the river churning in its bed, roaring with a powerful current ready to spill over its banks.

Tomorrow, after Uncle Barry's family arrives, there will be a disaster. It will be all over the news. There will be special reports about how the river overflowed and flooded the whole valley. The reports will tell how dozens of homes were washed away, and how hundreds of people were killed.

I can't change any of that, because Grandma already saw it. She saw my mom, my dad, my uncle, my aunt, and my cousins taken away by the flood. Then, finally, the waters took her as well. She saw it more than a month ago.

But on that day when we watched her in her bedroom,

holding on to her bedpost, torn by waters that we could not see, there was one name she didn't mention. She didn't mention me. And if I wasn't there, then at least one member of my family will have a future.

So tonight I take the high road out of town. And tomorrow I won't watch the news.

GROWING PAINS

I have no clue how I got the idea for this one.
And maybe it's better that way. . . .

GROWING PAINS

The scream stabbed into Cody Fenchurch's sleep, tearing a jagged hold in his dream. He had been dreaming he was tall—the tallest kid in school—towering over all the other kids who always teased him about his height. But great dreams like that never last, and Cody was dragged away from that happy fantasy, into the cold darkness of his room. He sat up, blinking in the moonlight, wondering who had screamed—and why.

Suddenly a second scream rattled his half-opened window, and Cody knew that both screams had come from next door. That's where his best friend, Warren Burke, lived.

Cody stared through his large window and could see right into Warren's room. He could see his friend sitting in bed and wailing. What was happening in there? It sounded like Warren was being torn to pieces.

Cody watched as the lights came on next door, and Warren's parents raced into his room. By then, Warren was running around, waving and thrashing his arms at empty air.

Soon Cody realized that his own parents were awake, too. He heard them whispering down the hall, talking about what was going on at the neighbors' house, and wondering what to

do. Then his dad poked his head into Cody's room. "You okay, sport?" he asked.

Cody assured his dad that he was, then he tried to go back to sleep. That's when Warren screamed again, and this time Cody heard him say something, too.

"Don't let them come back!" Warren shrieked. "Don't let them take me again! It's horrible! Horrible!"

Cody listened to Warren's mad ravings, and then he listened to Mr. and Mrs. Burke trying to calm him down. "It's only a dream," they kept telling him over and over again.

But that didn't seem to calm Warren down in the least. In fact, he continued to scream the rest of that awful, endless night, and Cody slept—or tried to sleep—with a pillow over his head.

In the morning, Warren was still screaming. And he was still screaming that next afternoon . . . when he was taken off to the hospital. As far as Cody knew, Warren never did stop screaming.

And that's how Cody Fenchurch lost his best friend.

———

"But you have to *try* to sleep," Cody's mom insisted. It had been three weeks since Warren Burke had been taken away, and once again, here Cody was, lying on his bed, his eyes wide open.

"You know what they say," his mother offered. "You grow when you sleep."

"I'm trying," said Cody, rolling over restlessly. "I always try."

His mother raised an eyebrow. "You're thinking about Warren, aren't you?"

"No," Cody said flatly. It was a lie, of course. How could he not think about Warren? He thought about him every time he looked out his window and saw his friend's empty room across the way. He thought about him every time he walked home from school—alone.

"Would you like to visit Warren?" Cody's mom asked.

Cody sat up in bed. "You mean they let kids visit other kids in the asylum?"

She wrinkled her nose, as if the word "asylum" had a stench to it. "They don't call those places asylums anymore, Cody," she informed him. "They're just hospitals—*special* hospitals."

Cody thought about that and looked out the window toward Warren's dark, empty room. For years he and Warren had talked to each other at night across the narrow pathway between their two houses, about all sorts of things—school, girls, sports—and growing up.

Growing up.

That had been a sore point with Cody. He and Warren had always been about the same height until fifth grade. But then Warren had started having what they called "growth spurts." One summer he even grew two whole inches.

But Cody didn't have any growth spurts. In fact, he hadn't grown a fraction of an inch in two years. While all the other kids in school were sprouting long, clumsy arms and legs, Cody remained unchanged.

Now, in the middle of seventh grade, Cody was the shortest kid in class, and Warren, if he hadn't been locked away somewhere, would have been the tallest. Cody remembered how ridiculous he used to feel walking home next to Warren. But Warren had never made fun of Cody's size—not like the other kids. That's why they had been able to stay best friends.

So now that his best friend went insane and was taken away, did Cody want to visit him? Did he *really* want to visit Warren after he had seen him scream for twelve straight hours?

Cody looked at his mom, who was standing at the edge of his bed. "Is it true that Warren's hair turned white that night?" he blurted out.

His mother offered him a slim smile and said wistfully, "That happens sometimes."

Harmony Home for Children did its best to be pleasant and inviting, but the disinfectant-scented linoleum couldn't hide the smell of decay, and the music pumped into the air couldn't hide the sounds of madness.

Warren was in a room at the end of a long hallway papered with balloons and teddy bears. It was the type of wallpaper that would have made Warren gag in his old, real life, Cody mused as he stepped into the barely furnished room with his mother. A nurse, who was required to stay during all visits, sat in the corner.

All that was in the room was a bed, a dresser with baby-proof latches, and Warren, crouched in his bed, staring at the wall across from him. He cowered as if there were a monster across the room, but there was nothing there but the same balloons and teddy bears that had invaded the hall.

The nurse smiled, as if it were her job to smile. "Stimulation is important for Warren," she said. "He needs to know people still remember him—that his old life is still out there when he's ready to go back to it."

Cody cleared his throat and held on to his mother like a small child. "What's up, Warren?" he asked.

But Warren didn't turn to look at him. Instead he just hummed to himself.

Cody tentatively let go of the death grip he had on his mother's arm and took a few steps closer.

Warren still didn't look at him, but he did speak.

"They let you in here?" he asked. "Why did they let you in here?"

Warren's voice sounded empty and far away. Cody noticed that his hair wasn't quite white but ashen gray, standing on end, and hopelessly tangled. This was not the Warren Burke that Cody knew.

"Yeah, sure, they let me in," Cody said, offering a lopsided smile. "You doin' okay?"

Warren shook his head and backed farther into the corner of his bed as Cody approached. "Don't let them get you!" he shrieked, his voice a wild warble. "Stay awake all night! Run when you see them coming! Don't let them take you to that place."

Cody could feel his own hair start to stand on end, but he

had to ask. "Who? Who's going to get me? And where am I supposed to keep them from taking me?"

Warren could only stare at Cody in horror.

The nurse, who didn't seem pleased with the direction of the conversation, pulled open the curtains. "Maybe we could all take a look at the view," she said. And then she turned to Warren. "Why don't you tell your little friend all about the walks we've been taking around the lake, Warren? Tell him how they help your nerves."

Cody looked out the window. The view might have been beautiful elsewhere, but not for the people here. The bars on the window could never let them forget where they were.

But Warren didn't seem interested in the view anyway. He just kept staring over at the wall as if waiting for something to happen.

Suddenly Cody's mother, who had been sitting quietly by the door, turned to the nurse and asked, "Is Warren getting any . . . better?"

"Oh, yes!" chimed the nurse, as if it were her job to chime. "He's growing stronger every day!"

"Growing!" said Warren, with a sneer in his voice. Then he snapped his eyes to Cody. "You're lucky," he said. "You're lucky you're so small. Growing as fast as I did was the worst thing that ever happened to me!"

"Now, Warren," said the nurse in her practiced, soothing voice. "Remember, we have to think positive thoughts." And she cast her eyes down to the little paper cup on the dresser to make sure he had taken his medication.

"I'll never have a positive thought again," said Warren. "Not after what I saw—not after what I *felt*."

Cody couldn't resist. "What did you feel?" he asked.

Warren's eyes went wide and his lips stretched back in a grimace, as if he were feeling it all over again.

"*Growing pains*," he hissed.

The nurse was beginning to act a little nervous. "Warren, why don't you take your little friend out to the rec room," she suggested. "You could play Ping-Pong, or a nice game of Scrabble."

But Warren wasn't interested in games. He reached out, grabbed Cody by the shirt, and pulled him close.

"*We grow when we sleep.* . . ." Warren whispered desperately in Cody's ear. And then, out of nowhere, he began to scream the way he had that first night—emptying his lungs, then gasping for air, and emptying his lungs over and over again.

Cody turned and ran, bursting out the door and racing down the long hallway. He didn't stop until he was outside, where Warren's screams blended in with the screams of all the other children who had gone mad.

A few days later, with the memory of the hospital still fresh in his mind, Cody visited the auto shop where his father worked. It was a restless place, where exhausted mechanics created automotive wonders. There were engines torn apart into a thousand small greasy pieces that would somehow fit together like a jigsaw puzzle. There were whole cars gutted to make room for

bigger engines that nature never intended. But strangest of all was the department his father managed, where they took big Cadillacs and made them even bigger.

As Cody stepped into the shop, his father was supervising one such procedure. A blue sedan, already stripped of its doors, was practically being sawed in half because the owner wanted five more feet of legroom. But today Cody hadn't come to watch them build a limo. He had come to talk to his dad.

"Did you ever know anyone who . . . uh, snapped . . . the way Warren did?" Cody asked when he had finally gotten his father alone in his small office.

"No," his father replied, but he had hesitated long enough for Cody to know that he was lying. His dad walked over and closed the door of his office, muffling the noise of the shop, then he looked Cody straight in the eyes.

"Don't tell your mother I told you this," he said, "or she'll blame me for giving you nightmares." He cleared his throat and began to pace. "I had this friend once, when I was about your age. Anyway, he went nuts, kind of the way Warren did. I wasn't there, but I heard about it—*everyone* heard about it, and there were lots of rumors."

He paused for a moment, then went on. "Some people said my friend got hit in the head too hard—his dad was a mean son of a gun. Others said he was never right in the head to begin with. Anyway, the story his parents gave was that he woke up screaming in the middle of the night, saying that the angels had come to take him. He kept on screaming, so they sent him away, and no one ever heard from him again."

"What do you think happened to your friend that night, Dad?" Cody asked.

His father scratched his neck and shrugged. "Probably nothing," he said. "And as for the things he said—well, it was just something made up by a mind that was about to go crazy . . . or already had."

Cody squirmed and felt his skin begin to crawl. "Maybe what happened to your friend is what happened to Warren," he suggested. "You see, after I ran out of Warren's room at the hospital, I sat out there on the porch of that Harmony Home place where they're keeping him, and I heard other kids screaming, too. I couldn't tell for sure, but they all seemed to be screaming about something that came in the middle of the night to take them away. Angels . . . monsters . . . aliens . . . whatever."

Cody's Dad looked at him for a moment, and then laughed, slapping him on the back. "You sure have some imagination," he said. "Not bad for a little guy."

Cody gave him a cold stare. "I'm not so little."

"Oh, don't be so sensitive," said his dad. "You'll grow soon— I can feel it in my bones."

They came at three in the morning.

It had been another sleepless night for Cody. He had counted about a thousand sheep and still hadn't so much as drifted off. He was about to start counting a new, larger flock of sheep . . . when they came. It began as a breeze he felt on the tip of his nose—but he remembered that his window was closed. Cody snapped his eyes open and looked across to the opposite wall.

A line had appeared—a thin black line—and it ran from ceiling to floor, spreading like a fissure or some kind of hole in space. Then, hands started to reach out of the hole—dozens of hands. And then, suddenly, there were people in the room! Cody tried to scream, but one large, heavy hand, cold and antiseptic-smelling, covered his mouth. Then several others grabbed Cody's arms and legs. He struggled wildly, but the hands were strong, and with little effort, they dragged him toward the hole, drawing him through the cold, dark fissure and into a bright white light.

All at once Cody felt himself being lifted onto something . . . then he was rolling, flat on his back, and suddenly he knew he was in . . . a hospital.

He was strapped down to a gurney and being rolled through clean white hallways. He kept his eyes fixed on a man with a clipboard, running alongside him. The man was clean-cut, clean shaven, and had spotless white teeth.

"I'm Farnsworth, public relations," said the man with a perfect smile. "It's good to see you again, Cody. It's been a while."

"I've never seen you before!" wailed Cody, fighting to get free from the tight bonds around him.

"Of course you have," said Farnsworth reassuringly. "You just don't remember."

"Take me back home!"

"In time, Cody."

The four hospital workers who had pulled him out of bed and through the hole in space now wheeled him down the impossibly long hallway like pallbearers with a casket. Farnsworth jogged alongside, making sure that everything went smoothly.

"Are you . . . an angel?" asked Cody.

Farnsworth laughed. "Heavens, no," he said. "None of us are. We're just the medical staff."

Farnsworth looked at his clipboard. "Things have been busy around here lately," he said. "We're backed up—almost a year behind—and you're way overdue."

"F-for what?" Cody stammered.

"A growth spurt, of course," answered Farnsworth.

They pushed Cody through a set of double doors and into a huge room that seemed to be the size of a stadium.

"Welcome to the Growth Ward!" Farnsworth announced.

In the room were thousands of surgeons, huddled together over patients . . . all of whom were kids.

Cody couldn't believe what he was seeing. It was like his father's auto shop, but instead of cars it was kids being taken apart and being put back together again—piece by piece. But what was most amazing of all was that these kids, in various stages of repair, were all alive!

And they were also awake.

Some screamed, others just groaned, and the ones who no longer had the strength to even groan just watched in terror as the "medical staff" dismantled them, then rebuilt them before their own horrified eyes.

"What are you doing to them?" shouted Cody. "What's going on here?"

173

"Bodywork and scheduled maintenance, of course," said Farnsworth over the awful wails around him. "How can a person be expected to grow without their maintenance appointments?"

"You're killing them!" yelled Cody.

"Nonsense, our surgeons are the most skilled in the universe," said Farnsworth cheerfully. "These kids will be patched up and back to their old selves by morning—and without a single scar from the experience."

"But I don't need surgery. I don't WANT surgery," Cody insisted.

"Why should you be different from everyone else?" asked Farnsworth. "And besides, you *do* want it." He smiled. "You do want to grow, don't you?"

Cody felt weak and sick to his stomach. "You mean . . . *this* happens to everybody?"

"Of course it does," explained Farnsworth. "Nobody remembers, though, because we erase it from their memory." Then the smile left Farnsworth's face, and he shook his head sadly. "Of course, every once in a while the memory erasing doesn't quite work. It's a shame, really—those poor kids are ruined for life, and all because they couldn't forget the Growth Ward."

Cody was still trying to digest what Farnsworth had just said, when he was rolled into a bright area where a group of surgeons waited. Their faces covered with masks, they anxiously flexed their fingers like pianists preparing for a concert. As Cody stared in horror at them, he noticed that there was something about those surgeons—something not quite right, but what was it? Keeping his eyes glued on them, Cody knew if he looked at them long enough, he'd figure out what it was that made them look . . . different.

"It says here, we're adding half an inch to your forearms today," Farnsworth said, glancing at his clipboard again. "And a whole inch to your thighbones. Good for you, Cody! We'll have you caught up to those other kids in your class in no time!"

Cody turned to see a silver tray next to the operating table. On it were a few small, circular bone fragments, no larger than LEGO pieces.

One of the eager surgeons grabbed a small bone saw from the tray and turned it on. It buzzed and whined, adding to the many unpleasant sounds of the great galactic operating room.

The surgeon said nothing and moved the saw toward Cody's leg, and the others approached him with their scalpels poised.

"No!" Cody cried. "You can't operate without anesthesia! I have to have anesthesia!"

Farnsworth chuckled. "Come now, Cody, where do you think you are, at the dentist? I think not! Growing pains are a part of life, and *everyone* has to feel their growing pains. *Everyone*."

Cody screamed even before the instruments touched his body—then he suddenly realized that it didn't matter how loud he wailed. For he had finally figured out what was wrong with those surgeons. They couldn't hear him. They had no ears.

I need to remember . . .

I need to remember . . .

I need to remember . . . what?

An alarm tore Cody out of the deepest sleep he had ever had. There was a memory of a dream—or something like a dream—but it was quickly fading into darkness. In a moment it was completely gone, and all that was left was the light of day pouring into his room.

"Wake up, lazybones," said his mother. "You'll be late for school."

Cody felt good this morning. No—*better* than good—he felt great, and he couldn't quite tell why. He stood up out of bed and felt a slight case of vertigo, as if the floor were somehow farther away from him than it had been the day before. His legs and arms ached the slightest bit, but that was okay. It was a *good* feeling.

"My, how you're growing!" his mother said as he walked into the kitchen for breakfast. "I'll bet you'll grow three inches by fall!"

And the thought made Cody smile. It felt good to be a growing boy.

ALEXANDER'S SKULL

Every once in a while I'll have a dream that becomes a story. I had dreamed that I received a package in the mail—the very package from this story. I woke up at two in the morning screaming. Since I couldn't get back to sleep, I wrote a story that took the dream to its logical conclusion.

By the way, if you read my novel *Red Rider's Hood*, you'll notice I borrowed the ending of this story.

Alexander's Skull

It started with my mom, many years ago.

My mom has a temper, you see, and one of the things that really got her up in a rage was the post office. If something took too long to arrive at our house, she would bawl out the mailman, as if it were his fault. If a card she sent missed somebody's birthday, she would go to the post office and demand her postage back.

The thing that irritated my mom the most about the post office was misdelivered mail, and she had a good reason for that one: the Mortimer Museum.

It was just dumb luck that the guy who founded that strange little natural history museum had the same last name as we did. We weren't related, my dad always reminded me. Still, without fail, a few times a year we would end up with a package at our doorstep that was supposed to go to the museum.

For my mom, it was just another postal nuisance—until the birthday incident. Then it became a regular obsession with her.

I was about four or so. It was my mom's thirtieth birthday, and we had relatives and friends from all over the county show up to surprise her. Everything was going along just fine until she started opening the presents—first the ones from people who were there, then the ones that had come in the mail.

Perhaps if she had looked at the address on the package, it might not have happened, but she didn't. So, right in front of more than forty guests, in the middle of a birthday party, my mother opened a box, reached in, and pulled out an armful of African centipedes.

The scream could be heard throughout the county. She took her hand, shrieking, and flung the centipedes across the room, where they landed on slices of birthday cake and in people's hair. The angry centipedes began to bite, and panic erupted. Needless to say, the party was ruined. The centipedes scattered so far across the room that we were still finding them in dark corners weeks later.

The centipedes, of course, were supposed to go to the Mortimer Museum for their exotic insect exhibit, and not to the Mortimer family. The post office, naturally, bent over backward and took full responsibility, offering to give my mother free postage for the rest of her life if she would just never mention it again. But it was too late.

From that day forward, we were at war with the museum and the post office. The poor mailman went to great pains to make sure we didn't get any of the museum's mail, but sometimes something slipped through. When it did, whatever it was—whatever it was—we kept it. Soon we had quite our own little museum in our basement: fragments of dinosaur bones, a meteorite, petrified wood.

But nothing we ever received was like the package we got one Halloween.

You have to understand, Halloween is a very special holiday for me. Most of the year I get teased for being sort of creepy and spending so much time alone, but on Halloween I can be myself and it's perfectly normal!

So that night I was in a rush to get out and stalk through the streets like a ghoul, striking terror into the heart of anyone foolish enough to answer their door, when a package arrived on our porch. I took it inside and quickly tore off the brown paper, pulled open the box, and like an idiot, reached inside to find out what it was.

My hand touched something cold, hard, and dirty. I quickly pulled my hand back and saw that it was covered with something black and sooty.

"Mom?" I called, feeling the shivers already climbing up past my elbow to my shoulder.

Mom came downstairs, took one look at the box, and heaved a big sigh. Then she peeled back the paper to reveal what at first looked like a dark rock. But when she reached in to pull it out, she came face-to-face with a human skull.

It was old—it must have been—because it was black and covered with ash. It was missing its jawbone.

"No way!" I said, not sure whether to be disgusted or excited. "It must be for the exhibit on Early Man."

Mom looked into its empty eyes bravely. "Splendid. Just what we need for Halloween. I'll go get a candle."

That night, the skull sat on our porch with a candle inside its empty head, like a human jack-o'-lantern.

Like the other things in our basement, this was something

we were going to keep—no matter how much the museum wanted it back. But the museum never came asking for it, and instead of ending up in the basement, it ended up in my room.

I can't say why I wanted the skull in my room. I was a little bit scared of it, but not as scared as I thought I would be. I liked the way it sat on my shelf and watched me. Also, since I didn't have many friends, it made me feel less alone.

My dad would look at the skull and shake his head. "Alex," he would ask, "how did you get to be so strange?" That's what he said when I first got Octavia, my pet tarantula, and when I decided that I would wear only black to school.

"If you're going to keep that thing, Alex," he said, "you ought to clean it."

So I did. I carefully wiped out the ash and polished the cold, hard bone until it was a smooth granite gray. Then I put it back on my shelf next to Clovis, my Venus flytrap.

Late at night, when I couldn't fall asleep, I would look at the skull. It seemed to be holding some kind of vigil in the dim moonlight, watching me as I watched it. *Who were you? I would ask. Were you a caveman? Were you killed by a mastodon during the hunt? Or are you the missing link?* The skull, to whom I wanted to give a name but somehow never could, never answered—it just sat there, watching silently.

Several weeks later it disappeared.

I spent an hour searching for it all around the house. Mom

wasn't very helpful. "You're so disorganized," she said. "I always told you you'd lose your head if it weren't attached to your neck."

The skull wasn't in the basement, or in any of the bedrooms or closets. I knew there had to be a sensible explanation. Turns out the explanation was so sensible it was disappointing.

You see, my dad is a dentist, and his office is right across the street in a little minimall. When I went out to see if he knew what had happened, I saw my skull sitting there propped up on the dental chair, like a patient who had been X-rayed one too many times.

"Sorry. I should have told you," said Dad. "I borrowed him to recalibrate my X-ray machine. It's been giving me trouble." He showed me a dozen X-rays of the skull, all blurry and out of focus. He took one more shot with his big camera and handed me back my skull.

"This should do it," he said. "Thanks."

When he developed the X-ray a few minutes later, the teeth were in absolute clear focus, just like any other dental X-ray . . . so much like any other X-ray that Dad seemed a little bit disturbed. He went over to the skull and picked it up from the pillow it was resting on.

"You say he was prehistoric?" asked Dad.

"Yeah," I said. "I mean, he must be. Why else would he be going to the museum?"

Then Dad flipped the skull over and looked at the upper teeth, all of which were still there. He poked at them with a dental instrument. "Since when did prehistoric man have dental fillings?" he said, raising his eyebrows at me.

That afternoon I went down into the basement and found the box the skull had come in. Inside, I found the original wrapping. The faint brown lettering was not addressed to the museum, as we had thought. It was addressed to me—Alexander Mortimer.

There was a return address, but no name. The return address simply read *475 St. Cloud Lane, Billingsville*.

It was a Saturday, so I decided to ride my bike over to Billingsville, only about ten miles away. I just had to see who had sent me this skull, and why.

Billingsville is a town with lots of old places and lots of new places. I got a map from the gas station, but try as I might, I couldn't find St. Cloud Lane.

"Ain't no St. Cloud Lane in Billingsville," an old-timer told me. "Not that I can remember, and I can remember quite a lot."

Eventually I gave up and decided to head home before it got dark. I rode through the winding trees of the new developments, wondering where on earth they were going to get all the people to fill these new homes.

That's when I saw it.

On a pole on a corner where two streets crossed were two signs—St. Andrew and St. Cloud Lane.

I sucked wind for a second, feeling kind of light-headed. Then I rode my bike down the lane. The entire street was filled with huge cement foundations, ready for construction crews. *The homes on St. Cloud Lane had not yet been built!*

It was dark by the time I got home, and the cold day had slipped into a frigid night.

"You missed dinner," said Mom. "Where were you?"

But I didn't answer her. I went right down into the basement and straight to the package the skull had come in. I looked for the postmark on the package. October 28. But the year was smudged out, and there was no way of telling whether the package was mailed this year, last year . . . or some year that had not yet come.

That night, back in my room, I stared and stared at my "friend" sitting on the shelf. I went up to him and looked deep into those hollow eyes, eyes that seemed so strange, and yet so familiar.

At three in the morning I slipped out of the house and crossed the street. Snow was falling and sticking to the dry ground. There would be several inches by morning. My feet left dark prints in the thin layer of white as I went to Dad's office. There, I unlocked the door with his keys and disabled the alarm.

The X-ray machine looked like a one-eyed beast in the corner of the examining room. I tried not to look at it. I went to my dad's office, and I looked around with my flashlight until I found the skull's X-rays still sitting on his desk. I took the most focused one and put it in my jacket pocket. Then I went to the files, found the folder I was looking for, and pulled it out. It was filled with dental records and X-rays.

I pulled out the skull's X-rays from my pocket and compared them to the X-rays in the folder.

They say you can identify human remains by dental records. It must be true, because the match was absolutely perfect.

I took a second look at the name on the file, and finally understood why it had been so hard for me to find a name for the skull. It was because the skull already had a name—it was the name that appeared on the file.

Alexander J. Mortimer.

As I reached up and felt my own cheekbones, and the shape of my eye sockets, and the ridges on my own front teeth, I finally realized why that head bone sitting on my shelf had, from the beginning, felt so very, very familiar.

In the morning Dad said we ought to take the skull to the police.

"They have ways of identifying these things," he said. "Who knows who it might be?"

But I told him that I had already gotten rid of it. "I gave it a proper burial out in the woods," I said, shrugging my shoulders.

He looked at me and shook his head. "How *did* you get to be such a strange kid?" he asked. Since my father was never the

type of person to mess with matters involving human skulls, he believed me, and it was never brought up again.

Only I didn't bury it.

I don't know who sent me the skull. I don't know how, but it was sent, and I am charged with its keeping. Dad thinks I'm spending too much time alone lately, and that maybe if we moved I'd make some friends. He's heard that there are some nice homes in Billingsville—and he intends to buy one. I already know what our address will be.

And so at night, when everyone else is asleep, I take the skull out of its secret hiding place beneath the floorboards of my room and I put it back on my shelf. Then I lie awake, gazing at my silent soul mate resting on that shelf and coldly wait for the day when I find myself on the other side of those dark, dark eyes, looking out.

CONNECTING FLIGHT

I tend to spend a lot of time in airports, since I travel a lot. I'm always amazed that airports actually function—there are so many things that can go wrong—and I'm not talking about the airplanes themselves—I mean all the issues with ticketing and booking. I once faced one of those computer glitches where two flights, one going east, and one going west, got confused and were scheduled to go out of the same gate at the exact same time. It got me thinking. I wrote the first draft of the following story while in flight. Freaked myself out, too.

Connecting Flight

The narrow, doorless hall seems to stretch on forever.

The bag slung across her shoulder seems full of lead.

And the image of her parents waving good-bye still sticks in her mind.

With a boarding pass in hand, Jana Martinez walks down a narrow, tilted corridor, toward the 737 at the end of the jetway.

She tries to forget the strange state of cold limbo that fills the gap between her parents behind her and her final destination—Wendingham Prep School.

It is only three hours away now—just a two-hour flight from Chicago to Boston, and then an hour's bus ride. Still, to Jana, this empty time between two places always seems to last an eternity.

She reaches the door of the plane, stumbling over the lip of the hatch, and a flight attendant grabs her arm too tightly. "Watch your step," the flight attendant says, trying to help Jana keep her balance.

Now, as she makes her way down the narrow aisle, Jana wonders if the flight attendant's overly strong grip will leave a bruise on her arm. She is sure the cruel strap of her carry-on bag will leave her black-and-blue.

The plane is divided by a single center aisle, and each row has three seats on either side. Jana finds her seat by the window on the right side of the plane. She has to climb over a heavy, pale woman to get there, and just as she finally settles in, her sense of loneliness settles in deeper than before.

I'm surrounded by strangers, she thinks. *I'm unknown to all of them . . . and unconnected.*

The plane is filled with people she's never seen before and will never see again—filled with hundreds of lives that intersect nowhere but on this plane. The feeling is eerie to Jana, and unnatural.

The woman beside her is several sizes too large for the seat, and her large body spreads toward Jana, taking over Jana's armrest, and forcing her to lean uncomfortably against the cold window.

"Sorry, dearie," says the woman, with a British accent. "You'd think people have no hips, the way they build these seats."

Jana sighs, calculates how many seconds there are in a two-hour flight, and begins to count down from seven thousand two hundred. She wonders if a flight could possibly be any worse. Soon she finds out that it can.

A woman with a baby takes the seat next to the large Englishwoman, and the moment the plane leaves the ground, the baby begins an earsplitting screech-fest. The mother tries to console the child, but it does no good. Grimacing, Jana notices an old man sitting across the aisle turn down his hearing aid.

"Why do I always end up on Screaming Baby Airlines?" Jana grumbles to herself, and the large woman in her airspace

accidentally overhears. She turns to Jana with a smile.

"It's the pressure in its ears, the poor thing," says the large woman, pointing to the wailing baby. Then she adds something curious. "Babies on planes comfort me, actually. I always think, God won't crash a plane carrying a baby."

The thought that seems to give so much comfort to the large woman only gives Jana the creeps. She peers out her window, watching as the plane rises above little puffs of clouds that soon look like tiny white specks far below.

"We've reached our cruising altitude of thirty-five thousand feet," and *blah, blah, blah*, drones the captain, who seems to have the same voice as every other airline pilot in the world. It's as if they go to some special school that teaches them all how to sound exactly alike.

The baby, having exhausted its screaming machine, can only whimper now, and the plump woman, who has introduced herself as Moira Lester, turns to Jana and asks, "You'll be visiting someone in Boston, then?"

"School," says Jana curtly, not feeling like having a conversation with a stranger.

"Boarding school, is it?" asks Moira, not taking the hint. "I went to boarding school. It's all the rage back in Britain. Not many of them in the States, are there?" And then she begins to spin the never-ending tale of her uninteresting family, all the boarding schools they attended, why they went there, and which classmates have become famous people that Jana has never heard of.

Jana nods as if listening but tries to tune her out by gazing out the window at the specks of clouds below. It is just about then that the feeling comes. It's a sensation—a *twinge*, like a spark of static electricity darting through her, that causes a tiny, tiny change in air pressure. It's like a pinprick in her reality—a feeling so slight that it takes a while for Jana to realize that she has felt anything at all.

As she turns from the window to look around her, nothing appears to have changed: Moira is still talking, the baby is still whimpering.

But as for Jana, she has a clear sense that something is suddenly not right.

"Something wrong, dearie?" Moira asks.

But Jana just shakes her head, trying to convince herself that it's only her imagination.

Then, about ten minutes later, Jana asks, "Where's the old man?" The sense of something wrong had been growing and growing within her, and now she has finally noticed something different.

The mother, bouncing her baby on her knee, looks at Jana oddly. "What old man?" she asks.

"You know—the old man who was sitting across the aisle from you. He was wearing a hearing aid."

The mother turns to look. Sitting across the aisle is a businessman with slick black hair. Certainly not old, and definitely not wearing a hearing aid, he sits reading a magazine in seat 16C as if he belongs there.

"Don't you remember him?" Jana persists. "He turned down his hearing aid when your baby was screaming."

The mother shrugs. "I didn't notice," she says. "Who notices anybody on airplanes these days?"

"Looks like there are some empty seats on the plane," suggests Moira. "Perhaps this man you're talking about moved."

Jana sighs. "Yeah, maybe that's it," she concedes, although not really convinced. She would have noticed if the man had gotten up.

"Excuse me," Jana says, and climbs over Moira and the mother and her baby, then heads down the aisle to the bathroom. There is something wrong, she knows it. Something terribly wrong. She can feel it in the pit of her stomach, like the feeling you get a few minutes before becoming violently ill.

Jana pushes her way through the narrow bathroom doorway and into the tight little compartment. Jana looks in the mirror, then splashes cold water on her face. *Maybe it's just the excitement of going back to school*, she tells herself. *Maybe it's just airsickness.*

But where is the man with the hearing aid?

She dries her face with a paper towel and makes her way back to her seat, looking in every row for the old man. She goes to the front of the plane. No old man with a hearing aid. What did he do? Jump off the plane?

When Jana returns to her seat, the mother and baby have moved to where she can lay her baby down on an empty seat—a few rows back on the other side of the plane. As Jana looks around, she notices that there are empty seats, and even empty rows on the plane now—but all the vacant seats appear to be on the side of the plane opposite her.

Jana stands there watching as several people from her side of the plane shift over to make use of the empty rows, making more room for everyone. How odd—the plane seemed crowded when she got on.

When Jana retakes her seat, Moira welcomes her back with a wide friendly smile. Jana forces her own smile, and as she settles in, she happens to glance out the window . . . then freezes.

"Moira," she says, "everything's covered in clouds!"

Moira glances out the window at the cotton-thick clouds rolling toward the horizon below. "Why, I suppose it is," she says.

"Excuse me," Jana says as she climbs back over Moira and crosses the aisle. She then leans awkwardly over the business-man and two other passengers to get a look out *their* window. She is certain she hadn't seen the clouds out of the other side of the plane on her way back from the bathroom.

Sure enough, from this window, Jana can see the ground—a patchwork quilt of greens and browns gilded by the afternoon sun.

"It—it's *different* on this side of the plane," she says, her voice shaky.

"So what?" asks the businessman, annoyed at the way Jana is still leaning across him. "We must be traveling along the edge of a front. You know—the line where cold air meets warm air, and storm clouds form."

Jana just stares at him, feeling her hands growing colder by

the moment. *It's a logical explanation*, she thinks, *but it's wrong.*

Quietly Jana returns to her seat. She pulls out the magazine in the pouch in front of her and tries to read it, but finds nothing can take her attention away from the clouds beneath her window, and the perfectly clear sky on the other side of the plane.

That's when the captain comes on the loudspeaker again.

"Just thought I'd let you know," he says in his every-pilot voice, "that we'll be passing Mount Rushmore shortly. If you look out the right side of the plane, you'll be able to see it on the horizon."

Jana doesn't bother to look, since she's on the left side. But she does notice that people on her side of the plane are chuckling, as if the pilot has made some kind of joke.

Then it hits her.

Geography was never one of Jana's best subjects, but she's sure that Mount Rushmore is not in Michigan—the state they should have been over right now! She turns to Moira. "Where is Mount Rushmore?" she asks, trying not to sound panicked.

"Can't say for sure," the heavyset woman replies. "I haven't been in the States long."

"This *is* the flight to Boston, isn't it?"

"As far as I know," says Moira. "At least that's what my ticket says."

Jana uneasily mulls over everything as she goes back to staring out her window . . . at nothing but clouds.

About an hour and a half into the flight, Jana has bitten her nails down to the stubs—a habit she thought she had broken years ago. That tiny tear in the fabric of her world that happened a while back has shred so rapidly, Jana wonders if it can ever be sewn back together again.

It is now dark outside her window. Jana reasons that that is perfectly normal. She has flown enough to know that when you fly east at dusk, the sun always sets behind you incredibly fast. It has to do with the curvature of the earth, and time zones, and that sort of thing. Perfectly natural . . . except that the sun is still shining on the other side of the plane.

The plane is filled with anxious murmurs. Perhaps Jana was the first one to realize things were screwy, but now everyone sees it.

"There's some explanation," one person whispers.

"We'll probably all laugh about it later," another says.

And indeed, some people are laughing already, as if laughing could make it all better.

Sitting there, with no nails left to bite, Jana wonders if it is always like this when things go wrong in midair. Do people not scream and wail the way they do in the movies? Do they get quiet . . . like this . . . or just whisper, or laugh? And if they do scream, do they only scream on the inside?

Jana calls the flight attendant over.

"Excuse me," she says, her voice quivering with panic, "but we have to land this plane. We have to land it *now!*"

The flight attendant smiles and speaks with practiced reassurance, as if Jana is nothing more than an anxious flier.

"We've begun our final descent," she tells her. "We should be on the ground shortly."

"Haven't you looked out the window?" Jana snaps at the flight attendant. "Haven't you seen what's happening out there?"

"Weather conditions up here," says the flight attendant, "aren't like weather conditions on the ground."

"Night and day aren't weather conditions!" shouts Jana. The nervous murmurs can now be heard around the cabin.

The flight attendant looks into Jana's eyes, grits her teeth furiously, and says, "I'll have to ask you to sit down, miss."

That look on the flight attendant's face says everything. It says, *We have no idea what's going on, but we can't admit that, you stupid girl! If we do, everyone will start panicking. So shut your face before we shut it for you!*

The flight attendant storms away, and Jana dares to do something she's been wanting to do since the sky began to change. She looks across the aisle to the businessman and asks him where he's going.

"Seattle," he says. "I'm going to Seattle—of course—just like you."

Several people on Jana's side of the plane gasp and whisper to one another, as if being quiet about it makes the situation any less horrific than it is.

"I thought this flight was going to Boston," say Moira.

"She's right," says another passenger behind Moira. "This plane is going to Boston."

The businessman swallows. "There must be some sort of . . . computer mix-up."

Jana sinks in her seat as the plane passes through the heavy cloud cover—on *her* side of the plane—and as soon as they punch through the clouds, she can see the twinkling lights of a city below. She doesn't dare look out the windows on the other side of the plane anymore.

In Seattle, Jana thinks, *it would still be light out.*

The truth was simple, and at the same time impossible to comprehend. Somehow, some grand computer glitch—not in any simple airline computer—got two flights . . . confused.

A flight like this will never reach the ground, she tells herself. *How can it?*

Suddenly the plane shudders and whines as the landing-gear doors open. People are looking out their windows at the night on the right side of the plane, and then at the day on the left. Cold terror paints their faces a pale white.

Across the aisle and three rows back, the baby screams again as they descend. To Jana, the screams are far less disturbing than the whispers and silences of all the other passengers, but not to everyone.

"Shut that child up!" shouts the businessman.

But the mother can do nothing but hold her baby close to her as they sit across the narrow aisle, waiting for the plane to touch down.

Across the aisle? Jana's mind suddenly screams. And then that sickening feeling that began almost two hours ago spreads through her arms and legs, until every part of her body feels weak. Jana glances at the empty seat right next to Moira and erupts with panic. She opens her seat belt, stands and shouts to

the mother, yelling louder than the woman's screaming baby.

"Get up!" Jana shouts. "You have to come back to this seat!"

"But we're landing," says the mother nervously. "I shouldn't unbuckle my seat belt."

"You're not *supposed* to be there!" Jana insists. "You started on *this* side. I can't explain it now—but you have to come back to this side of the plane—NOW!"

Terrified, the mother unbuckles her seat belt and, clutching her screaming baby, crosses the aisle the moment the tires touch the runway. Others who had moved to the empty seats on the left side sense what is about to happen. They race to get out of their seat belts and back to their original seats—but they are not fast enough.

In an instant, there is a burst of flame, and the world seems to end.

"Help me!" screams the mother.

Jana grabs the woman's hand while Moira grabs the baby. They fall into the seat next to Moira, and the mother shields her baby from the nightmare exploding around them.

Everyone screams as the plane spins and tumbles out of control—everyone but Jana. She glances out her window to see that nothing seems wrong. The plane is landing in Boston, just like planes always land.

But on the other side of the plane, the *left* side of the plane, there is smoke and flames and shredding steel. And, beyond the shattering windows, the ground is rolling over and over. In awe, Jana watches as the smoke billows . . . but *stays* on the other side of the aisle. In fact, Jana can't even smell it!

Moira leans into Jana. "Don't look!" she cries. "You mustn't look at it!"

And Jana knows that Moira is right. So instead, she holds Moira's hand and turns to look out her own window. Tears rolling down her cheeks, she watches the terminal roll peacefully toward her. She feels the plane calmly slow down, and she tries to ignore the awful wails from the other side of the plane . . . until the last wail trails off.

Then the captain begins to speak, uncertain at first, but then with building confidence. "Uh . . . on behalf of our crew, I'd like to welcome you to . . . Boston. Please remain seated until we are secure at the terminal."

The screaming has stopped. The only sound now is that of the engines powering down to a low whine. Slowly Jana dares to look across the aisle.

There she finds the man with the hearing aid staring back at her, aghast.

On the other side of the plane are all the people who had been there when they had taken off. Now that Jana sees their faces, she can recognize them.

Someone must have fixed the computer, Jana thinks, and then she turns to Moira. "Do you suppose that while we were watching the right half of that flight to Seattle—"

"—that the people on the other side were watching the left half?" finishes Moira. "Look at their faces. I can only imagine they were."

The mother, whose baby has stopped screaming and has fallen asleep, thanks Jana with tears in her eyes. Jana touches the

baby's fine hair, then smiles. Suddenly it seems that all those long stories Moira has told on the plane don't seem so boring, and in a way Jana longs to hear all of them again. In fact, she longs to hear every story of every person on that plane. *There are so many lives intersecting on an airplane*, she thinks. *So many stories to hear!*

Jana walks with Moira to the baggage claim, where suitcases are already flying down the chute and circling on the baggage carousel. There, Jana watches people from her flight greet friends and family who have been waiting for them.

"I just heard that a flight out west didn't make it," someone says. "It was the same airline, too."

But no one from Jana's flight says anything. How can you tell someone that you saw a plane crash from the inside, but it wasn't *your* plane?

"It's good that things ended up back where they belong," Moira says.

"There's nothing 'good' about it," says Jana flatly.

"No, I suppose not," Moira agrees. "But it's right. Right and proper."

Together, Jana and Moira wait a long time for their luggage, but it never comes. Jana has to admit that she didn't expect it to.

Not when all the luggage coming down the chute is ticketed to Seattle.

RALPHY SHERMAN'S ROOT CANAL

Ralphy Sherman is my one recurring character. Ralphy appears briefly in almost all of my books, and I give him his own stories in *MindQuakes, MindStorms,* and all of my other short story collections. Anyone who reads more than one of my books gets the added treat of trying to find Ralphy. It's kind of like *Where's Waldo?*

Ralphy is a teller of tall tales that just keep getting taller, and I have to admit, I have a lot of fun with him. For all of you Ralphy followers out there, you'll be happy to know that I'm going to be writing an entire Ralphy Sherman book.

Where did Ralphy get his name? That dates back to when I was in college. I had this friend who was a maniac, and often he dragged me into wild and questionable situations. One time we crashed a private country club. "But what'll we do if we get caught?" I asked. "Easy," said my friend. "We'll tell them we're the Sherman brothers. I'm Ronny, you can be Ralphy." When security came to question us (because we looked like two college students crashing a private club), we gave them the Ronny and Ralphy Sherman story. I really got into it. I went as far as to act all insulted when the guard accused us of making the whole thing up. I told him how upset our parents—highly respected members of the club—would be if they knew how terribly we were being treated. The security guard apologized, let us stay, and even gave us a coupon for a free buffet lunch. (Actually that's not true, he threw us out—but *Ralphy* would never admit to being thrown out!)

As for this particular story, it's true. Sort of. It was inspired by my son Jarrod's root canal—a process that was more painful for him than it should have been because the tag-team pair of endodontists couldn't get him numb, but they kept drilling anyway. They were eeeeeeevil. I promised Jarrod that I would write a story about his root canal, and who better to tell that story than Ralphy Sherman?

RALPHY SHERMAN'S ROOT CANAL

You probably won't believe this, but I swear it's true. It all started with a toothache. It was the kind of toothache you get after eating too much candy on Halloween night, not brushing your teeth for like a million years, and then going to sleep with entire chunks of taffy wedged in the valleys of your molars like snow in the Alps.

Okay, I'll admit that dental hygiene is not my personal strength. For a while last year, I did actually enjoy brushing my teeth when we had a nanny who bought licorice-flavored toothpaste—but unfortunately my sister, Roxy, and I scared her off. The replacement nanny refused to spring for the licorice stuff, because it was so expensive. Instead she bought this industrial dental solvent that tasted like toilet-bowl cleaner (don't ask me how I know what toilet-bowl cleaner tastes like—it's a memory best forgotten). Anyway, one taste of the new stuff and my brushing days were over.

Then came the toothache.

It was just small at first. A little irritation. It wasn't until a few days later that I noticed the hole. I didn't see it—I felt it. I mean, your tongue knows the feel of your own teeth the way

your eyes know the look of your room. If there's a single thing out of place, you know it.

From my tongue's perspective, this wasn't just a cavity, it was a sinkhole of epic proportions, and my tongue kept poking and exploring it of its own free will, with no orders from me. After a few weeks, the ache became a throb, and my tongue could no longer find the bottom of the hole.

Then I bit into a Now-R-Never.

Now-R-Nevers are these little square, almost-but-not-quite-chewable candies, imported from England. I believe they were invented by a secret society of British dentists back in the murky 1800s, when people were dying in the streets, and Charles Dickens was writing about dirty malnourished children with bad teeth. The bad teeth were because of the Now-R-Nevers, and for more than a hundred years, the dental industry has thrived thanks in no small part to this evil—but amazingly good-tasting—candy.

I knew from the moment I sank my teeth into the vicious little chew that there was a problem. It molded itself around my tooth, and pushed into the cavity until it hit something. Something deep. Something painful. Shock waves of agony pulsated through every inch of my body, radiating out of my fingertips. I reached into my mouth and attempted to dislodge the chew. It took a good ten minutes picking at it until it finally began to release its grip on my tooth. All the while, the pain rebounded through me like a Super Ball bouncing over all the synapses of my nervous system. Fortunately my father, who is often forced to endure pain on his many top secret missions, taught Roxy and me the fine Himalayan art of Kuri-Na—which is the mental control over pain. Unfortunately, I wasn't very good at it, and was screaming my guts out.

Roxy came downstairs with Püshpa, our current nanny, and they both watched with mild interest as I writhed on the floor like a demon child in the midst of an exorcism. Finally I pulled the Now-R-Never off, with a deep popping noise. As I lay there catching my breath, Püshpa leaned over me and gave me her cold eye of examination.

"Please to open your mouth," she said. Püshpa did not speak English all that well. She was from a small Eastern European country that no longer existed, but might exist again in a month or so, she hoped.

I opened my mouth, and Püshpa backed away, crossed herself, and made some gestures to ward off evil spirits. "You have bad hemorrhoid ache," Püshpa said. "You brush like good Jell-O-mold, your hemorrhoids be all clean and healthy."

To the untrained ear, this might make no sense, but it does to us. You see, Roxy and I decided that we would teach Püshpa English, but decided to teach it to her wrong. Roxy keeps an entire "Püshpeese" database in her computer so we can be consistent.

"Ha! It serves you left!" Püshpa said.

"Don't be infective to Ralphy," Roxy told her. "He's in a lot of champagne."

Roxy took a glance in my mouth, too, and raised her eye-

205

brows in thought. "Ooh! Can I do my science-fair project on your tooth?"

I wasn't too thrilled about the idea, as it would require me to sit at the science fair for three hours with my mouth open, but I owed Roxy big, from the time I crossbred her ChiaPet with a Venus flytrap, and it ate all the neighborhood cats.

Püshpa picked up the yellow pages, and tried to find me a fishmonger (which was Püshpeese for "dentist"). I proceeded to take elephant doses of Tylenol, and Roxy happily prepared her science project. She labeled her experiment "A Fistful of Molars" and made up a whole bunch of impressive but confusing graphs on the correlation between tooth decay and birth order in Western civilization.

The music may have started before the night of the science fair, but I had never noticed it before, since I had never held my mouth open long enough to hear it.

It was actually some little kid who heard it first. As I sat there with my mouth hanging open, next to Roxy's graphs and PowerPoint presentation, a six-year-old holding an I-heart-science balloon in one hand, and picking his nose with the other, turned to his mother and said, "Mommy, why is that boy singing?"

I wasn't singing, of course, and I looked at him like he was nuts.

His mother glanced at me with the resigned indifference of a parent forced to endure a child with an overactive but uninteresting imagination. "I'm sure it's coming from somewhere else, Jimmy."

"No!" Little Jimmy pointed his nose-finger dangerously close to my open mouth. "It's coming from there!"

I heard it now, too. It was a distant tinny voice. I thought it was from one of the other projects, but now I could feel the vibration in my jaw. The kid was right! The singing was coming from my cavity. I closed my mouth and the voice went away. I opened my mouth and the voice came back. It was kind of like opening and closing a music box.

The kid laughed. "Do it again! Do it again!"

By now a couple of other people had stopped to observe the "Fistful of Molars" exhibit.

"I know that song!" said one of the passing fathers. "That's 'Who's Sorry Now?' by Patsy Cline. It was my ex-wife's favorite song!" He leaned closer to listen.

Roxy was in heaven. "This is great!" She grabbed a piece of paper and a Sharpie, and relabeled her science project "The Amazing Human Radio."

I should point out here that it's not all that uncommon for dental work to pick up radio signals, and act as a receiver. In fact, on *America's Lamest Criminals*, there was this guy whose retainer picked up the police frequency, so he always knew how close the police were to the convenience store he was robbing. He got arrested the day he forgot his retainer at home.

A crowd began to gather around me. "Do you take requests?" one woman asked, and everyone laughed.

"My science project is in advanced biotechnology," Roxy told everyone, making it up as she went along. "Soon things like iPods and earphones will be obsolete, because this new

technology will deliver music right inside your skull."

She talked on and on about it, but I couldn't focus on her anymore, because the throbbing in my mouth was becoming sharper and sharper with the beat of every song.

When we got home, Dad was there. He had just returned from some top secret something or other, and was home long enough to change clothes and shower before his next assignment. He took one look in my mouth, declared it a federal disaster area, and demanded Püshpa take me to see a dentist, which confused her since to the best of her knowledge, a dentist had something to do with auto repair.

Dentists and I never got along. In fact, they usually requested that I never come back after the first appointment. I think this has something to do with my reflexes. See, I have this natural reflex that causes me to bite down with amazing force when someone puts something in my mouth, like, oh, say, a finger. Even though fingers can be surgically reattached these days, dentists did not appreciate the inconvenience, and I was listed on the American Dental Association Web site as Public Enemy number two. (You don't want to know what Public Enemy number one did.)

"Is because you are bad little Jell-O-mold, Ralphy" Püshpa told me, after the tenth dentist hung up on her. "If I were a fishmonger, I wouldn't help you either."

"Never mind, Püshpa. Just pick up the eggplant and call another."

It took days for us to find a dentist that would have anything to do with me. We finally found one willing to give me a phone consultation—but even then he sounded worried as he spoke to me, as if my voice might leap over the phone and gnaw off his ear.

"Tell me what you are experiencing," he asked.

"AAAAAAAAAAAAAAAAAH!" I told him.

"Yes. Well. Sounds like it's beyond my field of expertise. What you need is an endodontist."

Throughout the conversation, he kept telling me to turn down the radio, and I couldn't get him to understand that the music in my mouth was part of the problem. He hung up in frustration, but not before giving us the phone number of an endodontist who specialized in difficult cases.

As I understood, an endodontist was like a superdentist who ended the tireless march of oral bacteria like a can of Raid killed ants. Hence the title "End-o-dontist."

"Open up, let's see how bad it's gotten," Roxy said as soon as I got off the phone. I opened my mouth, and she peered inside. "Hmm," she said. "Smells like teen spirit."

I took a whiff of my underarms. I'm more of an Old Spice man myself.

"No, the song," she said. "'Smells Like Teen Spirit'—you know? Nirvana? Kurt Cobain?"

"Oh. Oh, right."

"*Here we are now, entertain us,*" sang Kurt.

"It sounds like an acoustic version," said Roxy—which was fine with me, because songs with lots of bass were more painful.

Roxy listened for a few moments more. "I didn't know they recorded an acoustic version," she said. "Interesting . . ."

The endodontic office was at the edge of the community beyond which were barren hills where only coyotes dared to roam. The small office complex had only two other tenants: a psychiatrist who specialized in Primal Scream Therapy and a school for the deaf.

The waiting room was empty and the whole place was decorated with some very odd pictures and artifacts. There was a little electric fountain that featured the *Titanic*, half submerged. There was a glass-encased thigh-bone that supposedly came from someone who died in the San Francisco Earthquake of 1906. There were matching posters of the atomic bombs going off in Hiroshima and Nagasaki. And in the center of it all was a sign that read REMEMBER THERE ARE WORSE THINGS THAN A ROOT CANAL.

Püshpa nodded her approval. "Is very comforting," she said. "It puts things in persp . . . in persp . . . what is word?"

"Perspiration," Roxie and I said in unison.

"Yes, yes. Puts things in perspiration."

From behind a door that said NO ADMITTANCE! came two large women with dark braided pigtails and shoulders like football players, which seemed even broader beneath their white dentists coats.

One of them smiled broadly. "Hello, we're the Von Suffrin sisters. We'll be working on your tooth today."

"Tag-team dentistry!" said Roxy, flipping the page of her magazine. "This should be good."

The smiling sister smiled a bit wider. The other one didn't smile at all. It's possible that the second sister was actually a man, but I'll give her the benefit of the doubt.

"Why don't I go get the room ready," said the sister with the Adam's apple. Then she disappeared behind the "No Admittance" door. The smiling sister sat down beside me, picked up a clipboard, and pulled out a pen from a pen holder shaped like Mount Vesuvius. She then proceeded to take down pertinent information, like name, birthday, and what I might like on my tombstone.

"Are you the next of kin?" she asked Püshpa.

"No," answered Püshpa, "I am the Jell-O-mold's nanny. Their schnauzer is out of town. Would you like to call him? I have eggplant in purse."

Dr. Von Suffrin, to her credit, didn't even blink. "I see. No, thanks. If I need to call, we have plenty of vegetables of our own." She turned to me. "Are you ready, Ralphy?"

Just then a scream came through the walls, a sound raw and bloodcurdling. It rattled the window and made the thighbone vibrate in its case.

"No," I answered.

"Oh, don't worry about that—it's just from the therapist's office next door. He has people scream to release their anxiety. You should try it sometime."

She took my hand firmly and led me through the door into the dark recesses of the Von Suffrin inner sanctum.

The room they led me to had state-of-the-art dental equipment, all done in shiny black plastic and black leather. It

looked like Darth Vader's dental chair. I sat down, staring face-to-face with an X-ray machine that looked like the head of a giant praying mantis.

As for the chair, it was comfortable. *Too* comfortable. It was clearly designed to lull a person into a false sense of security. There was a TV suspended from the ceiling that played the director's cut of *Jaws*. Beside the chair there was a whole host of chrome dental equipment that made my eyeballs begin to ache. In addition to the usual drills, mirrors, and poky things, there were some oddly shaped devices that didn't seem designed for human anatomy at all.

"Uh . . . what are those for?" I asked.

"Oh, those?" said the sister with the beard stubble. "Those are just in case."

The other sister held up a gas mask that looked large enough to swallow my entire head. "You can either remain conscious, or we can put you out. Which would you prefer?"

Well, I would rather have been unconscious, but I didn't trust the Von Suffrins. If they put me under, my organs might end up being auctioned on eBay.

"I think I'll stay awake."

"Suit yourself," she said. "Now let's have a look at that tooth."

I opened my mouth and presented her with the voice of Elvis Presley as he crooned "*Hunk-a-hunk-a-burning love . . .*"

She frowned, and turned to her sister. "Lucretia, could you come over here and have a look at this?"

"Certainly, Lizzy."

They both peered into my mouth, and looked at each other shaking their heads and alternately raising their eyebrows like they were communicating telepathically.

"What? What is it?" I asked.

"We've only seen this once before," said Lizzy. "You've got yourself an abscessed abyssal bacterial nexus."

"Is that bad?"

"That depends on your definition of 'bad,'" she said, pointing to a poster of Atlantis being swallowed by the sea. Lizzy smiled even more widely than before, then attached a metallic device to my head which she called "an appliance." It looked like a bear trap, and had teeth as sharp as Bruce the Shark, who was currently chewing Captain Quint in half on the plasma TV screen. Then she produced a hypodermic syringe about the size of an antiaircraft gun and injected a massive dose of novocaine into various points in my gums.

"Lucretia," she said, "we're going to need the big drill for this one." Lucretia nodded, put down her cigar, and went over to a padlocked cabinet.

I have had some painful experiences in my life. There was the "ice-pick incident" for instance, for which one of our former nannies was still serving prison time. Then there was the time I learned how unwise it is to dirt-bike through a cactus garden. But nothing in the known world could compare with the agony I endured at the hands of Lizzy and Lucretia Von Suffrin.

First off, all that novocaine numbed every nerve in my body, except for the nerve in my tooth. "How strange," said Lizzy, her smile growing ever wider. "Well, maybe if we keep drilling, we'll get past the pain. Eventually."

But there was nothing past the pain but more pain. I screamed long and loud—but it didn't matter—and now I knew why they chose to locate their offices here. My screams were camouflaged by the screams coming from the therapist's office—and for obvious reasons, no one at the school for the deaf was very concerned.

All the while, the music in my mouth kept getting louder and louder until it rivaled the grating drone of the drill—and when Jimmy Hendrix began wailing on his electric guitar, I was ready to be put out of my misery.

"I'll take that gas now," I told them, but it was no use. With my jaw locked in the "appliance," all that came out of my mouth was "I—AAH—YA—YA—OWWW."

"Patience, kid," said Lucretia. "It'll all be over soon." Then she pulled out a fresh drill bit that looked like it was meant for drilling for oil. It flexed like a plumbing snake.

Now the music was blasting louder than the drill, but Lizzy and Lucretia were too involved to care. "Almost there," Lucretia said. The long drill bit had completely disappeared into my mouth, and was in so deep, I thought it ought to be coming out of my . . . uh . . . toes. And as if to mock my pain, "La Bamba" blasted its joyful salsa rhythm into the room.

Wait a second . . . "La Bamba"?

That's when I finally made the connection. Richie Valens,

the guy who sang the original "La Bamba," had died in a plane crash. So did Patsy Cline, who sang "Who's Sorry Now?" And Jimmy Hendrix overdosed . . . Come to think of it, every song coming out of my mouth was sung by someone who died an unexpected, unpleasant death. But death was not the end for them, and now I knew there was a place where all tragically terminated musicians go . . . because I wasn't just pulling in some random radio station—my cavity was so infinitely deep, it had become a wormhole to an alternate dimension!

"Just a little bit further . . ." said Lucretia, practically on top of me now, her knee on my chest, and her entire hand shoved in my appliance-stretched mouth down to the wrist.

"*Para bailar la Bamba*," sang Richie Valens.

"We're almost there—I can feel it," said Lizzy.

"*Para bailar la Bamba se necesita una poca de gracia . . .*"

There was a whistling in the air now, like wind tearing through a forest, but neither of them heard it—Lizzy was too involved in her relentless drilling, and Lucretia was focused on holding down my jerking arms and legs. Soon the wind grew, drowning out the song, until it sounded like a freight train crashing through the room. Their pigtails were whipping in the wind—a wind that was funneling right into my mouth.

"Wait! Wait—I see something in there!" shouted Lizzy over the wind. "Oh my God! It's . . . It's—"

But she never finished because suddenly my tooth raged in pain, my mouth felt extremely full, and she was gone. Lizzy Von Suffrin, D.D.S., was sucked right into the wormhole.

Lucretia reacted with lightning reflexes, and grabbed onto the X-ray machine to keep from being drawn in as well. It was like a hole in an airplane at thirty-five thousand feet. In a rush of fluttering paper, crashing metal, and bouncing plastic, everything in the room, from the Atlantis poster, to the dental instruments, to the books and files on the shelves, were torn from the room, and right into the cavity. The "appliance" on my face crumbled like it was made of aluminum foil, tore loose from my mouth, and disappeared inside.

Lucretia held on to the arm of the X-ray machine for her life, her massive biceps straining for all she was worth, until the X-ray machine could no longer hold. It broke off, and she, along with the head of the X-ray machine, came flying toward me. I closed my eyes, bracing for impact, but felt only the throb of my tooth, and when I opened my eyes, she was gone, the wind had stopped, and the room was absolutely silent.

I looked around. There was nothing left in the room but me and the chair. All of that mass had sealed the wormhole.

The door to the room swung open, and I turned to see Roxy and Püshpa standing there, stunned.

"Ralphy!" said Püshpa. "What has happened here?"

Roxy looked at me, turning a little bit green. "Uh . . . Ralphy? There's something hanging out of your mouth."

My cheeks were still so numb that I hadn't felt it there. I reached up to see what it was. It was a single dark braided pigtail hanging out of the corner of my mouth like it had no better place to be.

Püshpa's eyes bulged so wide she began to resemble an anime character. "You ate them! You ate those nice fishmongers, you evil, evil Jell-O-mold!"

Püshpa turned and raced out that door screaming in a language that no longer existed (but might exist again in a few months), and we haven't seen her since.

Roxy sighed. "Well, she lasted longer than most, didn't she? How's your tooth?"

"Better," I told her. It was true. It no longer hurt. Roxie found a pair of scissors in the outer office and relieved me of the pigtail, which now hangs in my room next to various other trophies and ribbons.

Without Püshpa to drive, we walked home, but I didn't mind. I felt better than I had in weeks. All in all, I suppose I can't complain. The Von Suffrin sisters had performed a successful root canal, and in the end had filled my cavity. Literally.

As for Roxie's science-fair project, she took first place, and she's already planning her entry for next year.

That's when I'll be getting braces.

An Ear for Music

I have certain favorite pieces of classical music. There are several movements of Vivaldi's *Four Seasons* I love to listen to over and over again. One movement features fiery violins. The thought of "fiery violins," and the idea of music being able to influence environment, led to this story. My favorite part of the story is the identity of the old man. . . .

An Ear for Music

For Lee Tran, music was all there was, and all there would ever be. Nothing mattered but his music—and he let that thought swell his head as he stepped onto the stage of the huge concert hall, to the sound of thunderous applause.

The old woman was there.

Although the lights shone on his face, he could see her in the private box seat—a place reserved for only the wealthiest patrons of the arts. He could see the pearls around her neck, and her gown, which must have once been elegant, as she herself must have once been. But now she was old. Her face was wrinkled, her teeth yellow, and her thin gray hair wound in a bun so tight, it seemed to lift her ears toward the tip of her skull.

Lee pretended not to notice her. He knew how very important she was, but he wouldn't give her the pleasure of knowing that he cared.

The applause died down as he reached the front of the orchestra. With his bow in one hand and his violin firmly wedged beneath his chin, he waited for the conductor to signal the beginning of the concerto—a concerto Lee had written himself.

219

While other thirteen-year-olds played video games, Lee wrote music. It wasn't his first concerto, but it was the first one that was actually being played by an orchestra. It was also the first time Lee would be the featured soloist in front of so many people. It would have terrified him if he weren't so completely sure of himself.

The conductor brought down his baton, and the piece began with a thundering of brass and the pounding pulse of strings. In a moment the piece was mellowed by the smooth flow of woodwinds, and finally, above it all, rose a single violin, singing to the immense darkened hall.

It was Lee. While the fingers of his left hand flew back and forth across the strings and his right hand gently brushed the bow back and forth, he was creating sound so perfect even the conductor was in awe.

The piece was hard, filled with complex fingering and musical changes so grand, there were very few people in the world who could even play it. Lee was one of them. Although this was the first time he'd played with a major symphony, there had been rumors about him. Rumors that he was not only the greatest young composer of the century, but also the finest violinist known today. He was a fresh discovery in the world of music—and thinking about it made him play even better.

He became one with the violin, his passion flowing through him, flowing through the instrument . . . and as he played, the temperature in the concert hall began to rise.

First it rose a half degree, then a full degree, then two degrees at a time, until people began to feel uncomfortable. *Why is it getting so warm?* they were thinking. *Is the air-conditioning broken? Are there too many people crammed into the hall?*

These thoughts flitted through the dark hall, but they didn't linger for long. For the music was so perfect, so brilliant, that there was no room left in anyone's mind to think of anything else.

The piece grew to its fabulous finale, and Lee's fingers began to move so fast that they became a blur. The audience sighed in ecstasy and gasped in joy . . . and then they screamed in terror as the carpet beneath them burst into flames.

The fire exploded all around Lee, but he couldn't stop playing. Even as the emergency sprinklers began to gush icy water, and the entire audience raced toward the fire exits in panic, he continued to play. All the other musicians ran from the stage—all but Lee. He alone remained onstage until the piece was over, and when the last note was played, the only ones left in the burning concert hall were his parents, who were onstage with him trying to drag him out, and the old woman, the one who had been sitting alone in her box seat. Yes, throughout the fire, she sat there, applauding as the sound of fire engines grew nearer, and the smoke and flames rose higher.

The woman came to Lee's home the next day. She wore a molting fur coat that smelled of mothballs, and it also had a trace of smoke left over from the fire the night before. The

moment Lee laid eyes on her, he recognized the woman. She even wore the same clothes she'd worn to the concert.

Although she looked terribly out of place in the small, dingy apartment, the woman stepped in as if she belonged. Tall and intimidating, this woman somehow had a sense of royalty about her that Lee could not explain.

"Do you know who I am?" she asked his mother, who stood next to Lee staring at the stately woman.

"Of course we do, Madame Magnus," she answered. "How wonderful of you to come to visit Lee in his home." She cleared her throat nervously. "How terrible last night was," she began hesitantly, then didn't quite know what to say.

"Nonsense," said Madame Magnus. "The fire was put out, the concert hall was saved, and no one was hurt."

"But the show was ruined," said Lee's mother.

Madame Magnus smiled. "Ah . . . but what we *did* hear—it was heaven!" She turned to Lee. "You play like an angel, young Master Tran," she said. "More than an angel—a god."

Lee liked the sound of that but decided not to let it show. He shrugged. "I just play," he said simply.

Madame Magnus looked Lee over as if examining a horse. She touched his chin and lifted it, forcing him to look at her. Lee didn't like the feel of her fingers. They were like old newspapers left out in the rain that had crinkled up and dried in the hot sun.

"Play something for me, Lee," she said, as if it were a demand. "I would very much like to hear you again."

Lee did not like being treated like a trained seal, performing on request. He was an artist, and artists had to be treated with some respect. Even thirteen-year-old artists.

Most people couldn't understand what it meant to be a musician. Lee's grandfather had, but he was long dead now. It was his grandfather who had given Lee his first violin when Lee was only four. While other kids were drooling at cartoons, Lee Tran had created music.

Now that his grandfather was gone, there was no one else in the family who cared for music the way Lee did. His father was a poor man who worked hard and saw little in such frivolous things. As for Lee's mother, she had a tin ear and didn't know rock from Rachmaninoff. But one thing she did know— Lee had an inborn talent. And, thanks to her, Lee got his music lessons, even if the family had to go without food to pay for them.

In time, Lee became inseparable from his violin. Playing it was as important to him as breathing.

"No," he told Madame Magnus. "I don't feel like playing now."

Instantly his mother pulled Lee aside and whispered angrily into his ear. She spoke in her native Vietnamese so the old woman couldn't understand, but Lee suspected that Madame Magnus knew the language, and perhaps many others.

"Lee," his mother told him. "This woman, she is rich. She gives money to musicians, and the school she runs is the best."

"I don't care about her money," Lee said.

"But you care about your music. Study with her, and you'll become great."

"I already am great," answered Lee matter-of-factly. "And besides, what if she doesn't choose me for this special school of hers?"

"She'll choose you," his mother said with a certainty that Lee could not deny. Turning from him, she went to the shelf and took down his violin. "Play, my son," she pleaded. "Melt this woman with your music."

Lee opened the violin case. The instrument lay there in its velvet-lined case, a small silent creature, beautiful and powerful. But before he could play, Lee had to have the answer to a single question. He looked up at his mother and asked: "What caused the fire last night?"

His mother shrugged. "Electrical wiring?" she suggested. "Or someone smoking where they should not have been?"

Her guesses were logical, but Lee had his own idea about it, though he didn't dare say it out loud. The fact was, he had never played as well as he had last night, and although sometimes when he played he felt the room around him change, he had never seen his music produce a fire. So far he had noticed the lights dim or grow brighter when he played. Once he felt the air chill, and another time he had felt it grow warm. It always depended on the piece he was playing. But what he had felt last night was like nothing he had ever felt before. Did this Madame Magnus understand that?

"Play for her, Lee," his mother begged.

Finally Lee fit the violin into the nape of his neck and began one of his original melodies. It was dark and filled with solemn tones, and as he had done the night before, Lee forced his soul into the music, letting the sounds resonate through every bone in his body.

When he was done, and his musical trance cleared, Lee saw his mother and the old woman gaping at him. Outside, the sudden pitter-patter of rain was hitting the windows and rattling down the drainpipe from a sky that had been clear only five minutes ago.

The old woman smiled. "Will you come study with me at my school?" she asked.

Lee hesitated. Seeing the power he had in the moment, he milked it and held that power like a long musical note. Then he asked, "How good am I . . . really?"

"You are a master, young man," whispered the old woman. "You are among the best."

This was a good answer for Lee. Perhaps he would become famous. Perhaps he would become rich. He liked the idea of both. And if one of the steps along the way was studying with this ruined old woman, then he would take that step.

"Sure," he said. "I'll come to your school."

Madame Magnus clapped her hands together in joy. "We shall leave immediately," she said. "I pay all my students' expenses, and help support each of their families. Your parents shall receive five hundred dollars a week while you attend my school."

Lee's mother grabbed her heart. "You are far too generous, Madame Magnus," she said, her breath taken away.

But the old woman only smiled through her ancient stained teeth. "Oh, but he's worth much, much more."

———

The Magnus Conservatory of Music was on an estate in northern Vermont. It was a three-story mansion, completely hidden by the dense woods around it and far from the troubles of the big city. As he and his new teacher stepped out of Madame Magnus's limousine, Lee took a good look at the sprawling stately structure. It seemed odd to Lee that something so huge and so finely crafted could be so far from civilization.

"The upper floor is where I live," explained Madame Magnus. "The rest of it is filled with classrooms and lodgings for my students." She smiled at her new pupil. "I have chosen forty-nine students to work with. *You* are the fiftieth."

Another boy, perhaps a year or two older than Lee, with small, round glasses, came down the front steps to meet them.

"This is Wilhelm," said Madame Magnus. "He is your roommate. He is a star cellist who came all the way from Germany to study with me."

Before heading into the conservatory, Lee turned to look through a patch of woods, where he saw another building hidden deep within the tall trees. "What's out there?" he asked, pointing to the small wooden structure.

"The guesthouse," replied Madame Magnus. She said nothing more about it, but at its mention, Lee could see Wilhelm, who was already quite pale, grow even paler.

———

The work at the conservatory was grueling—the hours long, the classes hard. Madame Magnus taught all the musical classes herself, and for the "lesser subjects," as Madame Magnus called everything else, she had hired the finest instructors.

"Do you feel honored to be in my school?" she asked Lee after his first week.

Lee smiled slyly. "That depends," he said. "Do you feel honored to have *me* here?"

The old woman smiled back. It was a fine thing for Lee to finally have a teacher who thought the way he did—who knew music the way he did. Now he knew that Madame Magnus was the greatest music teacher that ever was. Only she could show him that path to greatness he so desired.

Yes, Madame Magnus knew her music. In fact, she could teach every instrument and knew exactly what to say to her young musicians and composers to inspire them all to greatness. But her course of instruction for Lee was strange indeed. She would not let Lee play any of the pieces he knew, nor let him play anything he wrote himself. Instead, she set him to work on dull exercises—scales and fingering practice—terribly mundane exercises that he had outgrown the first week he'd picked up a violin.

Next she had him play musical pieces that seemed specifically designed to be emotionless. Lee was confused. She spoke to him of passionate music, and of achieving flawless control of his instrument, yet she specifically kept him from playing pieces that would inspire him. Lee complied with her

wishes, and if he had been flawless before, these awful exercises made him beyond perfect.

Still, she kept his great musical abilities a secret from everyone else in the school, keeping him apart from the other students as if he were some kind of secret. Curious, Lee wondered what other secrets she kept.

Like the secret guesthouse.

More than once Lee had seen her personal butler go out there, and Lee began to feel a sort of kinship for the lonely little house kept separate from the rest of the school. For in a way, the guesthouse was like him, wasn't it? Everything inside it was kept hidden and locked up by Madame Magnus, the same way his talents were kept locked and hidden by her firm rule.

Once a week Madame Magnus's students gave her a personal concert, but Lee was not even allowed to play in these.

"You are only to watch," the old woman had told him, "and to listen."

Fuming, Lee would sit out in the audience with Madame Magnus, thinking of all the things he could do with the music that was being played.

I could bring forth flames or frost, he mused. *I could fill the room with steam or snow. Perhaps I could even drain the very air from the room.*

Could he do that? Lee would never really know as long as Madame Magnus refused to let him play.

During these weekly concerts he would watch the strange

old woman. There was something unsettling about the way she listened—the way her ears perked up at every note she heard. It was as though she absorbed the sounds, as though they flowed into her ears like water rushing into a whirlpool. Week after week he observed his teacher practically sucking in the music. It reminded Lee of something, but he couldn't put his finger on it.

"Have you noticed that when you stand behind Madame Magnus at a concert, the music suddenly doesn't sound right?" Lee asked Wilhelm one day. "It's as though somehow all the best notes have been sucked right out of it."

"Everyone's noticed it," Wilhelm answered in his heavy accent. "The woman, she gives me the shivers. Still, she is the best teacher there is. She has told me that my playing will make me famous someday, and I believe her."

Lee frowned. She had never said anything like that to him.

That night, just as Lee fell asleep, it occurred to him just what Madame Magnus reminded him of. She was like a vampire . . . but one that lived on something other than blood. *Is that possible?* Lee wondered. *Can someone actually live on music?* But the thought was lost in a swift current of nightmarish dreams.

———

"Somebody lives there, you know," whispered Wilhelm the next day during breakfast. "No one ever sees him come out, but he's there. Everyone knows it."

Wilhelm was talking about the guesthouse, of course.

Through the window of their room, the two boys could see its blackened windows.

"The lights never go on," said Wilhelm, "but one of Madame Magnus's servants brings a large platter of food out there three times a day." The thin, pale cellist leaned closer to Lee. "I think there's a monster in there."

Lee wondered about what Wilhelm had said, and that night he snuck out of the institute and crossed the distance through the woods to the mysterious little building. He just had to know if anyone or any*thing* lived there.

The guesthouse loomed in the woods, unpainted and covered with ivy. As Lee approached, its black windows seemed like dead eyes to him, and he began to wonder what nature of beast was kept there.

Making his way around the back of the sad-looking building, Lee pushed away the thorny bushes that surrounded it, bushes that seemed to be protecting the little house from trespassers. When he came across a broken window, his suspicions were confirmed—the windows weren't just dark, they were painted over so that no light could get in . . . *or* get out.

Lee took a step closer, and just as he put his face near the broken glass to peer inside, a hand reached out and grabbed him by the shirt! It was an ancient, pasty hand, and it held him in a desperate grip.

"*Leave this place*," rattled a raspy voice attached to a body Lee could not see. "*Leave and don't come back. Don't you know what she is?*"

Lee would have screamed if he hadn't lost his voice in fear. Standing frozen in the grip of the bony hand, he now could see the eye of an old man through the hole in the window.

"Nero played his violin," the wrinkled figure said in a voice that seemed to come from the grave. *"He played his violin, and Rome burst into flames. From Nero's flames she was born."* The voice grew in intensity. *"And all the masters who died before their time—they did not die!"* Then, as quickly as it had shot out at Lee, the hand pulled back into the jagged hole and disappeared into the darkness.

His heart pounding, Lee ran back to the conservatory, raced to his room, and hid beneath his covers, as if mere sheets and blankets could possibly shut out what he had seen. "Nero was an emperor of Rome," Wilhelm explained the next day in the library. He showed Lee a drawing in a history book. "He was powerful, arrogant, and legend has it that he played his violin while the entire city burned to the ground."

Lee looked at the article Wilhelm referred to in the encyclopedia. "But it doesn't say that Nero's playing actually *started* the fire."

Wilhelm shrugged. "Maybe it did, maybe it didn't. No one knows for sure."

Lee wondered how great a musician would have to be to be able to set an entire city on fire with his music. How evil such a person would have to be. And then he remembered what the old man behind the broken window had said: *From Nero's flames she was born.* Could he have meant Madame Magnus? Was *she* a creature born from those evil flames?

Lee closed the book and told Wilhelm what the old man had said about all the masters who had died before their time. "What do you think he meant by saying they didn't die?" he asked.

Wilhelm took off his glasses and rubbed his eyes. "I don't know," he said.

"Well, I'm going to find out," said Lee. "If Madame Magnus wants me in this school, then she can't keep secrets from me."

Wilhelm shook his head. "I wish I could be like you."

Lee looked at his friend. *But you can't be*, he thought. *Because you can never be the musician that I am.*

When Lee stormed up the stairs into Madame Magnus's private residence, she didn't seem shocked to see him, or even surprised. She only smiled that sly yellow-toothed smile of hers, then said, "To what do I owe this unexpected visit, young Master Tran?"

Lee got right to the point. "I want to know about the man in the guesthouse. Who is he, and why doesn't he ever come out?"

Madame Magnus looked at Lee from her high-backed velvet chair. "You've only been here two months," she said.

"What has that got to do with anything?" Lee demanded.

"Two months is a short time, but you are a fast learner. Perhaps you are ready."

"Ready for what?" Lee demanded.

But Madame Magnus only smiled. "Would you like to meet him? The man in the guesthouse?"

Lee wasn't expecting that. "Uh, sure," he said hesitantly. "Yeah, sure, I'd like to meet him."

And with that, Madame Magnus and Lee Tran walked into the chill of the night and far into the woods, until they reached the old guesthouse. The old woman unlocked the many locks on the door, and soon it creaked open into a musty world of old furniture that was kept in perfect condition. A grandfather clock ticked away, ominously marking the time.

"Did you think it would be a dungeon?" asked Madame Magnus, laughing when she saw the surprise on Lee's face.

And yet, in its own way, the place did have the feel of a dungeon about it.

There was music coming from a back room, and Lee wondered why he hadn't heard the music outside as they approached. Slowly he looked around, and then he understood the reason—the windows weren't just painted black, they were padded thickly, so that no sounds could escape.

Now listening to the music carefully, Lee noticed that it sounded familiar, and yet it also sounded totally new.

With Madame Magnus on his heels, he followed the sound into a back parlor, done in red velvet—the same red velvet, Lee noticed, that lined his violin case. There, hunched over a grand piano, sat the old man who had grabbed Lee through the broken window. He was pouring his heart into the music. Yet, as beautiful as the music was, it somehow seemed old and tired to Lee, not unlike the man himself.

As Lee listened to him play, once again the familiarity of the music tickled the corner of his brain. The music was romantic and sentimental, perfectly composed. It sounded like Gershwin, Lee finally decided. But this was nothing Gershwin had written in the short thirty-nine years of his life.

Lee studied the ancient figure still playing away at the piano. The old man could have been a hundred by the looks of him. He glanced up from the keys, and upon catching a glimpse of Lee, he sighed, then returned to his playing.

"I've brought you a young friend," said Madame Magnus to the old man.

"Is he the one?" the old man replied.

"The finest violinist alive, and the finest young composer in the world," answered Madame Magnus. And as his teacher said this, Lee held himself up proudly.

The old man just looked away, then returned to his music.

"You'll have to excuse George," said Madame Magnus. "He's not used to visitors."

And then Madame Magnus did something strange. She went to the piano and closed the lid over the keys so the old man could no longer play. "Time to rest, George," she said. "Time to rest."

The old man threw a sad look over at Lee and stood, his bones creaking. Then he went to lie down on the velvet sofa in the corner. He folded his hands over his chest, closed his eyes, and let out a singular long raspy breath. It didn't take long for Lee to realize that the old man had died.

Feeling panic beginning to set in, Lee turned in terrified

awe to Madame Magnus. But she said nothing. She simply walked over to the fireplace and took down a dusty violin case from the mantel.

"For you," she said, opening the case to reveal a Stradivarius violin that must have been hundreds of years old. "It belonged to Mozart himself," Madame Magnus announced. "Take it."

She held the violin out to Lee, and although he felt afraid to even touch it, he could not refuse the magnificent instrument. To play a Stradivarius violin was the dream of a lifetime. *Could this truly have been Mozart's?* he wondered as he took the beautiful wooden instrument into his hands.

Madame Magnus produced a handwritten manuscript of music, aged and as yellow as her skin. "Play for me, Lee," she said. "Play like you've never played before."

And Lee did.

For the first time in months he launched himself into a real piece of music. The Stradivarius was magnificent, and the piece of music glorious. It sounded like Mozart, but like no Mozart Lee had ever heard before. It was a rich musical tapestry full of life and youth and joy. Lee lost himself in it. He felt his soul plunging into the music. And as he played something happened—not to the room, not to the air, but to Madame Magnus herself. With every note it seemed the life of the music poured into her; the youthful, joyous tones seemed to drain into her flesh as if she were some musical black hole.

Lee couldn't keep his eyes off the woman, and although

terror began to fill him, he couldn't stop playing. No longer looking at the sheet of music, he played, his fingers flying over the strings, creating music fast and fiery—music that exploded out of the violin.

But nothing caught fire.

Now all the power of the music funneled right into Madame Magnus. Her eyes burned with its intensity. And to his horror, Lee saw that with each note, Madame Magnus grew younger—younger and more powerful.

Finally the piece ended, and Lee was drenched in sweat. Gasping for breath, he let the bow and violin fall to the floor, for they were burning his fingers.

Before him stood Madame Magnus, a young woman, now no older than twenty-five, and she threw back her head and laughed a hearty, horrible laugh.

Lee willed himself to run, but he just stood there, unable to move. Then, looking down at his legs, he saw that heavy metal shackles now fastened him in place.

"How marvelous!" Madame Magnus cried with delight. "How perfectly marvelous!"

"What's going on?" Lee demanded. "I don't understand!"

The young Madame Magnus smiled her sly smile, only now, on a much younger face, it seemed more than just sly—it seemed evil.

"Come, now," she said. "Don't play dumb with me, young Master Tran. You know precisely what's going on."

And Lee did, but he couldn't admit it to himself. He didn't dare.

"The other young musicians in this conservatory—none of them are good enough to feed me the truly powerful music I thrive on. I needed a great master—a *young* master, someone whose genius would fill my ears with the fresh fire of youth and make me young again. You are the one, Master Tran. *You* are the one I need."

Lee could only stand there, shaking his head. Not a single word rose to his lips.

"Oh, there have been others—*many* others," said Madame Magnus. "Mozart did not die young. He lived to be an old man . . . in my care, of course. And there was Schubert—he, too, grew old . . . with me. And of course you met dear Mr. Gershwin. As you saw, he didn't die young as the rest of the world thought . . . and neither will you."

"No!" screamed Lee. "I won't stay here!"

Then Madame Magnus stepped forward and looked deep into the boy's terror-stricken eyes. "You'll do *exactly* as I say for the rest of your life, young Master Tran. You'll play and you'll write music for no one but me. You'll feed me with your music as the masters before you did. And your music will keep me young and strong . . . until it is used up."

Madame Magnus picked up the violin and bow, then put them back into Lee's hands. "Now play for me," she said, any kindness that had once been there now gone from her voice. "Play me something *you* wrote. Something with *power*."

With no other choice, Lee tucked the Stradivarius beneath his chin and began to play, and instantly he felt his music swallowed whole by Madame Magnus's hungry, hungry ears.

I am the greatest, Lee told himself, fighting back tears of terror. *I am the greatest in the world!*

But that didn't matter anymore, since no one else would ever hear him play. Now his music would have to be enough, because now music was all there truly was for Lee Tran . . . and all there would ever be.

RIDING THE RAPTOR

This story is the forerunner to my novel *Full Tilt*. I was at Six Flags Magic Mountain, one of my favorite amusement parks, on an incredibly crowded day. Every roller coaster had a two-hour wait, except for one. It was as if no one saw this roller coaster. As I wove through the empty line to get to the front, the sun went behind the clouds and a cold wind started to blow. That got my imagination going. What if there was one roller coaster at every amusement park that not everyone saw? What if it could only be seen by those who were no longer satisfied by other thrill rides, and were now ready for the ultimate coaster? What would the ultimate roller coaster be?

RIDING THE RAPTOR

"This is gonna be great, Brent!" says my older brother, Trevor. "I can feel it."

I smile. Trevor always says that.

The trip to the top of a roller coaster always seems endless, and from up here the amusement park seems much smaller than it does from the ground. As the small train clanks its way up the steel slope of a man-made mountain, I double-check the safety bar across my lap to make sure it's tight. Then, with a mixture of terror and excitement, Trevor and I discuss how deadly that first drop is going to be. We're roller coaster fanatics, my brother and I—and this brand-new sleek, silver beast of a ride promises to deliver ninety incredible seconds of unharnessed thrills. It's called the Kamikaze, and it's supposed to be the fastest, wildest roller coaster ever built. We'll see . . .

We crest the top, and everyone screams as they peer down at the dizzying drop. Then we begin to hurl downward.

Trevor puts up his hands as we pick up speed, spreading his fingers and letting the rushing wind slap against his palms. But I can never do that. Instead I grip the lap bar with sweaty palms. And I scream.

You can't help but scream at the top of your lungs on a roller coaster, and it's easy to forget everything else in the world as your body flies through the air. That feeling is special for me, but I know it's even more special for Trevor.

We reach the bottom of the first drop, and I feel myself pushed deep down into the seat as the track bottoms out and climbs once more for a loop. In an instant there is no up or down, no left or right. I feel my entire spirit become a ball of energy twisting through space at impossible speeds.

I turn my head to see Trevor. The corners of his howling mouth are turned up in a grin, and it's good to see him smile. All his bad grades, all his anger, all his fights with Mom and Dad—they're all gone when he rides the coasters. I can see it in his face. All that matters is the feel of the wind against his hands as he thrusts his fingertips into the air.

We roll one way, then the other—a double forward loop and a triple reverse corkscrew. The veins in my eyes bulge, my joints grind against one another, my guts climb into my throat. It's great!

One more sharp turn, and suddenly we explode back into the real world as the train returns to the station. Our car stops with a jolt, the safety bar pops up, and an anxious crowd pushes forward to take our seats.

"That was unreal!" I exclaim, my legs like rubber as we climb down the exit stairs.

But Trevor is unimpressed.

"Yeah, it was okay, I guess," he says with a shrug. "But it wasn't as great as they said it would be."

I shake my head. After years of riding the rails, Trevor's

become a roller-coaster snob. It's been years since any coaster has delivered the particular thrill that Trevor wants.

"Well, what did you expect?" I ask him, annoyed that his lousy attitude is ruining my good time. "It's a roller coaster, not a rocket, you know?"

"Yeah, I guess," says Trevor, his disappointment growing with each step we take away from the Kamikaze. I look up and see it towering above us—all that intimidating silver metal. Somehow, now that we've been on it, it doesn't seem quite so intimidating.

Then I get to thinking how we waited six months for them to build it, and how we waited in line for two hours to ride it, and I get even madder at Trevor for not enjoying it more.

We stop at a game on the midway, and Trevor angrily hurls baseballs at milk bottles. He's been known to throw rocks at windows with the same stone-faced anger. Sometimes I imagine my brother's soul to be like a shoelace that's all tied in an angry knot. It's a knot that only gets loose when he's riding rails at a hundred miles an hour. But as soon as the ride is over, that knot pulls itself tight again. Maybe even tighter than it was before.

Yeah, I know what roller coasters mean to Trevor. And I also know what it means when the ride is over.

Trevor furiously hurls another baseball, missing the stacked gray bottles by a mile. The guy behind the counter is a dweeb with an Adam's apple the size of a golf ball that bobs up and down when he talks. Trevor flicks him another crumpled dollar and takes aim again.

"Why don't we ride the Skull-Smasher or the Spine-Shredder," I offer. "Those aren't bad rides—and the lines aren't as long as the Kamikaze's was."

Trevor just hurls the baseball even harder, missing again. "Those are baby rides," he says with a sneer.

"Listen, next summer we'll find a better roller coaster," I say, trying to cheer him up. "They're always building new ones."

"That's a whole year away," Trevor complains, hurling the ball again, this time nailing all three bottles at once.

The dweeb running the booth hands Trevor a purple dinosaur. "Nice shot," he grunts.

Trevor looks at the purple thing with practiced disgust.

Great, I think. *Trevor's already bored out of his mind and it's only this amusement park's opening day.* As I watch my brother, I know what'll happen now; five more minutes, and he'll start finding things to do that will get us into trouble, deep trouble. It's how Trevor is.

That's when I catch sight of the tickets thumbtacked to the booth's wall, right alongside the row of purple dinosaurs—two tickets with red printing on gold paper.

"What are those?" I ask the dweeb running the booth.

"Beats me," he says, totally clueless. "You want 'em instead of the dinosaur?"

We make the trade, and I read the tickets as we walk away: GOOD FOR ONE RIDE ON THE RAPTOR.

"What's the Raptor?" I ask Trevor.

"Who knows," he says. "Probably some dumb kiddie-go-round thing, like everything else in this stupid place."

I look on the amusement-park map but can't find the ride anywhere. Then, through the opening-day crowds, I look up and see a hand-painted sign that reads THE RAPTOR in big red letters. The sign is pointing down toward a path that no one else seems to be taking. That alone is enough to catch Trevor's interest, as well as mine.

He glances around furtively, as if he's about to do something he shouldn't, then says, "Let's check it out."

He leads the way down the path, and as always, I follow.

The dark asphalt we are on leads down into thick bushes, and the sounds of the amusement-park crowd get farther and farther away, until we can't hear them at all.

"I think we made a wrong turn," I tell Trevor, studying the map, trying to get my bearings. Then suddenly a deep voice booms in the bushes beside us.

"You're looking for the Raptor, are you?"

We turn to see a clean-shaven man dressed in the gray-and-blue uniform that all the ride operators wear, only his doesn't seem to be made of the same awful polyester. Instead his uniform shimmers like satin. So do his eyes, blue-gray eyes that you can't look into, no matter how hard you try.

I look at Trevor, and tough as he is, he can't look the man in the face.

"The name's DelRio," the man says. "I run the Raptor."

"What *is* the Raptor?" asks Trevor.

DelRio grins. "You mean you don't know?" He reaches out his long fingers and pulls aside the limbs of a dense thornbush. "There you are, gentlemen—the Raptor!"

What we see doesn't register at first. When something is so big—so indescribably huge—sometimes your brain can't quite wrap around it. All you can do is blink and stare, trying to force your mind to accept what it sees.

There's a valley before us, and down in the valley is a wooden roller coaster painted black as night. But the amazing thing is that the valley itself is part of the roller coaster. Its peaks rise on either side of us in a tangle of tracks that stretch off in all directions as if there is nothing else but the Raptor from here to the ends of the earth.

"No way," Trevor gasps, more impressed than I've ever seen him. "This must be the biggest roller coaster in the world!"

"The biggest *anywhere*," corrects DelRio.

In front of us is the ride's platform with sleek red cars, ready to go.

"Something's wrong," I say, although I can't quite figure out what it is. "Why isn't this ride on the map?"

"New attraction," says DelRio.

"So how come there's no crowd?" asks Trevor.

DelRio smiles and looks through us with those awful eyes. "The Raptor is by invitation only." He takes our tickets, flipping them over to read the back. "Trevor and Brent Collins," he says. "Pleased to have you aboard."

Trevor and I look at each other, then at the torn ticket stubs DelRio has just handed back to us. Sure enough, our names are printed right there on the back, big as life.

"Wait! How did—" But before I can ask, Trevor cuts me

off, his eyes already racing along the wildly twisting tracks of the gigantic contraption.

"That first drop," he says, "that's three hundred feet."

"Oh, the first drop's grand!" DelRio exclaims. "But on this ride, it's the last drop that's special."

I can see Trevor licking his lips, losing himself in the sight of the amazing ride. It's good to see him excited like this . . . and *not* good, too.

Every time DelRio talks I get a churning feeling in my gut—the kind of feeling you get when you find half a worm in your apple. Still, I can't figure out what's wrong.

"Are we the only ones invited?" I ask tentatively.

DelRio smiles. "Here come the others now."

I turn to see a group of gawking kids coming through the bushes, and DelRio greets them happily. The look in their eyes is exactly like Trevor's. They don't just want to ride the coaster—they *need* to ride it.

"Since you're the first, you can ride in the front," DelRio tells us. "Aren't you the lucky ones!"

While Trevor psyches himself up for the ride, and while DelRio tears tickets, I slip away into the superstructure of the great wooden beast. I'm searching for something—although I'm not sure what it is. I follow the track with my eyes, but it's almost impossible to stick with it. It twists and spins and loops in ways that wooden roller coasters aren't supposed to be able to do—up and down, back and forth, until my head gets dizzy and little squirmy spots appear before my eyes. It's like a huge angry knot.

Before long I'm lost in the immense web of wood, but still I follow the path of the rails with my eyes until I come to that last drop that DelRio claimed was so special. I follow its long path up . . . and then down . . .

In an instant I understand just what it is about this ride I couldn't put my finger on before. Now I *know* I have to stop Trevor from getting on it.

In a wild panic I race back through the dark wooden frame of the Raptor, dodging low-hanging beams that poke out at odd angles.

When I finally reach the platform, everyone is sitting in their cars, ready to go. The only empty seat is in the front car. It's the seat beside Trevor. DelRio waits impatiently by a big lever extending from the ground.

"Hurry, Brent," DelRio says, scowling. "Everyone's waiting."

"Yes! Yes!" shout all the kids. "Hurry! Hurry! We want to RIDE!"

They start cheering for me to get in, to join my brother in the front car. But I'm frozen on the platform.

"Trevor!" I finally manage to say, gasping for breath. "Trevor, you have to get off that ride."

"What are you, nuts?" he shouts.

"We can't ride this coaster!" I insist.

Trevor ignores me, fixing his gaze straight ahead. But that's not the direction in which he should be looking. He should be looking at the track behind the last car—because if he does, he'll see that there *is* no track behind the last car!

"The coaster doesn't come back!" I shout at him. "Don't you see? It doesn't come back!"

Trevor finally turns to me, his hands shaking in infinite terror and ultimate excitement . . . and then he says . . .

"I know."

I take a step back.

I can't answer that. I can't accept it. I need more time, but everyone is shouting at me to get on the ride, and DelRio is getting more and more impatient. That's when Trevor reaches out his hand toward me, his fingers bone white, trembling with anticipation.

"Ride with me, Brent," he pleads desperately. "It'll be great. I can feel it!"

I reach out my hand. My fingers are an inch from his.

"Please . . ." Trevor pleads.

He's my brother. He wants me to go. They *all* want me to go. What could be better than riding in the front car, twisting through all those spins and drops? I can see it now: Trevor and me—the way it's always been—his hands high in the air, wrestling the wind, and me gripping the safety bar.

Only thing is, the Raptor *has* no safety bar.

I pull my hand back away from his. *I won't follow you, Trevor!* my mind screams. *Not today. Not ever again.*

When Trevor sees me backing away, his face hardens—the way it hardens toward our parents or his teachers or anyone else who's on the outside of his closed world. "Wimp!" he shouts at me. "*Loooooser!*"

DelRio tightly grips the lever. "This isn't a ride for the

weak," he says, his hawk eyes judging me, trying to make me feel small and useless. "Stand back and let the big kids ride."

He pulls back on the lever, and slowly the Raptor slides forward, catching on a heavy chain that begins to haul it up the first big drop. Trevor has already turned away from me, locking his eyes on the track rising before him, preparing himself for the thrill of his life.

The coaster clackety-clacks all the way to the top. Then the red train begins to fall, its metal wheels throwing sparks and screeching all the way down. All I can do is watch as Trevor puts up his hands and rides. The wooden beast of a roller coaster groans and roars like a dragon, and the tiny red train rockets deep inside the black wooden framework stretching to the horizon.

Up and down, back and forth, the Raptor races. Time is paralyzed as its trainload of riders rockets through thrill after terrifying thrill, until finally, after what seems like an eternity, it reaches that last mountain.

DelRio turns to me. "The grand finale," he announces. "You could have been there—*you* could have had the ultimate thrill if you weren't a coward, Brent."

But I know better. This time, *I* am the brave one.

The red train climbs the final peak, defying gravity, moving up and up until it's nothing more than a tiny red sliver against a blue sky . . . and then it begins the trip down, accelerating faster than gravity can pull it. It's as if the ground itself were sucking it down from the clouds.

The Raptor's whole wooden framework rumbles like an earthquake. I hold on to a black beam, and I feel my teeth rattle in my head. I want to close my eyes, but I keep them open, watching every last second.

I can see Trevor alone in the front car. His hands are high, slapping defiantly against the wind, and he's screaming louder than all the others as the train plummets straight down . . . into that awful destiny that awaits it.

I can see that destiny from here now, looming larger than life—a bottomless blacker-than-black pit.

I watch as my brother and all the others are pulled from the sky, down into that emptiness . . . and then they are swallowed by it, their thrilled screams silenced without as much as an echo.

The ride is over.

I am horrified, but DelRio remains unmoved. He casually glances at his watch, then turns and shouts deep into the superstructure of the roller coaster. "Time!"

All at once hundreds of workers crawl from the woodwork like ants. Nameless, faceless people, each one with some kind of tool like a hammer or wrench practically growing from their arms. They all set upon the Raptor, dismantling it with impossible speed.

"What is this?" I ask DelRio. "What's going on?"

"Surely you don't expect an attraction this special to stay in one place?" he scoffs. "We must travel! There are worlds of people waiting for the thrill of a lifetime!"

When I look again at the roller coaster, it's gone. Nothing

remains but the workers carrying its heavy beams off through the thick underbrush.

DelRio smiles at me. "We'll see you again, Brent," he says. "Perhaps next time you'll ride."

As the last of the workers carry away the final rail of the Raptor on their horribly hunched backs, I stare DelRio down. I can look him in the eyes now, unblinking, unflinching.

"Tell your friends about the Raptor," he says, then he pauses and adds: "No . . . on second thought, don't tell them a thing. Wouldn't want to spoil their surprise."

Then he strolls off into the dense bushes after the workers, who are carrying the Raptor off to its next location. I just stand there. Nothing is left but the breeze through the valley and the distant sounds of the amusement park far behind me.

No, I won't tell anyone—ever. What could I possibly say? And if I encounter the Raptor again someday, I can only hope I will have the strength to stare DelRio down once more, dig my heels deep into the earth beneath my feet . . . and refuse to ride.

Trash Day

This story was a challenge. Literally. I was in a car with a friend, who was complaining that she had no ideas for stories. I said there are always ideas, and that you can write a story about anything. She said. "Okay, then I challenge you to write a story bout the next object you see." It was a Dumpster.

TRASH DAY

It began long before that *thing* arrived on their lawn.

In fact, it began long before Lucinda Pudlinger was born. There was no way to know all the strange and mysterious forces that had created the Pudlinger family. Nevertheless, all those forces bubbled and brewed together and spat out the Pudlingers on the doormat of humanity.

As for Lucinda, it had never really occurred to her how serious her situation was until the day Garson McCall walked her home from school.

"You really don't have to," Lucinda had told him, more as a warning than anything else. Still, Garson had insisted. For reasons that Lucinda could not understand, he had a crush on her.

"No," said Garson, "I really want to walk you home."

Lucinda didn't mind the attention, but she did mind the fact that Garson was going to meet her family. There was no preparing him for *that*.

As they rounded the corner on that autumn afternoon, the Pudlinger home came into view. It was halfway down a street of identical tract homes—but there was nothing about where the Pudlingers lived that matched the other homes.

True, they had a small front lawn like every other house on

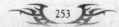

the block, but on the Pudlingers' lawn there were three rusting cars with no wheels—and a fourth piled on top of the other three. The four useless vehicles had been there, as far as Lucinda knew, since the beginning of time. While others might keep such old wrecks with an eye toward restoring them, the Pudlingers, it seemed, just collected them.

There was also a washing machine on that lawn. It didn't work, but Lucinda's mom had filled it with barbecue ashes and turned it into a planter. Of course, only weeds would grow in it, but then weeds were Mrs. Pudlinger's specialty. One only needed to look at the rest of the yard to see that.

As for the house itself, the roof shingles looked like a jigsaw puzzle minus a number of pieces, and the pea-green aluminum siding was peeling (which was something aluminum siding wasn't supposed to do).

The Pudlinger place didn't just draw your attention when you walked by it. No, it grabbed your eyeballs and dragged them kicking and screaming out of their sockets. In fact, if you looked up "eyesore" in the dictionary, Lucinda was convinced it would say *See Pudlinger*.

"Look at that place!" said Garson as they walked down the street. "Is that a house or the city dump?"

"It's *my* house," said Lucinda, figuring the truth was less painful when delivered quickly.

"Oh," replied Garson, his face turning red from the foot he had just put in his mouth. "I didn't mean there was anything *wrong* with it—it just looks . . . lived in. Yeah, that's right— lived in . . . in a homey sort of way."

"Homely" is more like it, thought Lucinda.

Out front there was a fifth rusty auto relic that still worked, parked by the curb. A pair of legs attached to black boots stuck out from underneath. As Garson and Lucinda approached, a boy of about sixteen crawled out from under the car, stood in their path, and flexed his muscles in a threatening way. He wore a black T-shirt that said DIE, and he had dirty-blond hair with streaks of age-old grease in it. His right arm was substantially more muscular than his left, the way crabs often have one claw much bigger than the other.

"Who's this dweeb?" the filthy teenager said through a mouth full of teeth, none of which seemed to be growing in the same direction. He looked Garson up and down.

Lucinda sighed. "Garson, this is my brother, Ignatius."

"My friends call me 'Itchy'" (which didn't mean much, since Ignatius had no friends). "You ain't a nerd, are you?" Itchy asked the boy standing uncomfortably next to Lucinda.

"No, not recently," Garson replied.

"Good. I hate nerds." And with that, Itchy reached out his muscular right arm and shook Garson's hand, practically shattering Garson's finger bones. It was intentional.

"Hey, wanna help me chase the neighborhood cats into traffic?" Itchy asked. "It's a blast!"

"No thanks," said Garson. "I'm allergic to cats."

Itchy shrugged. "Your loss," he said, then returned to tormenting the fat tabby that was hiding under the car.

"What's with him?" asked Garson as he and Lucinda made their way toward the house.

Lucinda rolled her eyes. "He's been bored ever since he got expelled."

What Lucinda neglected to say was how happy her brother was to be out of school. He'd planned on getting out ever since last summer when he'd gotten a job operating the Tilt-A-Whirl at the local carnival. It was that job which had given him his powerful right arm. Pull the lever, push the lever, press the button—if he worked at it hard enough, and practiced at home, Itchy was convinced operating the Tilt-A-Whirl could become a full-time career. With a future that bright, who needed school?

"Lucinda!" shouted Itchy, still under the car. "Mom and Dad are looking for you . . . and they're mad."

Lucinda shrugged. That was no news. They were always that way.

She turned to Garson. "You don't have to come in," she said, more in warning than anything else.

But Garson forced a smile. He was going to see this through to the end, no matter how horrible that end might be. And it was.

———

The inside of the Pudlinger home was no more inviting than the outside. It had curling wallpaper, brown carpet that had clearly started out as a different color, and faded furniture that would cause any respectable interior decorator to jump off a cliff.

Mr. Pudlinger was in his usual position on the recliner, with a beer in his hand, releasing belches of unusual magnitude. He stared at a TV with the colors set so everyone's face was purple and their hair was green.

"Where have you been?" he growled at Lucinda.

"Field-hockey practice," she answered flatly.

"You didn't take out the trash this morning," he said, grunting.

"Yes, I did."

"Then how come it's full again?"

Lucinda glanced over to see that the trash can was indeed full—full of the usual fast-food wrappers, beer cans, and unpaid bills.

"You take that trash out before dark, or no allowance!" her dad yelled from across the room. It must have slipped his mind that Lucinda didn't get an allowance. Not that they couldn't afford it—they weren't poor. It was just that her mom and dad liked to "put money away for a rainy day." Obviously they thought there was a drought.

Mr. Pudlinger shifted in his recliner and it let out a frightened squeak the way recliners do when holding someone of exceptional weight. It wasn't that Lucinda's dad was fat. It would have been perfectly all right if he was *just* fat. But the truth was, he was also . . . misshapen. He had a hefty beer gut, and somehow that beer gut had settled into strange, unexpected regions of his body, until he looked like some horrible reflection in a fun-house mirror.

"What does your father *do?*" Garson asked as they stepped over the living-room debris toward the kitchen.

"What he's doing right now," she replied. "That's what he does."

"No, I mean for a living," Garson clarified.

"Like I said, *that's* what he does." Lucinda then went on to explain how her father was hurt on the job six years ago, and how he had been home ever since, receiving disability pay from the government. "He calls it 'living off of Uncle Sam,'" said Lucinda. Of course, Mr. Pudlinger failed to tell Uncle Sam that he had completely recovered two weeks after the accident.

In the kitchen they ran into Lucinda's mom, who Lucinda had also wanted to avoid. The woman had a cigarette permanently fixed to a scowl that was permanently planted on her mouth, which was permanently painted with more lipstick than Bozo the Clown.

Lucinda reluctantly introduced her to Garson.

"Garson?" she said through her frowning clown lips. "What kind of stupid name is that?" Cough, cough.

"I'm named after my father," Garson replied.

"Yeah, yeah, whatever," she said, and spat her gum into the sink, where it caught the lip of a dirty glass. "You wanna stay for dinner, Garson?" she asked, batting her eyes, showing off those caterpillar-like things she glued to her lashes.

"What are you having?" he asked.

"Leftovers," she said flatly.

Garson grimaced. "Left over from what?"

Mrs. Pudlinger was stumped by that one. No one had ever asked that before. "Just leftovers," she said. "You know, like from the refrigerator."

"No thanks," said Garson. Clearly his survival instinct had kicked in.

Lucinda was beginning to believe that Garson would soon leave, and she would be spared any further embarrassment. But then her father called him over to the recliner.

"Hey, kid, I wanna show you a magic trick," Mr. Pudlinger said with a sly smile. Then he extended his index finger in Garson's direction. "Pull my finger," he said.

Garson did, and Mr. Pudlinger let one rip.

Lucinda watched tearfully as, moments later, Garson sprinted down the street, racing away from her horrible family. It was the last straw, the last time she would allow her family to humiliate her like this. Their reign of terror had to end.

Just as she turned to walk back into the house, a car swerved in the street, its tires screeching as it tried to avoid a cat. The cat, having missed being flattened, leaped into the arms of an elderly neighbor woman across the street. She turned a clouded eye at Itchy, who had just climbed out from under a parked car, laughing.

"You monster!" the old woman screamed, shaking her cane at him. "You horrible, evil boy!"

"Ah, shut yer trap, you old bat," Itchy snarled.

"You're trash!" the old woman shouted. "Every last one of you Pudlingers. The way you keep your house—the way you live your lives—*you're all trash!*"

That's when Mr. Pudlinger came out onto the porch. It was the first time Lucinda had seen him outside in months. He turned to Itchy, put a hand on the boy's shoulder, and as if

speaking words of profound wisdom, said, "Don't let anyone who's not family call you trash."

And then he went across the street and punched the old lady out.

When Lucinda's salvation finally came, it came thundering out of nowhere at five in the morning. That's when a mighty crash shook the house like an earthquake, waking everyone up.

Furious to have been shaken awake, Mr. Pudlinger shuffled out of the bedroom with Mrs. Pudlinger close behind, her face caked in some sort of green beauty mud that actually looked less offensive than her face.

"What's going on around here?" bellowed Mr. Pudlinger. "Can't a man get any sleep?"

Lucinda wandered out of her bedroom, and Itchy—a true coward when it came to anything other than cats and nerds—came out of his bedroom and hid right behind her.

Together the family shuffled to the front door and opened it to find yet another object on their front lawn—a Dumpster.

Dark green, with heavy ridges all around it, the huge metal trash container was one of those large ones they use in construction—eight feet high and twenty feet long. Yet it seemed like no Dumpster Lucinda had ever seen before.

"Cool," said Itchy, who must have already been calculating a hundred awful ways the thing could be used.

Mr. Pudlinger scratched his flaking scalp. "Who sent a Dumpster to us?" he asked.

"Maybe the Home Shopping Network," suggested Itchy.

"Naah," said Mom. "I didn't order a Dumpster."

But it clearly was meant for them, because the name "Pudlinger" was stenciled on the side.

It's like a puzzle, thought Lucinda. *What's wrong with this picture?*

But there were already so many things wrong with the Pudlinger lawn that the Dumpster just blended right in. Slowly Lucinda went up to it. It looked so . . . heavy. More than heavy, it looked dense. She looked down to see a tiny hint of metal sticking out from underneath. The edge of a car muffler poked out like the Wicked Witch's feet beneath Dorothy's house.

Mrs. Pudlinger gasped. "Look!" she said. "It crushed the Volkswagen Itchy was born in!"

Mr. Pudlinger began to fume. "I'll sue!" he shouted. And with that he stormed back into the house and began to flip through the yellow pages in search of a lawyer.

The Dumpster caught the sun and cast a dark shadow. As Lucinda left for school that day, she couldn't help but stare at the thing as she walked around it to get to the street.

It's just a Dumpster, she tried to tell herself. The way she figured it, some neighbor—some *angry* neighbor—had taken it upon himself to provide a container large enough to haul away all the junk her family had accumulated over the years.

But if that were so, then why didn't they hear the truck that had brought it here?

Before Lucinda knew what she was doing, she had put down her books and was walking toward the gigantic green container. Slowly she began to touch it, brushing her fingers across the metal, then laying her hand flat against its cold, smooth surface. As she touched it, all thoughts seemed to empty from her mind. It was as if the Dumpster were hypnotizing her. She giggled to herself for thinking such a silly thought and stepped away from it.

Then the Dumpster shifted just a bit, and the dead Volkswagen Bug beneath it creaked a flat complaint. *Anything that crushes one of our lawn cars can't be all bad*, thought Lucinda with a chuckle.

No, Lucinda decided, this thing was not evil—far from it. In fact, to Lucinda it seemed almost . . . friendly—certainly more friendly than anything else on their poor excuse for a lawn. And clearly it seemed to be waiting. Yes, happily waiting for something . . . but what?

Whistling to herself, Lucinda turned away. And as she strolled off to school, she thought about the great green metal box and the way it sat in anticipation, like a Christmas present waiting to be opened.

———

The neighbor's fat tabby cat was sitting proudly on the hood of one of the lawn cars when Lucinda returned home that afternoon. The Dumpster hadn't moved.

All day Lucinda hadn't been able to get it out of her mind. It was as if the thing had fallen into her brain instead of onto their weed-choked lawn. In fact, she had actually looked forward to coming home, just so she could take a good look at it again. There was something noble about the way it stood there—like a silent monolith.

But it isn't silent, is it? Lucinda thought. There were noises coming from within its dark green depths—little scratches and creaks, like rats crawling around. *Is there something alive in there?* she wondered. *Is there anything in there at all, or is it just my imagination?*

If it had been a Christmas present, Lucinda would have been able to shake it, feel its weight, and try to guess what it held. But there was no way she could lift a Dumpster.

Unable to stand not knowing what was inside, she ran to the porch, got several chairs, and stacked them one on top of the other. Then she climbed the rickety tower she had created and peered over the edge of the Dumpster.

As she had expected, it wasn't empty, and the shock of what Lucinda saw nearly made her lose her balance and tumble back to the ground. But she held on, refusing to blink as she stared down into the Dumpster . . .

. . . at her father, who sat in his recliner, watching TV.

"Dad?" she shouted. "Dad, what are you doing?"

"What does it look like I'm doing?" he asked, clicking the remote control with the speed of a semiautomatic weapon. "Get me the *TV Guide*, or you're grounded!"

In another corner of the Dumpster sat Lucinda's mother,

with her entire vanity and makeup collection before her. She scowled at her own reflection, took a deep drag of her cigarette, and began to apply a fresh layer of makeup.

"Mom?"

"Leave me alone," she said. "I'm having a bad hair day." Cough, cough.

In the third corner of the Dumpster stood Itchy. There was a lever coming from the metal floor, and a button on the wall. Pull the lever, push the lever, press the button. Pull the lever, push the lever, press the button—Itchy was working away.

"Have you all gone crazy?" yelled Lucinda. "Don't you know where you are?"

But it was clear that they didn't. Her father thought he was in the living room, her mother thought she was in the bedroom, and Itchy, well, he thought he was king of the Tilt-A-Whirl. They all were in their own private little heaven, if you could call it that. This Dumpster—this terrible, wonderful Dumpster—wasn't designed to haul away *things*—it was designed to haul away *people*!

"Well, are you coming inside or what?" asked her father.

Lucinda could have argued with them. And maybe, if she tried hard enough, she could have broken through their little trances and made them come out.

But if she tried hard enough, she could also keep herself from telling them anything at all.

That thought brought the tiniest grin to her face—a grin that widened as she leaped to the ground, into a tangle of weeds that cushioned her fall. Her smile continued to grow

as she stepped into the house, and she broke into a full-fledged laughing fit as she raced into her room and began to bounce on her bed.

The Dumpster was taken away sometime during the night.

———

The following week, Garson McCall stopped by to apologize for being so rude on his first visit. The startled look on his face didn't surprise Lucinda. She'd had many startled visitors during those first few days. One need only look at the carless, freshly planted lawn to know something had changed.

"Hi, Garson," said Lucinda in a dark, sad tone that didn't seem to match the brightness of the spotless house.

"Wow! What an overhaul!" exclaimed Garson as he stepped inside, his eyes bugging out at the new carpet and furniture.

Lucinda just shrugged.

A sixteen-year-old kid came bounding out of the kitchen to greet him, wearing a million-dollar smile that showed perfect teeth. "Hi, Garson, what's up?" the boy asked.

"Itchy?" Garson murmured in disbelief.

"Ignatius," the clean-cut boy corrected. "But my friends call me Nate."

In the living room a man who looked like an athletic version of Mr. Pudlinger was sipping lemonade and reading *Parents* magazine. In the kitchen a woman who resembled Mrs. Pudlinger, with several coats of makeup peeled away, was baking a pie.

"Garson, would you like to stay for dinner?" asked the

pleasant-looking woman. "We're having T-bone steak and apple pie!"

"Sure," said Garson.

Lucinda could practically see him drool, but the flat expression on her own face never changed. In fact, she didn't know if she *could* change it anymore.

"I can't believe these are the same people I saw last week!" whispered Garson excitedly.

"They're not," said Lucinda. "They're replacements sent by the Customer Service Department."

Garson laughed, as if Lucinda had made a joke, and Lucinda didn't have the strength to convince him it was true.

"Listen, Garson," she finally said. "I'd like to talk, but I can't. I have to study."

"Study?" Garson raised an eyebrow. "On a Saturday?"

"I have to get an A in math," Lucinda replied.

"And science," added the new Mrs. Pudlinger cheerfully.

"Don't forget English and history," Mr. Pudlinger sang out. "My daughter's going to be a straight-A student, just like her brother!"

Lucinda sighed, feeling herself go weak at the knees. "*And* I have to be the star of the field-hockey team. *And* I have to keep my room spotlessly clean. *And* I have to do all my chores *perfectly* . . . or else."

"Or else . . . what?" asked Garson.

Then Lucinda leaned in close, and with panic in her eyes, she desperately whispered in his ear, "Or else it comes back for me!"

Mrs. Pudlinger turned from her perfect pie. "Lucinda, dear," she said with a smile that seemed just a bit too wide, "isn't it your turn to take out the garbage?"

"Yes, Mother," Lucinda replied woodenly.

Then Lucinda Pudlinger, dragging her feet across the floor like a zombie, took out the trash . . . being horribly careful not to let a single scrap of paper fall to the ground. Ever.

CRYSTALLOID

When I was first writing the two collections that many of these stories come from, the publishers wanted a story that the artist could use to create a really great cover. I wanted to create a really interesting, unique monster; something scary, but classy at the same time. I had the image in my mind of a creature made entirely of crystal. With that in mind, I set out to write "Crystalloid."

CRYSTALLOID

The Sand Trap had already claimed a neighbor's dog. At least that was the rumor. They said the poor animal had gone down slowly, like it had been sucked into quicksand. It must have felt the same way a dinosaur felt when it got stuck in a tar pit and sank inch by inch into hot, black eternity.

Of course, nobody believed the rumor. Quicksand? On a beach? No such thing! No, that stuff was only in the Amazon or deep in the Congo—and anyone foolish enough to poke around in places like that deserved whatever they got.

But I believed it. People didn't make up things like that—not unless they were particularly twisted. That's what made me trek down that long strip of empty beach near my grandma's old beach house. I had to check it out for myself.

I'd been living with Grandma almost four months now. It was my dad's new girlfriend's idea, and at first, I was just supposed to spend the summer.

"It's for Philip's own good," she had said, sounding so caring, as if the real reason she wanted to get rid of me had anything to do with helping me. Anyway, she convinced my dad it was a last-ditch effort to keep me out of trouble. After all, ever since my dad and mom split, I had developed a

special talent for getting rid of his girlfriends. Maybe my dad figured if I were out of the picture, that wouldn't happen anymore.

Anyway, it worked. They spent the summer together in Europe, and I kept out of trouble—if you don't count that first day, when I got mad and shattered a bunch of glass figurines in Grandma's crafts shop.

In fact, I've done so well out here, my dad and his girlfriend decided to leave me in this lonely part of the world for good. Or at least it seems that way.

So, since it looks like I don't have a choice, I've been trying to make the best of it, and I've actually grown to like the desolate beaches better than the crowded city I used to live in. Of course, the kids at school out here are kind of time-warped back a dozen years or so. But I can put up with that. After all, I have little mysteries to spice up my day—like pets disappearing in the Sand Trap.

The rumor about the dog had been going around school for a day or two before I actually decided to check it out. It was early on a Saturday morning, and as I left the house, a wall of storm clouds had stalled on the horizon. They seemed to be taunting the little beach community, sounding off dull thunder every now and then, but keeping their distance, like an army waiting to attack.

"You have no business going out on a day like this," Grandma warned me. "The wind'll blow you halfway to tomorrow."

Of course, that didn't stop me. Weather never did. And

neither did warnings. Besides, I loved going out when it was cold and windy. I didn't tell Grandma I was going to the Sand Trap though . . . or that I was taking a bucket.

As I trudged along the smooth shoreline, I breathed in the ocean spray that chilled me inside and out, then I opened my shirt and let the cold of the day fill my body with goose bumps. People didn't understand why I liked to feel cold all the time. I couldn't explain it, either.

A few hundred yards down the strand, I finally came to the weird, perfectly round patch of sand on the beach behind Grandma's house. Everyone called it the Sand Trap because it was always a few inches lower, and a few shades lighter, than all the other sand around it. But what was really weird was that the Sand Trap washed away every day in high tide, then always came back to re-form itself—once again, perfectly round. And, when you looked down at it long enough, you could swear the sand was moving. But that was just an optical illusion—I was sure of it.

I stood before the Sand Trap for the longest time, building up my nerve to do what I had decided to do . . . and then I stepped into it.

Instantly I noticed that this sand was finer than the rest of the sand on the beach—and it was colder, too. But was it quicksand? I didn't think so; after all, I didn't start sinking.

And so I got down on my knees in the Sand Trap, and I stared into it until I could see the sand slowly start churning. Then I dug my hands into it and filled my bucket to the brim. I had wanted some of that strange sand ever since I heard it

existed, and now, at last, I was going to have some of it for my very own.

―――――

The windows in Grandma's workshop are always wide open because of the heat from the furnace and blowtorch. You see, Grandma is a glassblower. She creates bowls and jars and dainty little crystalline figurines that she sells in a crafts shop right next to her house.

That first day, after I had smashed that shelf of figurines, Grandma, instead of yelling at me, sat me down and showed me exactly how much work it took to make just one of the delicate pieces. She also told me how good Grandpa had been at it. "He had always wanted to teach you," she told me, a bit of sadness in her voice, "but you never had the interest."

But after living with Grandma for a while and watching her work the glass, I did develop an interest. There was something about the molten glass that fascinated me, and I grew to love learning the craft.

At first, all I could make were lopsided glasses and mystery ashtrays—everything with sides that didn't quite stay up was a mystery ashtray. But that was three months ago. I've gotten much better at glassblowing now, and I spend most of my free time in that workshop making things.

The things I make aren't cute little animals, though. Mine are powerful beasts. Tigers with angry eyes. Dragons breathing crystalline fire. Glass sharks with bloody teeth. Grandma sells them in the shop, too. She even gave me my own shelf to display my creatures, and she labeled my shelf PHANTASTIC PHENOMENA BY PHILIP.

Now, Grandma never knows what to make of my creations, and she just eyes them with a look that's half proud and half worried. "I guess it's better to get your monsters out of you than to keep them inside," she told me once, laughing nervously.

Well, there are lots more where those came from, I wanted to tell her. And then I thought of the Sand Trap and said nothing. As far as I knew nobody had ever blown a glass creature from *that* sand.

As soon as I had dragged the bucket of strange sand to the workshop, I began to work with it. First, with the fire turned full blast, I quickly melted the sand into a thick semiliquid. Next I wrapped it around my glassblowing pipe. It wasn't muddy and speckled like other unpurified glass, but instead it burned a clean white-hot. Then I held out the stick and watched as it dripped down the stick, inching toward my fingers like the *Blob*.

"You will be incredible!" I told it. "You will be like nothing I've created before." And with that, I put my lips to the end of the tube and blew into the pulsating mass of hot liquid glass.

Grandma almost screamed when she saw it later that week. Her face went white, and at first I thought she was going to pass out. Then I realized she was just stunned by

my creation. I grinned, entirely pleased with myself.

"Do you like it?" I asked.

She caught her breath. "Philip . . . I don't know what to say." She dared to venture closer. "Is this what you've been working on all week?"

"Pretty cool, huh?"

Grandma grimaced. "Well, it sure is something. . . . I just don't know what."

To me, it was everything I'd imagined it would be. The glass creature stood there capturing the late afternoon sun, sending out daggers of light in all directions. Two feet tall, with claws that were sharp and menacing, it had shiny muscles on its hind legs that bulged, looking as though they were ready to pounce. When you looked at it long enough, you would swear you could see it moving.

Its animalistic face was like nothing on earth that I'd ever seen. It had a long snout, and a menacing grin filled with row after row of razor-sharp teeth. Its nostrils flared; its large eyes seemed to follow you around the room. The thing could scare a gargoyle right off its rooftop.

"My masterpiece!" I told Grandma.

"Uh, maybe you've been spending too much time blowing glass," she suggested. Then she left to make dinner, and I closed up the shop—which gave me more time to admire my creation.

"You need a name," I told my crystalline beast as it sat there on a wooden countertop, for it was too large to fit on my display shelf. I thought and I thought, but no name I came up with seemed right. "Perhaps you're something best left nameless, huh?"

Outside I could hear a chill wind blowing, sending shivers up my spine . . . just the way I liked it.

———

I awoke the next morning to the storm that had been looming offshore for days, and was now finally rolling in with a vengeance. I slept with the window open, so the sill and the carpet beneath it were drenched. My toes and fingertips had grown hard from the cold, the numbness inching up through the rest of my body, which shivered uncontrollably.

In fact, I was so cold that I put on warm clothes, which I never do. Then I closed the window, which I never do, either. I ventured downstairs, fully believing that I was heading for the kitchen to cook something hot for breakfast. I was surprised when I realized which direction my feet had turned—I was out the side door, and heading into Grandma's shop.

As I opened the door, bolts of lightning flashed in the distance, illuminating the place before I could flick on the light. I could see the glass beast reflecting that cold white flash. Then, just before the lightning bolt vanished, I caught a glimpse of my creature's eyes staring at me.

Quickly I turned on the light. My glass beast stood there just as beautiful and menacing as it had the day before, hunched and ready to spring. It leered at me with its large eyes and many rows of teeth. As I neared it, looking deep into its glassy mouth, I swear that I could smell its breath, all salty and wet, like the sea. I moved my hands across it. It was cold as ice and smooth as whalebone. I slid my fingers down the ridges of its curved back, feeling its crystalline sharpness. Then, leaning toward it, I whispered . . . *"I made you."*

Saying it somehow made me feel powerful. *"I created you,"* I said, my voice stronger this time. Then, as I peered into its clear glass heart, I thought I saw something move . . . but it was only the reflection of Grandma opening the door behind me.

"Philip, what are you doing here?" she asked. "We don't open for an hour."

I turned to her with a start, feeling a bit embarrassed and guilty for being caught admiring my own handiwork.

"Come have breakfast," she said with a grin. "It'll still be there when you come back."

Then the look on her face changed. It became curious, then concerned. She walked closer to her prize showcase, where her most precious creations were kept—colorful swans, dainty unicorns, and other kinds of graceful creatures—and the concern on her face deepened. Something wasn't right in that case. And I realized what it was the same moment that Grandma did.

Every one of her most precious creations was missing its head.

I looked into my grandmother's face and saw a look that wasn't anger—it was sorrow. In fact, it was pain. "Philip, what did you do?" she exclaimed.

My first response was the same sorrow as hers, but it was

quickly overcome by fury. I gritted my teeth and felt my face going red. "Why do you think it was me?" I shouted, my voice practically a growl.

Her eyes were full of tears. "Who else was in this shop, Philip? All the windows are locked. Do you think neighborhood kids would come in here and do such a thing? No—we have nice children in this neighborhood—*nice* children," she repeated, as if I wasn't one of them. It made me furious. It made me want to take what was left of those pretty glass sculptures and wreck them all.

"Maybe somebody did it before you left yesterday!" I shouted. "Maybe they were like that half the afternoon, and you just didn't notice. How often do you look over there, Grandma?" I stared her down. "How often?"

She looked away, proving that I had won, but I didn't let up.

"Why would I do something like that to you, Grandma?" I pressed, and then I thought back to that first week when I smashed that whole shelf of figurines. "I mean . . . why would I do that *now*? I like it here. I don't want to get sent away."

That clinched it. She finally believed me. One thing about grandparents, when you give them the truth, they can tell. Still, the question remained: Who broke the heads off those figures?

"I guess it must have been some tourist kids," Grandma finally said, shaking her head. Then she headed for the door. "Come have breakfast," she said as she left, not saying another word about it.

I could have believed it, too—that it was some bored tour-

ist kids. I could have believed that there were people mean enough to do things like that . . . because at times I had been one of them. But somewhere deep down, even though I couldn't admit it to myself quite yet, I knew the answer was much closer to home. And as I sat down quietly to eat my bowl of cereal, I couldn't help but think back to my crystalline creation on the heavy wooden counter . . . and how, as I had left the little shop, I could swear it winked at me.

We sold it that afternoon. I was kind of upset. I never thought it would actually sell. If I did, I would have hidden it. It was mine, and I had no desire to see it in someone else's hands. But a large man with a big black hat took one look at it, let out a deep belly laugh, and slapped his fat wallet on the counter. "How much?" he asked.

I swallowed hard. "It's not for sale," I told him. Maybe I didn't say it forcefully enough.

"Name your price," he countered.

Then Grandma had to open her mouth, thinking she was doing me a favor. "Two hundred and fifty dollars," she said. "Not a penny less."

The man raised an eyebrow.

I sighed with relief, certain that no one would pay that much for a piece of glass.

But the man pulled out the cash, placed it in my grandmother's hands, and she placed it in mine. "You earned this," she said proudly.

The man laughed out loud again. "Never seen something so ugly that looked so beautiful," he said. "My wife'll kill me." And then he laughed once more as he carried out my prize beast.

As it turned out, his wife never had the chance to kill him.

———

Whatever happened, happened sometime during the night. All I know is that the next day the papers said something about a man disappearing. They didn't have a picture yet, but I knew who it was. Even before I read the papers, I knew.

You see, that morning I awoke with a spot of sunlight reflecting in my eyes from a piece of sculptured glass sitting on my dresser. It was my own grinning glass beast.

Again, I had left my window open and was half frozen. My teeth were practically chattering out of my head. I wanted to scream in terror when I saw that my creation was back . . . but at the same time I was glad to see it.

As I stared at the glass beast, I could swear that it was closer to me than it originally was. Was it creating some optical illusion the way it did back when it was just weird sand in the Sand Trap?

No, I finally decided, it wasn't closer—it was . . . *larger*. At least six inches larger than before. And it wasn't just taller, either. It was broader as well, and its muscles were thicker than those I had given it. In fact, now I could even see fine

glass ridges, like tiny veins, in its huge, bulging muscles.

"Come down for breakfast, Philip!" Grandma called from downstairs.

I looked at the thing, wanting to hate it, wanting to tell it to go away. But I couldn't. The truth was that I didn't want it to go away.

"I can't let her see you," I told my beast, "so I'm going to lock you in here, okay?" Not waiting for an answer—afraid I might actually get one—I quickly left and locked my door.

After school, I went straight to the shop. I didn't want to think about the glass beast in my room. I just wanted to sit there at the register and smile mindlessly for what few tourists and passersby came into the shop on that cold September day.

As I walked in, Grandma gave me a big smile. "You little sneak," she said, wagging her finger at me. "To think you kept it from me all this time!"

I didn't know what she was talking about, and I've learned the best thing to do when you're clueless is to keep your mouth shut until you have a clue.

"I needed to get in to your room to collect your dirty laundry, and I was wondering why you locked your door," she went on with a grin. "Anyway, I used my old passkey, and do you know what I found in there?"

I gulped a gallon of air. "What?"

"This," she said, and pointed to the showcase that used to

hold her now-headless creations. In their place was a large, crystalline punch bowl carved with such care and sharp precision, it looked like it had been cut out of diamond. It must have cost thousands of dollars.

"When'd you buy this?" I asked her, staring at the rim of the bowl, which had fine beveled edges . . . like teeth.

She laughed. "Stop trying to be funny, Philip. I know that you made it. I just didn't realize how talented you were!" she exclaimed, giving me a hug. "Tell me, how long have you been hiding this masterpiece in your room?"

All I could do was keep silent, trying to figure out what was going on.

I looked at the bowl's perfect surfaces, each cut like a gemstone; its shape perfectly round. I could never make anything like this. Still, there was something familiar about it. I touched it, running my finger down a deep ridge in its surface design.

Cold as ice, I thought. *Smooth as whalebone.*

Then I shuddered so hard I shook nearly every piece of glass in the room.

But Grandma didn't even notice. She was busy putting a five-hundred-dollar price tag on the punch bowl.

It sold that same day to a couple driving south, whose names I made a point to forget.

With my bedroom window open, I waited for it that night. The temperature had dropped, and I could feel myself almost disappearing into the cold.

I heard it before I saw it—a hissing, slithering sound through the window, down the cold, coiled radiator, across the wall, and onto my dresser.

So perfect, I thought. *So beautiful.* And then I let myself relax, like a father who had been waiting for his child to return home.

Fascinated, I watched it take shape once more—its old shape—the beast I had created. I fell asleep staring at it across the room, mesmerized at how the moon, its blue light twisting through the flapping blinds of my open window, painted my beast in fine neon lines.

———

In the morning when I awoke, it was something new. A chandelier, with glass arms, and dangling from those arms were a hundred beautifully shaped, sharp crystalline spears. It was too heavy for me to carry down the stairs all by myself, but somehow I managed it—probably because the chandelier's many arms actually helped itself through the hall, like the arms of an octopus.

Grandma looked at it with a sense of apprehension and a vague sense of dread—the kind of dread you feel before you know enough to feel fear.

"You . . . *you* made this?" she asked.

"Of course I did, Grandma."

She looked into my eyes, trying to catch me in a lie, but she couldn't, because in a way, I wasn't lying.

"You must have worked all night," she said to me coolly.

"No," I told her. "Actually this is something I've been working on for a while. I've been, uh, hiding it . . . like the punch bowl."

"You've been hiding a lot of things from me in that room," she said.

When I just shrugged, she let it go. I knew she was fishing for a lie, but she found only half-truths. Lucky for Grandma she was a firm believer in old sayings like "What you don't know can't hurt you" and "Let sleeping dogs lie."

I strung the chandelier up from a beam in the corner of the shop, and all day long its dangling crystals sang in the breeze like a wind chime whenever someone walked in. It was as if the thing were trying to draw attention to itself. But it didn't have to do that. Even in the darkest corner of the room, it stood out over everything else in the shop.

It was Mr. Dalton who took an interest in it later that day. He owned an antiques shop a few miles down the road, and usually kept his nose too high in the air to step into a tourist shop like ours. But that nose must have gotten wind of some unusual glass sculptures we'd had in the shop lately, because he'd been here twice, earlier in the day, and here he was sniffing around again.

He'd come in first at around ten, pretending not to look at the chandelier, then again after lunch, with a magnifying glass. Finally he returned a third time as we were getting ready to close for the evening, clearly ready to talk business.

"How much do you want for it?" he asked as he ran his finger along its six glass arms, marveling at the fine-cut design of its dangling shards, each sharp as a razor.

"It's not for sale, Mr. Dalton," said Grandma without even looking at it. "It's—"

"Seven hundred dollars," I blurted out. It was mine, and I could sell it if I wanted to. Or at least I could "rent" it.

Mr. Dalton laughed a practiced laugh—the kind he gave whenever he was bargaining with someone.

"Come, now," he said. "Don't be ridiculous, son. After all, it may be unique, but it's full of imperfections. There are flaws in the design, and—"

"No, there aren't," I countered, staring him straight in the eye. "It's perfect . . . absolutely perfect. Seven hundred dollars, or no deal."

He gritted his teeth through his congenial smile, furious to be outbargained by a fourteen-year-old. "Very well," he said. Then he paid me in cash, probably figuring he would sell it in his own shop for over a thousand.

As I helped Mr. Dalton carry the chandelier out of the shop, Grandma looked at me, trying to read something in my face. But lately it seemed my face was unreadable, even to me as I stared at myself in the mirror each morning.

"Would you mind riding with me to my store?" Mr. Dalton asked after we'd put the chandelier into the back of his van. "I could sure use your help carrying it in."

Figuring he'd sort of paid for my help already, I hopped into the front seat, and we took off.

It was as I was carrying the chandelier from Mr. Dalton's van to his shop that I thought I heard it breathe through the tinkling of its many dangling crystals. It sounded like the rush of the ocean when you put your ear to a shell.

Once inside Dalton's shop, we hoisted the chandelier up with a rope over a beam, right in the center of the room. It took a while, and by the time we were done, it was already dark outside. The antiques shop was lit with dim yellow incandescent lights that glimmered off the hanging chandelier, casting tiny spots of light around the room like fireflies.

I hung around, waiting for something to happen.

"It's not that far," Mr. Dalton said to me after a few moments. "I suspect you can walk home from here."

I shrugged, glanced at the chandelier again, and waited.

"I hope you don't think you're getting a tip for bringing it over," he said coldly. "I've already paid through the nose as it is."

And that's when it happened. The crystalline monstrosity jerked itself off the rope and fell.

Spinning out of the way just in time, Mr. Dalton looked with wonder, which quickly built into horror, at the chandelier. It had landed on the ground like a cat, barely making a sound. Then, two crystalline spheres hanging in its center turned toward the terrified man. And both he and I knew at that moment that those spheres were the thing's eyes.

Amazed, I watched it skitter on the wooden floor like a giant glass spider and then spring across the room, landing right on top of Mr. Dalton. He sputtered something I couldn't hear, but he didn't have a chance to scream as the chandelier's glass arms swung inward, and its hundred dangling crystals

became teeth as sharp as the shards of a broken bottle.

It was feeding.

I couldn't watch a moment longer, and I ran to the next room, stumbling over furniture, smashing my shins. Quickly I slammed the door behind me, then collapsing in an old high-backed chair, I turned the chair around so I didn't even have to see the door.

That's when I spotted an old-time radio, large and wooden, across the room. I raced over and turned it on, found a station, and cranked up the music full blast, drowning out the sounds coming from the other room. For five minutes I sat there . . . then ten . . . then twenty. Finally I dared to turn off the radio.

There was silence in the other room, and soon my curiosity began to match my fear. Slowly I made my way back in, opening the creaking door, terrified of what I might see.

But when I finally looked in, I saw no sign of Mr. Dalton— not a button, not a shoelace . . . and the creature—my creature—sat there in the very center of the room. It had resumed its old form now—the gargoyle beast that I had first created. I could hear it breathing a heavy satisfied breath, and I could see its chest rising and falling.

Slowly the beast moved toward me, but I didn't run. My feet were frozen, and I couldn't move. It came up close and brushed against me, purring like a cat. I reached out and stroked its icy mane. The second I touched it, my fear began to drain away, replaced by numbness. In fact, I could feel the creature draining away everything I had ever felt.

Everything good, everything bad—all of it was slipping away into a cold emptiness. It was like sinking into quicksand.

Am I its master? I wondered. *Or is it the other way around?*

As the monster circled around me, I could see just how big it had grown. It was as big as me now, and I felt helplessly drawn to it.

I climbed on its back, and it leaped out an open window, carrying me home with such powerful smooth strides, it felt like I was floating on air. I could almost feel myself dissolving into it, becoming a part of it.

———

Grandma never mentioned the crystalline beast to me or to anyone. She didn't even say a word about it when the police came by to see if we had seen Mr. Dalton on the day he had disappeared. We told the officers the truth—that the man had bought a chandelier, and that I had helped him carry it back to his place.

That was a month ago, although it feels like another lifetime. In fact, everything that came before my creature feels like another lifetime to me now.

Grandma doesn't talk to me much anymore. She tolerates me in the house, and at the breakfast table. She'll ask me to pass the butter and stuff, but she takes no further interest in my comings and goings . . . or to the comings and goings of other things in the house. She asks no questions, and locks herself in her room most of the time. Perhaps I should feel bad about that, but I don't feel much of anything anymore. Except cold.

My dad came to visit today, with his girlfriend, who I've been told is now my stepmom. She's the same one who first suggested I be sent away to live here—the same one who convinced him that a college fund for me was unrealistic, and the money was better spent on their summer trip to Europe.

Dad's out jogging now, and my new stepmom is upstairs drawing a bath. "Oh, how beautiful," she'd said when she'd first stepped into the guest bathroom. "A bathtub made entirely of glass."

"They don't make them like this anymore," I had told her, running my fingers along the Art Deco design of its sharp beveled edges.

Now I sit downstairs listening to loud music. I am icy cold as I let the music flow through me, like the icy wind blowing through the window that I always keep open. My veins are like glass, growing numb, and I feel myself feeling nothing . . . while upstairs, my beautiful crystalline bathtub slowly fills with water.

SHADOWS OF DOUBT

No story to this one, just a creepy bit of poetry . . .

SHADOWS OF DOUBT

In the blink of an eye, you might suddenly feel
That your world's been invaded by all things unreal.
They slink up behind you, and don't make a sound,
But there's nothing to fear . . . if you don't turn around.

In the pit of your stomach there rests a device
That can calculate how fast your blood turns to ice;
It measures the temperature nightmares will start,
Then divides it by beats of a terrified heart.

At the foot of your bed lies a blanket of fear,
You might think it's quite safe, but it's always quite near.
When its steel-woolen quilting wraps 'round you one night,
You will learn that it's not only bedbugs that bite.

At the top of the stairs there's an attic I've found,
That remained even after the house was torn down,
And it's filled with the cobwebs of lonely old dreams,
Which have grown into nightmares that swing from the beams.

At the mouth of a cave lives a shadow of doubt;
If you dare to go in, will you ever come out?
Are there creatures who lurk where it's too dim to see?
Can you hear when they move? Are you scared yet? (Who, me?)

At the edge of the earth flows a river of fear,
And it pours into space day by day, year by year.
As you shoot the cold rapids, and stray far from shore,
Do you notice your lifeboat has just lost an oar?

In the eye of the storm stands a ghost of a chance,
And around her all spirits are destined to dance.
She turns a cold gaze toward an unlucky few—
Don't dare to look now, for she's staring at you.

At the end of the world stands a giant steel door,
And what lies beyond it, nobody's quite sure . . .
Is it crystal-clear heavens, or night blazing hot,
And which is more frightening: knowing or not?

In the face of the future we fly on our own,
Hoping our wings never turn into stone.
If you fall from that sky to the sea, will you drown?
Well, there's no need to worry . . . unless you look down.

At the back of your mind, there's a hole open wide,
Where the darkness is creeping in from the outside.
You can light rows of candles to cast the dark out,
But it's always there hiding . . .

                              . . . in shadows of doubt.